RAW DATA

RAW DATA

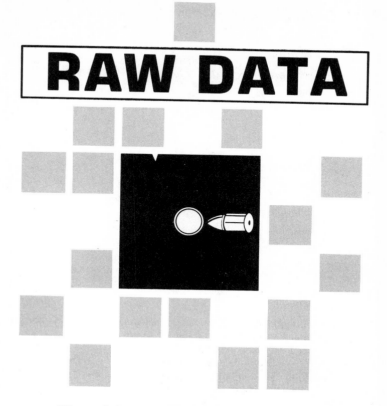

Sally Chapman

ST. MARTIN'S PRESS ■ NEW YORK

To my parents, Carl and Velma Chapman

Design by Diana Andrews

Library of Congress Cataloging-in-Publication Data

Chapman, Sally
        Raw data / Sally Chapman.
                p.   cm.
        ISBN 0-312-05953-1
        I. Title.
PS3553.H295R3   1991
813'.54 — dc20   91-7397
                                                     CIP

First Edition: June 1991
10 9 8 7 6 5 4 3 2 1

Special thanks to Mark Fisher of IBM, Jim
Osbon of SSTG, Joel Harms of the San
Francisco Police Department, Tom
Abraham of the Santa Clara County
Sheriffs Department, the Marin County
Office of the FBI, and to Holly Cooper.

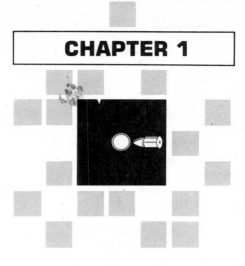

CHAPTER 1

When the bloodied remains of what was once Ronald Gershbein turned up inside the Research and Scientific Division of International Computers, Inc., everyone in Silicon Valley was understandably piqued. Sure they were used to the computer industry's ups and downs, people becoming millionaires one day and bankrupt the next. They were blasé about the corporate gossip, tired of tales of drugs and alcohol, bored with the stories of the divorces, the affairs. But a murder in the central computing complex of ICI, the largest and most prestigious computer firm in the world? That was sinking to a level of tawdriness that bordered on plain sleaze, not to mention the havoc all that blood wreaked on truly state-of-the-art circuitry. As one software executive phrased it: "There goes the neighborhood."

Joshua, one of thirty programmers working for me, discovered Gershbein's body about nine, Wednesday morning. I was in my office absorbed in a heated conference call with East Coast manufacturing. Joshua ran in panting and looking pale.

"Joshua, what is it? I'm really busy." I put a protective hand over the phone receiver. Joshua was a high-strung, overreactive type who had been known to become hysterical over water cooler malfunctions, and I knew better than to take him too seriously.

"Julie, he's . . . he's dead," Joshua garbled, sniffling and clutching the side of the doorway like Greta Garbo in *Camille*.

"Who's dead?" I asked. Joshua just stood there shaking, and I saw the situation would require my full attention. I made a quick excuse to my caller and hung up. Walking over to Joshua, I put a steadying hand on his shoulder.

"You'll have to tell me what's wrong, Josh. Try to calm down so we can talk. Take a few deep breaths. That's right. Now, is the operating system on the fritz again?"

Joshua's lips moved but emitted no sound, then he pointed a trembling finger upward.

"The computer room?" I asked. Joshua nodded frantically. I sighed and grabbed his arm, leading him briskly down the hall, up the stairs to the main computer room on the third floor, where I pressed my security password into the electronic keypad outside the door. We walked inside the antiseptic-looking, white-walled room filled with large, square metal machines devoid of ornamentation except for a few simple switches and blinking lights. I tried to describe a computer room to my mother once as a room filled with big meat freezers. Even the air was chilled to keep down machine temperatures. I shivered and surveyed the area. Everyone seemed to be standing around looking ill and stricken, but then they looked like that a lot. No one looked dead.

"In here," said Alan, a white-coated operating systems analyst. He opened the door on the back of the ICI 9000 and gestured toward it like he was displaying a new dishwasher on a TV quiz show. I looked inside and choked. There was Ronald Gershbein curled up in a fetal position, crammed in among the wiring looking very out of place and very, very deceased. Brown stains had spread across his white short-sleeved shirt. It took me a second to realize it was blood. *Who would do such a thing to Gershbein* was the first thought that raced through me. He was the guy in the office everybody liked. He was good at his job, he helped out other people when they needed it, he never got involved in any petty office feuds. I had completed his quarterly performance review with him the day before. The meeting had gone well, things had seemed okay with him. Looking back on it, Gershbein had appeared a little distracted, but he was just that way sometimes.

I turned my head from the gruesome sight, fighting back nausea. It was then I felt my knees begin to buckle underneath me, but I caught myself by grabbing the edge of a desk. I felt like sobbing or screaming or running out of the room far away from the sight of Gershbein's body. I couldn't connect the man who had been my friend and employee with the masklike face inside the computer. Yet horribly, it was he. Everyone's eyes were upon me, and I knew they were looking to me to take charge of the situation. That's me, Julie Blake, your basic take-charge, be-all-you-can-be kind of gal. Only my insides were turning to oatmeal. I closed my eyes for a second and steadied myself. The worst thing I could do was fall apart in front of my employees.

Alan looked at his former coworker without emotion. "We were getting a lot of operating system errors this morning. Couldn't understand it. Joshua opened the back to check out the thermal conduction module and there was Gershbein. If you look closely here," Alan said dryly, tapping his index finger against the bloody stain on Gershbein's shirt, "you'll notice a hole. I'd say it was a gunshot."

I stared at the bloody corpse a moment then turned

away, my skin beginning to crawl. The insides of my stomach continued to clench up and I felt something rising in my throat. I prayed I wouldn't throw up in front of everyone. "I just can't believe this," I muttered.

Alan nodded. "Me either. The circuits are shot, completely gooed up. I don't know how field engineering is going to clean up this mess, but I guess I had better go tell them," he said in an annoyed tone. He started to leave.

"I want everyone in this room to stay put," I said as loudly and authoritatively as I could manage. "I don't want anyone to go out of this room and I don't want anyone to come in. And don't make any calls and tell anyone about this. Not yet."

I curled my fingers into fists to keep my hands from shaking. I wasn't sure why it would make any difference if people remained in the room or not. Gershbein looked like he had been dead awhile, so the killer had had plenty of time to escape. Keeping people where they were just seemed the right thing to do. I must have remembered it from an old episode of *Kojak*.

I saw Alan push up one of Gershbein's stiffening legs, check the bloodied wires underneath, and shake his head morosely. The sight made me feel sicker than I already was.

"Alan, stop that. Go sit down and do some work."

"How can I? The computer's down."

"So go read a manual or something," I said. He shuffled off to join the others who were now huddled over a disk drive, some whispering, some weeping. I went into a small side office, grabbed a phone, and dialed my boss's four-digit extension with trembling fingers.

"Brad Elkin." He sounded annoyed at the interruption. Elkin was a serious A-type personality, but then, who wasn't?

"You better come to the computer room right away. We've got a problem. A big one," I said. Elkin could tell by my voice that it was urgent.

"I'll be there as quickly as I can."

I sat in a chair and tried to calm myself before I called

the police. I couldn't remember my professors in the Stanford MBA program ever discussing this type of problem. It was then I remembered that Gershbein had a wife and baby. His wife's name was Darlene or something. I couldn't recall her name, and just then it seemed very important that I remember it. I was going to have to call her, but I wasn't ready. Not yet. I was still too shaky and I didn't want to blurt out the news to her before I was in better control. But calling the police couldn't wait.

I had never reported a murder before. It was one of those things you saw in movies or TV but never anticipated doing yourself. I took a deep breath and dialed 911. A dispatcher in the sheriff's office answered and asked if I had an emergency.

"Yes, I need to speak to the chief of police." Always go straight to the top is my policy. The dispatcher said that he couldn't connect me to the police chief. I asked him why not, and he explained that his job was only to dispatch emergency vehicles. He gave me the Sheriff's Department's direct phone number. Once I got through I asked the too-cheerful receptionist for the police chief. She put me on hold and I listened to Barry Manilow croon "I Write the Songs."

"This is Lieutenant Dalton," a man answered in a smooth, unpolicelike voice. He wasn't exactly the chief of police, but he would have to do.

"Lieutenant Dalton, this is Julie Blake. I'm with ICI."

"ICI? You know, I read that article in the paper last week about ICI's new disk drives," he said happily, as if he should have gotten brownie points for the act of reading. "Very impressive access times."

"Thank you, but—"

"We have an ICI 3000 series running right here in the police department. We're all state of the art here in Silicon Valley."

"Great news, but—"

"We have sixty megabytes of memory, two strings of disk drives, and a relational data base."

"Glad to hear it, but you see—"

"How can I help you, Ms. Blake?"

"Someone here has been murdered. We found him inside our mainframe."

"No kidding?" he said with unconcealed excitement. "Okay, don't let anybody leave. And whatever you do, don't let anybody touch anything. We'll be there right away."

Lieutenant Dalton sounded way too eager, like a kid who had just found out he gets to go to camp. It didn't seem right, but I had to give him the benefit of the doubt.

"I'd appreciate your help. And please, could you come in an unmarked car? No need to advertise this thing. You understand, of course."

"Of course," Dalton replied with the respect naturally accorded a representative of the single largest employer in Silicon Valley.

"I'll have someone meet you in the lobby."

We hung up. When I walked back to join the others, two systems analysts were studying Gershbein's body and heatedly discussing the trajectory of the bullet, while Joshua, apparently having fainted, lay spread-eagled across a 5234 communications controller. Two other programmers in the room stood in the corner farthest from Gershbein where they now held on to each other, their eyes and noses red from crying.

"Is there any way it could have been a suicide?" Joshua asked feebly, apparently recovered.

Alan rolled his eyes. "Sure, Josh. Gershbein shot himself in the chest, put the gun away to avoid clutter, then crawled inside the back of the computer and closed the door behind him. Don't be an idiot."

"All of you be quiet," I told them. The room became silent. I loved that part. I spoke, they listened. "Has anybody touched anything?"

"Not anything that we hadn't already touched before," said Joshua. "Like the keyboards, the control panel on Larry, and well, I guess we touched Gershbein." Larry was a nickname for the ICI 9000. I saw Joshua beginning to sniffle again so I sent him to the lobby to wait for the police.

After Joshua walked out, my boss Elkin walked in wearing an expression of restrained astonishment. Tall and silver-haired, Elkin represented professionalism and quiet strength to me. I was relieved to see him.

"Julie, it's a zoo here. There are four police cars outside and an ambulance, all with their sirens blaring. Who's hurt?" Elkin questioned with admirable calm. So much for my request that they arrive *sans* sirens. Was everything around me falling apart?

"Where are the police?" I asked.

"They're signing in with the security guard."

"You mean they have to get visitors' passes?"

"We don't make exceptions to security procedures, not even for police. They'll be here soon enough. Now tell me what happened. Joshua was in a panic out in the lobby, but he wouldn't tell me what was happening because he said you told him not to talk to anybody."

"Gershbein is dead. Shot," I told him, my voice finally gaining some steadiness. There was a moment of silence.

"Where is he?" Elkin finally asked with slightly less composure than he had previously displayed. He followed me over to the ICI 9000 and I showed him Gershbein. Elkin winced and ran his fingers through his hair. In the five years I had worked with Elkin I had never seen him ruffled. I noted with admiration that even with this disaster he was still in control.

"Do we know how it happened?"

I shook my head.

"I better go tell Garrett," said Elkin. "He's going to find out soon anyway and it's better if he hears it from me. We'll need advice from headquarters. Nothing like this has ever happened here before," he said, shaking his head. He looked at me. "I think Garrett should be the one to contact Gershbein's family. Can you handle the police on your own?"

"Of course," I answered. I watched Elkin as he walked off, then jumped like a cat when I realized I was leaning on Larry, ICI's most powerful supercomputer and currently Gershbein's tomb. Running a hand over Larry's metal casing, I almost felt sorry for the machine caught in the middle of this tragedy. Over the past few years the Project 6 team had started talking about Larry as if he were a person, referring to how he was feeling each day, his likes and dislikes, his favorite temperature, his insatiable appetite for fresh data. It was a game we played, but we all had a fondness for Larry, this powerful, hulking information cruncher we worked with every day. Sometimes in the back of my mind, irrational as it was, I thought maybe Larry really was more than just a machine. At that moment it struck me that if he had eyes to see, Larry could have told us who had killed Ronald Gershbein.

I glanced once again at Gershbein's corpse then quickly turned away. Murder was something that happened in dark alleys in the bad parts of town, a distant event you read about in the newspaper or saw on the evening news and shook your head over. It wasn't something that happened in your office. My mind reeled with questions. I tried to remember if Gershbein had been acting strange recently or if he had seemed upset. Sifting through the past week's events, I tried to think of any office feuds or gossip, but I came up with zero. It ran through my head that maybe his murder had something to do with the project we were working on, but I pushed it out of my mind as quickly as it had entered. No need to jump to conclusions, I told myself. I needed a lot more information.

The door opened and the police swept in, complete with badges and guns and crisp blue uniforms, all of them looking surprisingly clean-cut and WASPish. I noted with satisfaction that two of them were women.

"Ms. Blake, I'm Lieutenant Dalton," a shortish, dark-haired man said to me. He was the only one of them not wearing a uniform, probably because they didn't come in a European cut. In his gray suit and blue suspenders he looked too squeaky clean and too well dressed, more like a dance instructor than a cop who handled homicides. When he spoke I detected a slight aroma of breath spray. He extended his hand, gave me a handshake that lasted too long, then let his eyes roam all over me as if I were goods in a window display. I sized him up as self-impressed and pseudo-suave. I wasn't exactly oozing sensuality in my blue business suit, tortoise glasses, and my hair pulled back into its usual grim pony tail, but I could see his surprise that I was young and relatively attractive. Why did everyone assume that because you've reached an executive level in a large corporation and you're a female, you're supposed to look like something wrestled on *Wild Kingdom?*

I led the lieutenant to Larry and opened the back. He and the six officers he brought with him stared at Gershbein a moment. Curled amid the computer circuitry, Gershbein looked like a space traveler from another world.

"How did he fit in there?" asked a policeman, scratching his head.

"We were expecting a memory upgrade in a few days, so there was plenty of free space inside for Gershbein," Alan quickly chimed in. "The ICI 9000 series is completely site-upgradable. It's the best machine we build. This morning, even with a corpse in it, response time was subsecond," he said proudly. "Although I did notice a degradation in throughput."

The police looked at Alan as if he were an alien from the planet Goonbob.

"One of the programmers found Gershbein just as you see him," I told the police. "No one has moved anything."

Lieutenant Dalton looked at Gershbein more closely, then told one of his men to get everyone out of the room. Three police officers carrying small metal cases moved in toward Gershbein. One woman began taking photographs of the body while the two men inspected the room and scribbled in notebooks. Dalton ushered me into the small office.

"How long will it take you to find out who killed him?" I asked after closing the door to ensure our privacy.

Dalton sat in the chair behind the desk. "I can't answer that. At this point it could have been anybody. You know how these things are."

"No, I don't. All I know is that one of my employees has been murdered, and you've got to find out who did it."

"We'll do the best we can, Ms. Blake."

"What does that mean? What procedure do you go through in a case like this? Do you have a manual you follow, because I'd like to see it," I said in an angry voice I didn't intend. I guess finding a friend and employee murdered made me irritable. I'm funny that way.

"We approach it like this," answered Dalton. "First we secure the crime scene. We gather what evidence we can, then we question the victim's family, friends, and, in this case, his coworkers. We look for who had a motive and an opportunity to kill the victim."

"What's your success ratio?"

"Ms. Blake, I'd like to ask the questions here. That's how I do my job, if you don't mind." Dalton looked offended. I have this tendency to assume that no one but me is completely competent to get anything done correctly. Sometimes it annoys people.

I tossed Dalton a placating smile. "Sure, of course. You go right ahead. I'm sorry. It's just that this has been upsetting, more than upsetting, and I need to know that something is going to be done about it."

Dalton took out a pocket-size pad of paper and began jotting earnestly to make sure I knew the wheels of justice were turning. He started asking me questions, and I filled him in on what I knew about the morning's events.

"Okay, what was Gershbein working on?" he asked after we had gotten the background information out of the way.

I hesitated before answering. "It's a confidential project."

"What kind of project is it?" Dalton looked at me with fresh interest.

"It's confidential," I repeated. "I can't discuss it with someone who doesn't have security clearance. I suppose you'll need some information about it, but I'll have to check with my management first."

By Dalton's expression I could tell he was dying to know more, but he maintained his cool, detective-like composure. He settled back in his chair and crossed his legs. Somehow I never pictured a cop crossing his legs.

"What is your position here?" he asked.

"I'm a V.P., head of the research project."

A smile crossed Dalton's face and I imagined him in a sharkskin suit trying to teach me the cha cha.

"You're kind of young to be in a job like this, aren't you?" he said. "You look like you're just out of college."

"I'm ten years out of college and I assure you quite qualified for this position. Aren't you supposed to be asking me questions relating to the murder?"

"Yes, of course. Let's see," he said, stumbling on the words and quickly studying his note pad. "What was your relationship to Gershbein?"

"I was his manager."

"What was his position here?"

"Research program analyst. The best I had."

"Did he have any enemies at work that you know of?"

"No, I've never heard of any problems like that."

"Have you ever heard any office gossip about Gershbein's life-style?" asked Dalton. He saw my puzzled look. "You know, drugs, booze, gambling, sex stuff?"

"No, I never heard anything like that. Listen, Gershbein was quiet, reserved, and seemed to be very happily married. I guess you never know anyone completely, but as far I do know he never did much of anything except tinker with computers and software. His background was thoroughly checked out before he was allowed to transfer to my department."

Dalton's eyes lit up. He could restrain himself no longer. "I guess you're working on some pretty secret stuff," he said like a little kid talking about spaceships and laser guns.

I just looked at him and nodded. It was pretty secret stuff, all right. My responsibility was a confidential ICI project owned jointly by ICI, the Defense Department, and another Silicon Valley firm called Comtech, and I certainly wasn't going to divulge its secrets to Lieutenant Dalton.

It had been the Defense Department's idea to keep the whole thing secret. The project objective was to develop carbon-based memory material, the functional equivalent of a silicon chip that would be the size of a single molecule. We would have our final designs in a couple of weeks—that is, if a murder investigation didn't get in the way.

It bothered me that even with Gershbein's brutal murder, I was still thinking about my work and how it would be affected. But then, my work was my life these days, and it seemed to come before everything else.

"I'll tell you this about Gershbein," I said to Dalton. "The government checked out everything about him before he joined the team. In our work secrecy is important, and they knew every scrap of his history—who were his friends, who weren't his friends, what brand of underwear he wore, and what wine he drank—before they okayed him to work on this project. I'm sure of it because they did the same thing to everyone, including me."

The look on Dalton's face told me that what I had just said wasn't what he had wanted to hear.

"Is there any way someone could have gotten in here last night without signing in at the security desk?" he asked me.

"I don't think so. Second-shift operations people leave about nine P.M., and after that there's usually no one around, except for whoever is working late. You have to insert an ICI badge in a badge reader to enter the building. In addition to the badge entry, anyone who enters or leaves after eight at night is supposed to sign in and out at the security desk." I thought a moment. "But someone could have stayed in his office after regular working hours, I suppose. Then he could have waited until Gershbein was alone and killed him."

Dalton looked puzzled. "But how did this person get out?"

"Simple," I said. "He could have hidden in the building until morning, then walked out with nobody noticing."

I think Dalton might have squealed and clapped his hands, but he was interrupted by a knock at the door. An officer who looked like Dudley Doright stepped in. He seemed shy about interrupting.

"Lieutenant, we found blood in between the keys at one of the terminals."

"You mean he was killed while sitting at the terminal?" I asked.

"It looks that way. The killer tried to wipe off the keys, but it seeped between them. We can't be sure it's the blood of the deceased until we test it."

"How's the questioning going?" asked Dalton.

The officer suddenly looked peevish. "The answers I'm getting are kinda strange. These guys don't act normal. We're having trouble keeping them away from the computer, and when Rodriguez started dusting the computer for fingerprints a couple of those guys in white coats tackled him and started yelling something about air particles," he told Dalton. "Those are some weird guys out there." He cocked his thumb and pointed it in the direction of my employees.

"Those weird guys are the most highly skilled, brightest people in the business," I told him, the mother lion protecting her cubs.

"Any leads yet?" Dalton interrupted quickly in hopes of avoiding a fistfight between Dudley Doright and me.

"Yeah, we checked the sign-out sheet at the security desk in the lobby and only one of the programmers other than the deceased, a Joshua McCormack, was signed out after eleven last night. Fred can't be sure until we get the body to the lab, but he's guessing that the time of death was last night somewhere between nine and eleven. We're going to take McCormack in with us now for questioning."

I jumped up. "You think Joshua killed Gershbein? That's ridiculous," I told him.

Dalton gave me a patronizing look. "He was in the building last night. We have to check it out."

"But Joshua wouldn't hurt anybody. And it doesn't make sense to think he would shoot someone, stuff him in the computer, and then casually sign out at the security desk before making his escape."

"Stranger things have happened, Ms. Blake. Besides, we have to check it out. It goes in the official records," he said solemnly, as if the official records were the Koran. Dalton quickly dismissed the officer and told me we would be continuing our discussion later. We walked back into the main computer area where they were taking out what was left of Gershbein covered and on a stretcher. I saw Joshua in the corner, his face white, and I walked over to him. He looked at me with puppy-dog eyes.

"Julie, I swear, I didn't shoot Ronald. He was sitting at the terminal working when I left. I spent most of my time in the other wing of the building. God, I even signed a petition last year opposing handguns. What are they going to do to me?" he blurted.

"If they start slapping you around at the station just remember it's a violation of your civil rights," said Alan. "I hear they know how to hit you so the marks don't show. Be sure and let me know, okay, Josh? I like police stuff."

I glared at Alan until he walked off. I turned to Joshua.

"Exactly where were you last night, Josh?"

"In the east wing working on the production control program."

"You were there the whole time?"

"Just about. I came into the computer room a little after nine to get some books. I saw Gershbein sitting at a terminal, but he looked busy so I didn't say anything. Right after that I left the computer room and went back to the east wing."

"Did you see anyone else in the building?"

"No, it was getting pretty late. Everyone was gone."

"So no one in the east wing saw you and could confirm that you were there?"

"I don't think so. Jeezus, Julie, what are they going to do to me?"

"Nobody's going to do anything to you. I'll call our attorney and he'll send someone to go with you to the police station. Just don't worry. I'll look into it. It's going to be okay."

Joshua looked slightly calmer when he walked out with one of the female officers. I wished I could believe my soothing words as much as he did. I used the closest phone and called the ICI attorneys' office. They agreed to send someone to meet him at the station. As I hung up the phone I felt a tapping on my shoulder. It was Dalton.

"We're going to have to move everyone out of this room, at least until tomorrow," he said. "One of your guys hit my fingerprint man over the head with a big round thing when he tried to get prints off the surfaces inside the computer. We can't have that."

"I'll make sure my group cooperates from now on," I told him. "How are your people doing? Have they found any clues yet?"

"Not yet. These things take time."

"But aren't there fingerprints or something that you've found? What about fibers? Aren't you supposed to look for fibers from the killer's clothing?"

"Trust me, we know how to gather evidence."

"Of course you do. I'm sorry. You'll get back to me as soon as you do come up with something?"

"Sure. One more thing. My men are checking with the security folks, but I wanted your opinion on this. Is there any way a person outside of ICI, like one of Gershbein's family members for instance, could have gotten in here last night?"

I shook my head. "No, not on their own. All doors are locked and are only badge-operated at night, except the door at the security desk where there is always a guard. And entering the computer area requires inputting a password into a security keypad."

"What if an ICI employee went to a side door and let someone in? Is that possible?"

"Sure, but I think it's unlikely anyone who works for me would do that."

"It's unlikely that anyone would wind up dead inside

a computer," Dalton answered. I thought maybe he wasn't as stupid as I thought.

"Well, I'll be on my way then," he said. "I'll be calling you. We're going to need access to your department's personnel records."

"Of course."

"Well, not to worry, Ms. Blake," he said, raising one eyebrow in a manner I assumed was supposed to be suave. "We'll have this thing cracked in no time. All of our files of criminal records are computerized on the ICI 3460," Dalton added with zest. I faked a smile. The 3640 wasn't one of our most reliable models.

It took another hour to get people cleared out of the computer area and for things to return to some normalcy, then I gave my computer staff the afternoon off. That was a first, but then so was murder in the computer room.

It was two-thirty before I got back to the office. My secretary, Mrs. Dabney, handed me a stack of phone messages as I passed her desk. I noticed her magenta lips puckered with annoyance.

"Some policeman in a suit came in here and asked for Ronald's personnel file, but I wouldn't give it to him. I told him he could arrest me if he wanted and slap me right in the slammer, but that file is ICI confidential and it's not leaving this office." She looked at me over the top of her rhinestoned glasses and gave her graying bob hairdo an affectionate pat.

"It's okay," I told her. "You can give it to him. Send it over by courier."

Mrs. Dabney looked around to make sure we were alone, then leaned her small, wiry body forward on her elbows and rested her chin on laced fingers. "So what did he look like?" she asked in a voice that sounded like a petite cement mixer. "Was there much blood?"

I gave her a reproachful look. It didn't stop her.

"Joshua McCormack doesn't look like a killer, but then you never know, do you? You think you know people. You work with them every day, and then something like this happens and you realize you didn't know what went on behind their faces. Personally I always thought there was something in Joshua's eyes." Mrs. Dabney looked to me for a reaction.

"Do you have anything else for me?" I asked wearily.

She held out a manila folder. "Just this. It's the background info on that Ruskie professor, the one from Leningrad. He'll be here day after tomorrow. I already put it on your calendar."

I took the folder, thanked her, then entered the safe confines of my office, shutting the door behind me. I started to open the folder, but instead tossed it to the side of my desk. It wasn't important. A Soviet professor was to tour our research facility as part of an international technical exchange program. He wasn't to see anything confidential or even anything of remote importance. As far as I was concerned it was useless public relations, the last thing I had time for, especially now.

Sitting in my leatherette executive swivel chair, I closed my eyes and pondered my situation. At thirty-four I was the youngest person ever to reach the level of vice-president at ICI and was currently the leader of one of the company's most important projects in its history. On top of that, I now also had the distinction of being the only project leader to have a corpse turn up on company premises. But I was more worried about poor Gershbein and what effect his murder would have on my project. ICI was very concerned with its image, and there was bound to be plenty of negative publicity attached to a murder. The best way to deal with it was to catch the murderer and close the books on it as quickly as possible. That was a problem for the police, but I didn't have much confidence in government bureaucracies.

Who would want to kill Gershbein? He was what people outside the business called a computer nerd. He wore Hush Puppies and pen protectors and loved to sit glued to a terminal for hours laboring over some intricate piece of programming. I understood people like Gershbein. I was one of them. I had traded in my pen protector for pearls and

· 17 ·

my Hush Puppies for sensible heels, but inside I was still as enraptured by technology as any of them. And that made it even harder for me to understand how someone like Gershbein could possibly get mixed up in the worst end of a murder. Who would want to kill a harmless programmer? I remembered again about Ronald's wife and new baby, and I felt my ulcer start its familiar internal combustion. Opening my desk drawer, I pulled out my Maalox, took several swigs from the mouth of the bottle, and waited for the chalky liquid to soothe the furnace in the pit of my stomach. With my hands to my temples, I clenched my eyes shut and thought about Gershbein. Garrett was going to break the news to his wife, but I knew I should make a personal call that day after work. There was something inside me that didn't want to. The human nuance was so unpredictable. You couldn't plan for it, couldn't flowchart it, couldn't break it down into logical components, confine it within definable parameters. I imagined how Mrs. Gershbein would react when I went to see her. I had met her once at an office United Way drive. She was tall and blue-eyed, kind of quiet. Just then I remembered her name. It was Dorothy. What would I say to her? Would she blame me?

While I agonized, Charles Stafford, a fellow ICI manager and also my fiancé, breezed into my office sporting his typical corporate uniform—dark suit, red power tie, starched white shirt with his initials embroidered on the cuff—looking as polished and clean as a freshly manicured nail. His light-brown hair and hazel eyes matched my own coloring, and my best friend Max loved to comment how Charles and I looked like two WASP dolls made by Mattel. Charles took one look at me then lifted me out of my chair and wrapped me in his arms. I breathed in his delicious aroma laced with expensive soap and Polo cologne.

"I heard about Gershbein. How awful," he said. I held onto him a moment then left his embrace to close my office door so we could have some privacy. Suddenly my legs felt too weak to carry me and I sat back down in my chair, grateful that I could at last drop my professional façade.

"Charles, I feel so horrible about Gershbein. I don't understand how something like this could have happened," I blurted, forcing back the tears that had been threatening to emerge all day.

He bent down and wrapped his fingers around mine. "You look drained, sweetheart. I know you're worried sick."

I nodded and gave his hand a squeeze.

With a weary sigh, Charles placed himself in the mauve chair in front of my desk and leaned back, stretching his arms and legs with the self-assurance of a male cat confident of his turf. "It's so hard to believe that something like this could happen here at ICI," he said. "It makes me really angry. A cop gave me a ticket last week for not making a full stop at a stop sign; meanwhile murderers are running around loose killing people. And what's the point of having all this security, the badge readers and everything, if somebody can somehow just walk in off the street and murder someone?"

"But that's just it," I said. "How could it have been someone off the street? No one can get in here."

Charles's eyes widened. "You're not thinking it was an ICI employee who killed Gershbein?"

"What else can I think?"

"Julie, just about everyone here has graduate or post-graduate degrees," he said with an incredulous look.

"You don't think people with graduate degrees are capable of murder?"

"I certainly don't think it's likely. Well-educated people commit securities fraud or tax evasion. They embezzle from pension funds. They don't murder."

"I wished I shared your confidence."

Charles leaned closer to me. "What can I do to help you, sweetheart?" he said, his voice lowered to a whisper. "I don't like seeing you upset like this. What if tonight I gave you a nice massage by candlelight while you sip chardonnay and listen to Vivaldi?"

I watched the sly smile on his face and thought for the one-hundred-and-thirty-third time how much he looked like Mel Gibson. I had never attracted a man like him before. I was the girl in high school that few people ever noticed, except during exam time when people struggled to sit next to me so they could steal looks at my test answers. Since I was fifteen it had always been the intellectual, unexciting geeks who had pursued me, the type whose clothes never quite fit, the type who created prizewinning science projects in school. They saw me as no-nonsense and studious, which I was. That image put me on the social fringes in high school; now it put me into a sought-after career and into the arms of a man my mother described as dashing.

"Julie, I don't want to sound cold, but you have to start thinking about damage control. A murder in one's department doesn't exactly enhance one's résumé."

"I'm not concerned about myself, Charles," I told him. "I'm concerned about the project and poor Ronald Gershbein and what happened to him, what's going to happen to his wife and child."

Charles twisted uncomfortably. "I'm sorry. That did sound hard and I didn't mean it that way. Look, I know it's terrible, but I never even knew the guy. You're what's important to me and I just don't want you to get hurt, that's all. Be realistic. The man is dead, gone, zeroed out. There's nothing you or I can do about it except make sure you don't get hurt in the aftermath."

"It's okay. Look, Charles, I need to get back to work. I've got to contact our public relations person in San Francisco and see how this situation is going to hit the papers."

"Of course." Charles leaped up and headed for the door, then stopped and looked back at me. "Julie, you really do looked wrecked. Let me at least take you to dinner tonight. There's a place at Half Moon Bay I want to try. I can get away after eight."

I smiled at him. "I wish I could, but I've decided to visit Gershbein's wife right after work. Do you think you could come along with me?" I looked hopeful.

"Sorry, sweetheart, but I can't. I'd like to be with you but I'm working until at least seven-thirty. Why not ask Max to go? She always loves a disaster."

"I wish you wouldn't talk about her that way. She is my best friend."

He made a face. "I try to forget. Well, gotta run. I'll call you tonight after you get home. I love you." He kissed the air then slipped out. I forgave him for his coldness about Gershbein.

The phone rang. Elkin had the FBI on the speaker phone in his office and they wanted a full report on everything that had happened. I told Elkin I'd be right there. I grabbed my notebook and a ballpoint, then took another swig of Maalox before heading out the door.

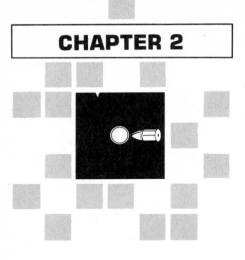

CHAPTER 2

"If you ask me, Ronald Gershbein was a corpse long before they found him cooling the circuits of that computer," said Maxine LaCoste as she snaked her way through the Highway 101 rush-hour traffic. The steering wheel of her lipstick-red Porsche vibrated beneath her fingers as she pressed her purple Charles Jourdan pump more solidly on the accelerator. With a dramatic swerve to the left she veered around a cement truck that dared to stand in her way. I gripped my seat for a false sense of security.

"What baffles me is why anyone would want him dead. I liked Gershbein, but let's face it, he was the quintessence of boring—the walking, talking human equivalent of a bowl of bran. I can't remember him ever talking about anything that didn't have to do with computers. You know, that's what happens to people around here," she warned with a wagging finger. "They devote so much of their time to fiddling with the insides of machines that they wake up one day and *poof*, they've become machines themselves. Gershbein's wife probably had to make sounds like a disk drive to get him in bed with her. I can't imagine who would want to kill the guy," Max said, her frequent hand gestures leaving the steering wheel alarmingly unattended.

"That's my point." I had to raise my voice to be heard over the sounds of Stevie Wonder on her German CD stereo. "What could Gershbein have been involved in that would make someone want to kill him? Murders are committed because of money or passion."

"In which case it's got to be money. I can't see him in the middle of a hot love triangle, unless it included some sort of electronic device. How kinky."

"Maybe Gershbein was having an affair, maybe with the wife of someone in the office, and he was killed by a jealous husband."

"But what about Joshua McCormack? He's single and he's the big suspect, isn't he?"

"That's because he's the only one they know was in the computer room with Gershbein last night. But Joshua isn't a killer. Besides, what's Joshua's motive?"

"Who the hell knows what motivates Joshua? Maybe Gershbein sat on his keyboard or stole his pen protector."

"I don't think those are motives for murder, Max."

She thought a moment. "Okay, maybe it was one of those fanatics you read about who thinks computers are evil. Or maybe it was somebody who finally cracked up after having his charge account screwed up by a computer for years. He figured the best way to fight back was to kill one of the people responsible for computers, so he blasted a programmer. Seems logical. I've wanted to shoot one many times." She laughed.

I gave her a look to let her know I didn't buy the theory.

She frowned at me. "Jules, you've got to relax. You're

all tightened up, your face looks tense, and little wrinkles are showing around your eyes. Why do you feel like you have to take charge of everything? It's not your fault Gershbein was killed."

I took a deep breath of the Santa Clara air and leaned my head back against the seat. "I don't know, Max. Maybe it was."

"What are you talking about?"

"I gave him his quarterly performance review yesterday. I was thinking about it this afternoon and I remembered that as he was leaving the office, all of a sudden he stopped. He said he had something else he wanted to discuss. But I had another meeting so I put him off. Maybe he needed to talk to me about something important, something related to why he was killed."

Max gave her hair an aggravated toss. "Maybe he just wanted to talk to you about a raise or a way to increase Larry's throughput, or maybe he wanted to lodge a complaint about the ICI cafeteria. You know, they had some tapioca there the other day that looked like some sort of bodily excretion. The important thing to remember is that it could have been anything. Don't feel responsible."

"But if something that could provoke a murder was going on in my department, I should have known about it. And I would have if I had taken a few extra minutes to talk to him."

Max sighed as she blasted her horn at the car in front of her.

"That's just your Puritan-work-ethic-mea-culpa complex talking. For all you know, his murder could have had nothing to do with the office. In fact, most likely it didn't. Most likely it was just some crazy person who walked in and shot Gershbein. And there's nothing you can do to change it."

"I can find out who did it."

Max raised one eyebrow into a perfect arc. "Forget it, my friend. That's a job for the police."

"The police don't seem totally competent to me."

"No one seems totally competent to you but you. Look at it in managerial terms. You have to delegate authority in order to get the job done. Think of it as giving the police an opportunity to excel. But you keep out of it. You've got to stop carrying the world on your shoulders and get a little enjoyment out of life or you'll be dead from a heart attack at thirty-five, and then what would poor Charles do? You're the only woman who ever loved him for himself and not his profile." She winked and giggled. I had to smile.

"Just think of all the advice you've given me over the past three years. And I've never taken any of it," I joked. "Doesn't it bother you to waste your wisdom on me?"

"Of course not. Persistence is my forte. You know that. I think of you as my project. I'm determined to get you to relax and loosen up, and I don't care how long it takes."

"Could be years."

"So you'll be a very relaxed and loose seventy-year-old. Together we'll pick up elderly guys and play strip checkers."

I laughed then leaned back in my seat and tried to get rid of the stress filtering through my body. The conference call with the FBI had been formal and tense. Apparently Garrett had called our Defense Department contact and he had called in the FBI. The FBI wanted to leave the murder investigation to the police, at least for now, but they made me go over every detail of the morning's events, even though they had already gotten most of the facts from Lieutenant Dalton. Their questions droned on for over an hour, and I walked out feeling drained and guilty by association.

I took a deep breath and tried to get my mind off murder. With the windows down, the wind whipped Max's long black hair against her cheek and pinkened her pale skin. I watched her face and thought once again how beautiful she was.

Max embodied a sensuality that made me feel bland in comparison. I was short, my features even but unexciting. I knew I was attractive, at least attractive enough to interest the Lieutenant Daltons of the world, but when I looked in the mirror I saw myself as clean-cut and professional looking and without the sensuality I so admired in Max. She was long, flowing, deep-hued silk; I was a gray flannel business suit. She was bubbling French champagne. Next to her I felt like warm beer. Still, she was my closest friend and I enjoyed being her pet project. She made me laugh and encouraged me not to take life so seriously. Charles was as intense about work as I was, and sometimes Max was my only relief from my sober-mindedness. And I knew deep inside she wasn't nearly as tough as she pretended. I watched her glance at me, her expression suddenly somber.

"I don't want to give you anything else to worry about, but I was in Hanson's office today when he got a phone call from Garrett about the project. I gathered from Hanson's end of the conversation that something was very wrong, and they weren't talking about Gershbein's murder."

I gave Max a hard look. "That's impossible. If there was anything wrong with the project I would be the first to know. Absolutely. What did Hanson say on the phone?"

"Nothing really. It wasn't what he said. It was *how* he said it. It was his tone of voice and the look on his face, like a sick weasel, that made me think there was a problem. But you're right. I'm sure I just misinterpreted it."

Max pulled the Porsche at the the curb of 214 Hackberry, home of the newly widowed Mrs. Gershbein.

"This probably won't take too long," I said as I dropped my purse, retrieved it then fumbled with my coat. I tried to think of what my first words to Gershbein's wife would be, but my mind drew a blank. I noticed Max chuckling at me.

"You're Wonder Woman when it comes to logic and circuits, but when it comes down to dealing with human emotions you crack completely. It's quite interesting."

"Spare me the psychoanalysis and just get out of the car. By the way, I appreciate you coming with me." I stepped onto the curb.

"No thanks necessary," she replied with a smile.

I closed the car door and we faced the Gershbein home. It was a simple, one-story tract house with a neatly trimmed yard and a pale stucco façade. The whole subdivision was done in the same Spanish design, and the houses looked like hundreds of Taco Bells lined along the streets. I glanced at the newly sodded grass in front of the house and my stomach clenched. It had only been a week ago that Gershbein had proudly told me about his new lawn. I walked to the door and paused. Looking at Max, I noticed that she too looked uncomfortable. That made me feel a little better. Misery loves company and all that. I rang the doorbell.

The door opened and revealed a large, red-haired woman of about thirty, wearing a pink cotton sweatsuit and a pair of very red eyes. She was at least five inches taller than Ronald had been, and the first thought that struck me was what an odd-looking couple they must have made.

"Mrs. Gershbein, I'm Juliet Blake and this is Maxine LaCoste. I called you earlier."

She hesitated at first, then she nodded and opened the door for us. Her large frame and long thick red hair reminded me of some Amazon goddess, and I pictured her dressed in animal pelts, lifting up Gershbein and clutching him to her breast.

Max and I walked inside. The room was sparsely decorated with a collection of simple furniture that could only be described as neo-Sears modern, but the large assortment of books on the shelves made the room more hospitable. In the corner on a desk sat Gershbein's personal computer and a stack of software manuals. My gut tightened again when I saw a few baby toys scattered on the chairs and realized that the baby would never know its father. The house was clean but happily cluttered, as if its occupants were too absorbed in other activities to worry much about interior decorating. I liked houses like that. My eyes were drawn to a table holding a collection of photographs of friends and family. Ronald and Dorothy must have been happy together.

"Have a seat." She motioned to the couch. Max and I pushed aside a stuffed dog and a rattle and sat down. "It was nice of you to call and ask to visit me. I've had so many calls from Ron's coworkers. You don't expect sensitivity from a company as large as ICI. Would you like a cup of coffee?"

"No, thank you. We don't want to take up much of your time," I said, struggling for conversation.

"It's okay. My sister is taking care of the baby." Dorothy Gershbein sat on a sofa across from us and looked at me with a directness that told me the conversational ball was in my court. My fingers toyed with the hem of my skirt.

"Mrs. Gershbein," I began.

"Call me Dorothy."

"Dorothy, I'd like to express the company's and my own grief over the tragic death of your husband."

Max kicked me. I sounded like a funeral director, even to myself. All I needed was "Swing Low Sweet Chariot" as theme music. That was the one sentence I had memorized so I decided I had better start winging it, but Dorothy spoke before I had the chance.

"I want you to know that I don't blame ICI for what happened," she said. "I guess maybe I should. I mean, if the doors had been locked better or something, maybe it wouldn't have happened." Dorothy had lost eye contact with me and her eyes fell across the living room as if its contents looked different from how they ever had before.

"I wish I could tell you . . ." I began, but she held up a hand and stopped me.

"It's okay. I'm not going to sue you or anything. Ronnie loved ICI. I really think his happiest moments were when he was working. I used to be jealous at first. I mean, it was hard on me. He always spent such long hours at the office. But then I saw how some of my girlfriends' husbands were unhappy with their jobs and they brought that unhappiness home with them. Ronnie loved his job. He was a happy man, happy with his work and his family. We have a ten-month-old baby. Did you know that?"

Tears slipped from Dorothy's eyes and she pulled the bottom of her sweatshirt to her face and wiped, then noisily blew her nose, leaving a shiny streak on the shirt's edge. I got up from my chair and sat down on the sofa next to her. I placed a tentative arm around her shoulder, not sure if she wanted that kind of contact from me, but she smiled.

"Crying makes me feel better, so I'm just letting myself do it if I feel like it," said Dorothy.

"You go right ahead," Max said. "Let it out."

The three of us were quiet a moment in case Dorothy needed to let it out some more, but she seemed calm. I was the one who broke the silence.

"I really admired Ronald," I told her, and meant it. "He was a great guy and a superb technician."

Max nodded. "Even the people at Comtech had a lot of respect for him."

Dorothy nodded. "Thanks. He thought a lot of you too. He mentioned you quite often and in glowing terms."

"Really?" I said, flattered. I figured that was enough small talk because Dorothy looked pale and like she needed a rest. But there were still questions I wanted to ask.

"Have the police talked to you yet?" I asked her.

She nodded. "They were here an hour asking questions, but I don't think I told them anything too useful. I wasn't that worried when he didn't come home last night. You see, he called me and told me he would be working really late. And a couple of times during the past few weeks he's pulled all-nighters at the office. I got worried when he didn't show up this morning at least to shower and change his clothes."

I wondered why Gershbein would be working all night. There wasn't any reason for it that I could think of.

"Look, Dorothy, I'm sure the police have gone over this, but I want to ask you again because I knew Ronald very well and I can't figure this thing out." I took a breath. "Do you know of anybody who would want to kill him?"

I saw Max roll her eyes and I could have kicked myself for making such a quick and brutal change of subject, but after hearing my question Dorothy seemed to come more alive, her posture becoming more erect, her voice stronger.

"No. I told the police, Ron had no enemies. He was the most adorable man in the world. No one would want to harm a hair on his head." We both smiled at her last remark since Ronald's head was bald as a baby's behind.

I dug further. "But what about his work? Was he arguing with anyone at the office?"

She paused a second. "No, nothing like that. I already told you, he loved his job and he seemed to like everybody there. We went to the ICI family dinner this year and he seemed really friendly with everyone."

"Dorothy, there was a reason he was killed. There has to be. It would be hard for a stranger, a person outside of ICI, to get into the building. Even if he could, he wouldn't randomly shoot someone then take enough time afterward to conceal the body inside a computer."

"What are you getting at? Are you saying it was a friend of his who killed him? Someone he worked with?"

"I'm saying that his murder was carefully planned. The person knew when Ronald would be alone. The person knew his body would fit inside the computer. Someone who didn't know much about computers would never think to open the back of one and use it as a hiding place, would he?"

"I guess you're right. Somehow it makes it all seem worse."

"But it will also make it easier for us to find the killer. But we have to figure out why someone would want your husband dead."

Dorothy stood up, walked toward the desk, and touched the keys of the small computer.

I pressed on. "Dorothy, it's important that you tell me if there was anything unusual going on with him."

"There was one thing," she said. The pitch of her voice had lowered, and I leaned forward to hear her.

"What is it, Dorothy?"

She turned toward me. "Sometimes Ronnie would get nervous about a project. I could tell because he would work late, smoke a little more, eat less. But mostly I knew because he would talk about the project constantly. He would eat, drink, and sleep it. It would bore me to death because I couldn't understand the technical terms he threw around.

Computers don't really interest me much. I'm in retail merchandising. Did you know that?"

"I think Ronald mentioned it to me," I fibbed.

"Anyway, the past few months Ron seemed anxious about something at the office. It was the same old symptoms. He worked late, would hardly eat, had a lot of trouble sleeping. It seemed worse than the other times, only this time he wouldn't talk about it. Not a word. I even asked him to tell me about it, which I never had to do before, but he wouldn't. Before he had always talked his head off about work."

"You don't have any idea of what it might have been about?"

"No, I don't. I wish I did." Her face saddened once more and she dropped into the chair in front of the computer, her shoulders slumping.

I could tell she was going to cry again and I felt I was only making things worse for her. I stood up to leave and Max followed suit. "We've taken up enough of your time. If there's anything I can do for you, let me know, Dorothy. I really mean that."

"Wait a minute," she said, reaching inside a desk drawer and pulling out a stack of computer printouts. "Ronnie spent a lot of time looking at this the past month. The paper is a lot wider than the paper he uses on his home computer, so I guess it's from the office. I suppose you should have it." She held it out and I reached for it and thanked her. Flipping through it quickly, I recognized it as a printout of Larry's security system software. It astonished me that Gershbein would have it at home because it was considered highly confidential software and restricted to ICI premises. Gershbein wasn't the type to break rules.

Dorothy walked us to the door. She seemed smaller to me now, as if our discussion of Ronald and her subsequent tears had shrunk her, made her cave in upon herself. I wanted to embrace her, to dry her tears and tell her that things would be okay, but I knew they wouldn't. Besides, if I were her, sympathy wouldn't be what I wanted. There would be other words I needed to hear.

"We'll find out who did this to Ronald. I promise," I told her. Dorothy looked at me and at last I saw some fire in her eyes.

■ □ ■

The blood between the keys had turned an ugly, muddy brown. I didn't want to touch it. I wasn't even certain why I was there, bending over the terminal, just staring at the dried blood. I guess I felt it held the secret to what had happened to him. I stood in a storage area near the computer room where engineering was keeping the terminal until field maintenance could pick it up. I could see scratches on the keyboard where the police had scraped off blood to take for laboratory testing. There was still the dark grimy residue from the fingerprint powder.

What was it that Gershbein had wanted to talk about the day before? The question gnawed at me. Perhaps Max was right and it had only been a minor business issue. Otherwise, why did he wait until he was practically out the door before bringing it up? Because it was so minor he had forgotten about it, or because it was something he was struggling with and he had to build up his nerve before mentioning it? And I had cut him off because, as usual, I was racing off to my next meeting. I wondered how many of life's important moments I missed because I was too busy to take the time to listen and take notice.

After leaving Dorothy Gershbein I had endured a lecture from Max about keeping my nose out of murder investigations and letting the police do their job. I thanked her for sharing then had her drop me back at the office. I wanted to look at the security software that Gershbein had taken home with him. It was a blatant security violation that he could have been fired for. Why would he have done it? I looked over the program, but everything seemed okay. I should know. I had written it myself four years earlier.

It struck me that if Gershbein had been signed on to

the terminal the night he was killed, then the audit log would show the exact time of night he had accessed the computer system. I sat down at a terminal in the computer room, entered my i.d. and password, and brought up the audit log. Scrolling through the listing, I found what I needed. The log showed that Gershbein had signed on to Larry at 10:05 and signed off at 10:23 P.M. He must have died only a few moments later. Next I looked for Joshua's log-on i.d. It showed him logged on to a terminal in the east wing, far from Gershbein, from 9:15 until 11:20. It also showed that he had entered a large number of transactions.

I made a mental note to call the police the next day to tell them what I had discovered. It might get Joshua off the hook and help establish a more precise time of death for Gershbein.

At nine-thirty I got in my car and drove the fifteen minutes down Highway 101 to my home. I put my car in the garage, fumbled with my house keys, and let myself in through the kitchen door. As I walked through the dark kitchen, the sound of my footsteps on the tile echoed, magnifying the unwelcoming emptiness of the house. It was at times like these I wished I had a cat. I turned on the lights in the living room, illuminating the bare white walls and nondescript furniture that was the bland result of some hasty shopping at Macy's. Everything in the room blended together in various shades of an uninspiring beige, giving the whole place the warmth and ambiance of a very sanitary public rest room. But I, like the Gershbeins, had no time for interior decorating. I was seldom at home anyway. Sometimes those bland rooms looked to me a little like my life, everything in neutral hues, with few splashes of brightness of color, but I usually managed to push those thoughts out of my mind. You want some excitement and color in your life, Julie? I asked myself. Well, you got it today. Murder wasn't my idea of a nice break in routine.

I didn't approve of feeling sorry for myself. My life was, after all, an enviable one. I had worked hard in high school, hard in college, hard in grad school, and hard at my job so

I could move steadily upward in my career. It had paid off. I had the job I had always wanted. The *Chronicle* had even included me in an article about young superachievers in Silicon Valley. I had achievements, respect, a bright future. I had Charles.

The superachiever sighed with fatigue and dropped her purse, coat, and briefcase on the couch and went to the kitchen. A rumbling in my stomach reminded me that I had forgotten dinner. I opened the refrigerator, its white light cutting through the darkness, and I searched for something edible. Inside sat a bit of wilted lettuce, a candy bar, and some Chinese takeout growing an interesting green, fuzzy mold. I checked the lid of a carton of vanilla yogurt. The expiration date was two days before, but how can you tell when yogurt goes bad? I took a spoon out of a drawer, leaned against a cupboard, and ate the yogurt while standing up. To cap off my meal I poured a small glass of iced white wine. Sipping the cold liquid, I savored its relaxing effects and I felt better. Still, better wasn't good enough. I felt drained and exhausted and my anxiety level was as high as the ozone layer. I knew from experience that in this state I wouldn't get to sleep for hours, and with all the pressure I was under I needed a good night's rest. Music. That would do it. Something to get my mind off my troubles.

I popped a CD into the stereo and the voice of Frank Sinatra filled the living room. Old songs were my favorite and had been since I was a teenager. When my friends were listening to The Grateful Dead, I was dreamily immersed in Mel Tormé and Nat King Cole. With one hand around my wineglass and the other pressed daintily against my chest, I began to dance around the couch. During graduate school I had taken an Arthur Murray course with a girlfriend. We had done it as a joke, and it was a way of ensuring we got out of the university computer room at least one night a week. Most of the dance steps I had forgotten, but one of the instructors had been a little German man with shiny blue eyes and a thick accent. I could still hear his "one, two, chay, chay, chay" ringing in my ears. I cha-chaed with my unsuspecting television, a well-heeled armchair, and a floor lamp with substantial savoir faire. After I danced with most of the living-room furniture, I poured myself more wine, moved into the bathroom, and stripped off my clothes to Sinatra's rendition of "One More for My Baby." I drew a hot bath filled with fragrant bubbles from some bath potion Max had given me for my last birthday and, like plunging back into the womb, dropped my body blissfully into the water. The foaming, perfumed bubbles enveloped me up to my neck and the feeling of relaxation combined with the wine made me feel light-headed. My nightly bath was one of the few times I had during the day to be alone and unhurried. As I closed my eyes to savor the delicious feeling, the phone rang.

I jumped, then smiled. It had to be Charles. Always thinking ahead, I had brought my cellular phone into the bathroom in case he called. Picking up the receiver, I felt very Doris Day, sitting in a bubble-filled tub about to speak to my lover on the phone. I put some bubbles on my nose.

"Hello," I purred into the receiver.

"Julie, it's Brad. Sorry to bother you so late, but I tried to call you earlier and you were out."

All the Doris Day drained right out of me. Brad Elkin wouldn't be calling me this late if it wasn't urgent, and I felt awkward talking to my boss while I was nude.

"Julie, we're having an emergency meeting of everyone on the project tomorrow at nine. I know this is short notice, but please bring all your system security records for the last sixty days."

"What's going on, Brad? Does this have to do with Gershbein?" I could tell something was wrong. Very wrong. In the five years I had headed Project 6 I had never been asked for the security records, the listings of who accessed Larry and what files they had gone into.

"No, Julie. We've got another problem on our hands, but I can't go into it on the phone. I know that's not a very good explanation, but security is tight on this thing. Everything will be explained tomorrow. I'm really sorry for calling you so late, but you understand?"

"No, I don't."

"We'll talk tomorrow."

"Wait a minute," I said to him but he had already hung up. He had sounded so distant. My stomach suddenly felt like molten lava and I remembered with annoyance that I was out of Maalox. I got out of the tub and dried off.

Elkin had been relatively calm that day about Gershbein's death. Now he was suddenly rattled enough to call me at home to schedule an emergency meeting. Something bad had happened.

But what could be worse than murder?

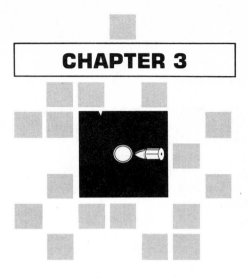

CHAPTER 3

Silicon Valley, like the tiny chip for which it was named, is in appearance a small, uninspiring, unremarkable place. Its land is flat, its buildings low and unimaginative as if its architects had played with too many toy blocks as children, their creative vision stunted by the unrelenting intrusion of square, boxlike designs. But like the silicon chip, its appearance belies its power, for within its parameters ideas are born and technology is nurtured that has revolutionized the world.

It wasn't the power of the technology itself that fascinated me as much as the power of the minds behind it. It drew me there and held me its willing captive. I wanted to know it, to be a part of it, to affect it with the force with which it had affected me. There had never before been a morning that I didn't look forward to the day's work, but that particular morning as I drove to ICI my eagerness was mixed with a feeling of dread that the feces were about to hit the corporate fan.

My father, a lieutenant colonel in the air force, died when I was six. I have no concrete images of him in my mind, my memories vague and wistful, like recollections of a dream. But when I find myself in a bad spot I sometimes like to imagine what stalwart advice my father would have given me and all the things he would have said to bolster my spirits. As I exited the freeway that morning at dawn, I imagined him telling me, "Julie, you're brighter and more capable than all of them. You can handle anything. Now go out there and kick some ass." It made me feel better.

Elkin set the meeting for nine, but by eight forty-five the executive briefing room was swimming with white-shirted employees wearing anxious, expectant faces. Everyone knew something was up. I had gotten out of bed at five that morning and hustled to the office by six in order to put together the security access files Elkin had requested. They now sat in the file I clutched under my arm. Having not slept much the previous night, I entered the briefing room feeling tired and haggard, certain I looked even worse.

As with all ICI meeting rooms, the executive briefing room was outlined in a muted blend of corporate grays with no vivid colors that could distract one from whatever business was to be discussed. The lighting was indirect, drifting down from the ceiling in a soft glimmer, giving the room a dreamlike quality in sharp contrast to the glaring fluorescent brightness of the rest of the building. Fifty chairs, each ergonomically designed to keep its users comfortable but alert, were lined up in perfect rows facing a podium that stood in the front of the room. On the wall above the podium hung a photograph of ICI's founding father, Harold T. Gordon, with the company's motto, "Opportunity for Individuals," carved on a brass plaque beneath the frame.

As soon as I walked in I searched the room for Elkin

or Garrett. I was going to ask them what was going on, but neither man had arrived. If they followed their usual tactics they would saunter in at the last minute to avoid a barrage of questions.

I noted with dismay the absence of coffee and doughnuts, always a sign that a meeting was called to announce something unpleasant. In the back corner Max stood talking animatedly with a systems engineer who gazed at her like a dog might gaze at filet mignon. Interesting, I thought, that Comtech personnel were invited to the meeting. I waited impatiently until I caught Max's eye, then motioned to her. Max nodded in response, ended her conversation, and glided over. She wore a soft gray skirt, the kind that swirled and floated when she walked, and a pale-pink silk blouse with an embroidered front and padded shoulders. It was a studied divergence from the style of most of the professional women I knew. We all wore tailored, dark suits with the standard bows at the throat, the conventional sensible shoes. Women were still the minority at the top of the industry, and once we had made it we always tried too desperately to look as if we belonged. Max had her own style.

"So whose head will roll this morning?" Max asked.

I struggled to smile. "I just hope it's not mine." Neither of us laughed. I grabbed Max's arm and steered her away from the others. "Okay, tell me. Do you know what's up?"

"Only that it's something big. It's all hush-hush, which always means something bad has happened." She saw the look on my face. "But I'm sure it has nothing to do with you. You're the fast tracker, remember? You can do no wrong."

I tried not to show my disappointment. Confidentiality was not as strict at Comtech as at ICI, and Max often knew the inside gossip before I did. But I would know soon enough.

All conversation softened as Brad Elkin walked into the room, followed by John Garrett, the ICI director who reported directly to the chairman of the board. The room's chatter had turned to a respectful quiet not because of Garrett's presence, because they were all used to seeing top brass due to the importance of Project 6. It was Elkin who caught everyone's attention. Tall, broad-shouldered, with a head of thick silver hair and crisp blue eyes, he had a powerful presence and an electricity that crackled in a crowded room. He and Garrett stopped near the front to greet an engineer. They didn't even look at me as they walked by and I sensed they were avoiding me. Having never been the type to wait for an invitation, I walked up to them.

"Brad, I need to talk to you," I said, interrupting their conversation.

Garrett seemed peeved, but Elkin smiled at me. He looked tired.

"Good morning, Julie," he said. "I can't talk to you now, but I'll see you after the meeting."

"I think we need to talk now."

Garrett shot me a venomous look. "It's time to start. Let's go," he said, and the two men moved toward the podium, leaving me standing there feeling confused and foolish.

Yes, I was a fast tracker, and at ICI fast trackers were looked upon with a certain amount of awe, even from those higher on the corporate ladder. But I had been around long enough to know that I would hold my position only as long as I was a consistent winner. At my job level ICI had no patience for losing, and it took only one mistake to ruin a career.

People began moving to their seats, so I took a chair next to Max near the back of the room, holding my notebook and my file in my lap. I was a born notetaker and carried my trusty five-subject college notebook everywhere. It was a joke in the office about whether I carried it with me to the ladies' room. I didn't.

Elkin stood at the podium and Garrett sat in the first row. When Elkin cleared his throat the room became quiet. That impressed me. I wondered if you could learn it through practice.

"Before we begin today, I want to take a moment and express the grief we all share over the tragic loss of our co-worker, Ronald Gershbein. If together we could take a moment of silence to commemorate in a small way the passing of our friend," said Elkin. The room fell silent, heads bowed.

Then the rear door flew open with a loud *whack* as it rebounded against the opposite wall. All heads turned.

"Okay, I'm late. I couldn't help it," the newcomer said. I watched the typical entrance of Wayne Hanson, the twenty-eight-year-old entrepreneur, Harvard dropout genius who had founded Comtech four years earlier. During the past few years a hyperactive nervous system and a world-record sugar addiction had to have killed off a few million of his brain cells, but luckily for ICI, Hanson still had plenty to spare. Wearing ragged sandals, stained khaki pants, and a torn V-neck sweater pulled haphazardly over a shirt and tie, Hanson looked better dressed than usual as he burst through the room like water from a firehose.

"Superboy has arrived," Max whispered. Hanson leaped to the front of the room, noisily knocking over an empty chair, then he plopped down next to Garrett. He pulled a somewhat flattened Hostess Twinkie from his shirt pocket and began to gobble it, unconcerned with the crumbs that sprinkled like fairy dust on Garrett's Brooks Brothers suit. Garrett looked at Hanson as if he were something dead he had found in the basement, but he knew Hanson had to be tolerated because Hanson was the brainchild and inspiration behind Comtech. And ICI needed Comtech. Silicon Valley was like Hollywood in its heyday, filled with big money, new ideas, misused power, and young genius. It was in its way a glitzy industry, a high-stakes game where people made and lost fortunes overnight and you were only as good as your last product. Winning the game was everything, and Hanson was currently a very big winner. He could dribble all the Twinkie crumbs he wanted on John Garrett because Garrett yearned to be president of ICI, and he knew Hanson could help him get there. Garrett brushed the crumbs off his suit and shot Hanson a brittle smile. Elkin looked on calmly.

It was with two very different sets of eyes that Max and I watched Elkin from the rear of the room. I had always respected Elkin as a protégé respects her mentor. Since he had transferred me into Project 6 five years earlier, I knew there was something admirably different about him. He didn't play the corporate game like everyone else. He wore the cool, polite composure that ICI demanded of its top executives, but he was missing the subtle insecurities, that touch of humbled fear that most ICI executives shared. Elkin showed few vulnerabilities, and I studied him because I wanted to learn from him. It was the general assumption that Elkin would take Garrett's job as head of the research facility by year end when Garrett would be due for a new position. I was secretly betting that I would fill Elkin's job.

Max also kept a keen eye on Elkin, not because of his corporate integrity but because, as she described it, she had a most definite urge to spend about eight hours alone with him in a motel room.

The brief silence made briefer by Hanson's arrival, Elkin embarked upon the morning's business.

"I want to thank all of you for attending this meeting on such short notice," he began, knowing that it would have been grounds for dismissal if someone on the project had failed to show for the hastily called meeting. "I believe you all know that the Defense Department has a keen interest in the success of Project 6 and is watching us very closely. Naturally the confidentiality of our project has been of the utmost importance, and it was the government's trust in ICI that allowed us to continue with such a sensitive task."

Usually ICI execs loved it when the company waved the red, white, and blue, but I noticed Garrett shifting nervously in his seat. He looked agitated.

"The Defense Department informed us late yesterday that a security specialist from the National Security Agency is being sent here to investigate Project 6," Elkin announced. A nervous rumble swept across the room.

I felt the blood rush to my face. "Because of Gershbein's murder?" I asked too loudly. Everyone looked at me and I felt Max's hand on my arm.

Garrett turned and gave me another one of his infamous looks, but I met his eyes and we had a short staring match. I won. The word "murder" was much too vulgar a term to be spoken within the hallowed halls of ICI. I guess I should have phrased it as Gershbein's "passing into the great beyond" or his "untimely demise."

"There are two reasons the NSA is concerned about the project. One of those reasons is the death of one of our employees," Elkin responded. "The other reason is that they believe the preliminary structural designs for molecular memory have been leaked."

You could hear thirty-seven mouths drop open. As for me, I felt as if I had been kicked in the stomach. How could information have leaked? It was impossible. Multiple levels of security were employed in every area of the project, from the operating system within Larry down to the external security procedures used by the janitorial staff.

I saw a few heads turn once more toward me. Everyone knew that as head of the project I had responsibility for data security. I forced myself to look calm. I didn't want anyone to know that this was the first I had heard of the data leaks. Why hadn't Elkin told me beforehand? The fact that he and Garrett were letting me hear the news with everyone else was a breach of department precedent. Any problem like this should have been discussed with me in detail before it was announced to the staff. The procedure is outlined in the management manual, but apparently the manual had been tossed out in this case. Did they think there was a connection between Gershbein and these supposed data leaks? Then I remembered the security code that Dorothy Gershbein had given me the day before.

"Naturally we are in the process of implementing new security procedures beginning at the systems level," Elkin continued. "We will be conducting interviews with each of you on the project, going over all procedures in detail. Even the most minor security breaches will be noted. Please have all systems management logs, calendars, and other materials associated with the project available at these interviews. A representative from the NSA will be present at all of these. This is disturbing, I realize, and a troublesome break in the routine of the project, but these leaks are not only a threat to ICI confidentiality but a punishable federal offense. We will be distributing new magnetic badges and entry codes tomorrow. Let me say that we are all extremely pleased with the progress of Project 6 and that this is only a temporary setback. Things will be back to normal in no time. Thank you for your cooperation."

Typical, I thought, for Elkin to close the meeting with an upbeat note and a smiling flash of teeth. Everyone in the room sat dumbfounded for a few seconds before slowly filtering out.

Elkin walked over to Garrett, who gave him a tap on the back, and the two men walked toward the door. Before leaving, Elkin stopped in front of me.

"We need to meet."

"You bet we do," I told him.

"How about my office in ten minutes?" He looked at me with a pleasant smile.

"Sure," I replied, hoping the sweat on my face didn't show. "Nice girls don't sweat. They glow," my mother told me when I was a kid. Wrong, Mom. Nice girls *do* sweat. You even sweat blood sometimes when the pressure is on and everything you worked for hangs by a thread. Mom had imparted her street savvy to me for all of life's events that she deemed critical, which included husband handling, hiding figure flaws, and accessorizing with scarves. Unfortunately this wisdom had left me bereft of information with which to face my particular daily realities, and I found myself facing each new problem with only my wits to assist me. But the caliber of this crisis would tap resources I never knew I had. I was trying to think of what my father would have said to me in this situation when a hand grabbed my shoulder.

"Fix this problem and fix it quick," blurted Wayne Hanson, waving his Twinkie-crumbed hands threateningly in my face. I braced myself. ICI employees followed the unspoken rule of never expressing criticism openly, preferring to berate each other behind each other's backs. Comtech people had the luxury of complete self-expression.

"Are you hearing me, Julie?"

"Not now, Wayne," I said. Wayne's small nose and mouth were twisted in anger. His forehead furrowed, his red hair stood up comically, and I thought he looked like a pissed-off Pomeranian.

"Don't screw with me. I've got two hundred thousand shares of Comtech stock going public in thirty days and this security foul-up could ruin everything. It's your responsibility, Julie," he snarled. "It's your—"

Max grabbed Hanson by the arm, and his mouth slammed shut.

"Sweetheart, we need to chat. Now," she told him. "Can you spare him, Julie?"

Max dragged him into the hall. He looked angry and befuddled, but he followed obediently. I owed her one.

I took a breath, walked outside the conference room, and saw Charles leaning against a wall, waiting for me. Since Charles's department wasn't directly involved with Project 6, he had not been invited to the meeting, but I could tell by his face that he had already heard the news. Holding my arm, he led me into an empty meeting room then shut the door behind us. I looked at the wall, my body numb, but my brain already sifting through events to determine how and why the project had gone wrong and if Gershbein could have played a part in it. The unthinkable had happened. Naturally security leaks were always a possibility when working on new technology in a company as large as ICI. But Project 6 was different. It had to be different. Security and backup had been put in place at every level. Could anyone have tapped into Larry? Only a handful of people had access to Larry, and fewer had access to the really sensitive data within him. There were layers of passwords that were changed monthly. To break in seemed impossible.

"Julie, listen to me." Charles's voice brought back my attention. "You'll get through this. Elkin's ass is on the line and he might try to make you a scapegoat. He might. But you can work with him, play ball with him on this thing, and you'll come through intact. If he makes you look bad then it hurts him too. He was the one who hired you for this project, the one who's been singing your praises these past few years. Not to mention that he's close to getting promoted to Garrett's job. He's not going to make it look like his judgment is that bad if he can help it. That's your ace."

I took a deep breath. "But where did the leak come from?" I asked, knowing he couldn't answer. What I did know was that I couldn't stop until I found out.

■ □ ■

I marched down the hall and up the stairs to Elkin's office. The door was closed. I took a moment to prepare myself for the worst, then I knocked.

"Come in." Elkin's voice sounded light and friendly. I stepped in and, upon finding him alone, shut the door with just enough force to let him know I wasn't feeling humble.

"Why wasn't I told about the data leaks before this morning?"

Elkin didn't look surprised by my directness. He knew I would never walk in like a dog with my tail between my legs. He had taught me better than that. "Security reasons, Julie."

"Security like hell, Brad. I'm head of this project. It's my responsibility and it's my right to know what's going on. And why is the NSA involved? We're already going to have the FBI breathing down our necks. What is the NSA's interest in this?"

"The molecular memory designs were leaked to the Soviet Union."

His last statement jolted me. It took every ounce of my self-control to keep my voice steady. "And you're just telling me all this now?"

Elkin motioned for me to sit, but I remained standing.

He paused, pressing his hands together in front of him, and I knew he was carefully choosing his words. I searched his face to try to gauge what he was thinking, but it betrayed nothing. It never did. It crossed my mind that he would have been a pretty good poker player if he had been the type to go in for games.

"I'm sorry you feel like your power has been taken away in this situation, Julie, but you've got to understand that things here are a little more important than corporate protocol," he said. "I don't need to tell you that people are looking at this project with a very watchful eye. They're upset about these leaks, and that's on top of what happened to Gershbein. And we're not just talking about ICI execs. As I mentioned in the meeting, the NSA is very interested. If the Soviets have gotten our molecular memory architecture at this point, it's possible that they can get the whole thing. That's about all I can say right now. But you have to understand the seriousness of this."

"I understand the seriousness."

"I'm not sure you do. Do you realize that with everything that has happened there's a good chance headquarters is going to close down the project?"

"And waste five years of work?"

"Don't be naive. There's a man dead and a government security leak here. I've been in disasters before. Nothing ever like this, but I have enough experience to predict that soon everyone is going to start pointing fingers at everybody else. No one is going to want to take the blame, especially not top management. The easiest way for everyone to save his ass is to close the project down and pretend it never happened."

The situation seemed to be deteriorating with each moment that passed. My legs got that rubbery feeling again so I sat down in a chair. Headquarters closing down the project was something I couldn't imagine. What I felt at that moment must be what it feels like to have your husband suddenly say he's leaving you. Without warning someone tells you he's taking the biggest part of your life away. My heart pumped, my body tensed, and my mind raced with ways I could save the situation. I had to keep the project going, at least temporarily, until I could fix things.

"Have you heard anything definite yet from headquarters?" I asked, my voice remaining firm although my insides had turned to Cool Whip.

"Not yet, but it's inevitable. It's a matter of time."

"We have to keep that from happening, Brad. We're so close to completion. We're only weeks away."

"Julie, we've got a security leak here. What do you want me to do?"

I leaned forward in my chair and put my hands on the edge of his desk. It was a subtle form of aggression I had learned from a book on negotiating. "You can stall them. Give me two weeks. I can fix the data leak problem."

"Julie, we've got the FBI and the NSA already working on that." He leaned back in his chair as if to evade me. He must have read the same book. "You know there's a project starting up in the Poughkeepsie plant. It's a new disk drive prototype. I'm sure they would be glad to have you working on it."

Anger swelled inside me, but I managed to keep it at a controlled boil. I wasn't about to get sent off to Poughkeepsie like a kid being shipped off to prep school, and I didn't want Elkin's or anyone else's patronizing. I was stronger and more capable than all of them, and if I wasn't, I could fake it.

"Listen to me, Brad. I understand our computer and our software inside and out. And there's no one, including the FBI and the NSA, who can solve this data leak problem faster than I can."

"You may not believe this, Julie, but I'm thinking of you. Project 6 is turning into a disaster area. Once you're through the NSA questioning I can transfer you out of here and maybe save your career."

"If you want to save my career you can leave me right here where I've put in twelve hours a day for the past five years. Just give me some time. Then you can transfer me to Poughkeepsie, Boise, or Beirut if you want."

Elkin sighed. My radar said he was softening. I made my final play.

"Respect me enough to let me make this decision for myself. Two weeks, Brad. All I'm asking for is to keep the project going for two more weeks. I'll find the leak, I'll plug it, and Project 6 can continue."

Elkin thought a moment. "I'd have to go to Garrett for approval, and he'll be against it."

"You can handle Garrett."

Elkin looked away from me. I thought perhaps I had lost.

"Okay, Julie. I think I can manage two weeks. But handle things quietly. And don't pull me into it. I'm having a few career problems of my own as a result of this. I don't need any more."

I exhaled with relief. "Thanks, Brad. You won't be sorry."

"I'm already sorry," he said, but he smiled at me.

"Tell me one thing more, Brad. Why didn't you tell me about the data leaks before this morning?"

"The NSA specialist told Garrett and me that no one should know until the general announcement was made."

"Where is this NSA person now?"

"In the next office waiting to talk to you."

"I don't even get a chance to catch my breath, do I?"

"I'm sure he planned it that way. It's time for you to go in. His name is Vic Paoli. I don't have him figured out yet, but we have to cooperate with him completely. Do you have your files?"

I held out the stack of papers in my hand.

"Good. Then let's go."

We both got up from our chairs and walked out into the hallway.

Elkin stopped before opening the office door. "You know that I always support you one hundred percent, don't you?"

I prayed I could believe him.

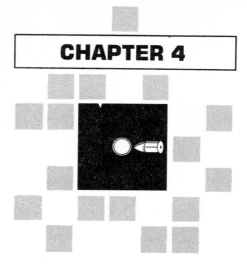

CHAPTER 4

I like men. In fact, I like them a lot. I like the way they look and sound and feel. I really like the way they smell, especially on their necks, that little part somewhere between their Adam's apple and the nape of their hair, the spot where they splash cologne after they've showered. When Elkin opened the door for me and I walked into the office, I smelled a wonderful male aroma of musk and spice mingled with just a hint of mothballs. But before I had the chance to explore it, there was a solid clicking sound behind me. I spun around to find myself facing a closed door, leaving me on the inside and Elkin safely out in the hall.

"Could you run down and get me some coffee? I could really use it," a cheerful voice said. I wondered why everybody was in a good mood but me. I turned around and faced the possessor of the aroma. He looked in his mid-thirties and he sat sprawled lazily in a chair with his feet propped on the desk. The smell of mothballs came from a suit that looked like it had been wadded up in the back of his closet since high school. I noticed the holes in the soles of his Weejuns and his socks that had "Celtics" written on the sides. He smiled and his whole face flashed like somebody had turned on his headlights.

"I don't bring coffee," I told him.

"I figured that. Too bad. Well, I told Elkin not to bother with introductions. You know who I am and I know who you are, so I thought it best we got right down to biz."

"You're Vic Paoli?" I asked, just for something to say. I was in a lousy frame of mind and not interested in cute conversation.

"Bingo. And you're Juliet Blake. See, all that graduate school wasn't for nothing. Have a seat, Julie." He gestured toward a chair with a sweep of his hand, then laughed, making his blue eyes crinkle up at the corners. He was a husky man with curly brown hair that was rumpled from him running his fingers through it. He had a thick neck, broad shoulders, and a slight strain in his shirt fabric that indicated a muscular body, and all of this was crowned with a baby face that didn't quite fit with the rest. His body and his attitude was that of a hockey player and his face the face of a cherub on the label of a baby food jar. There was something about him I found revolting, yet I wanted to tell him about it while sitting on his lap. It increased my nervousness, which was already substantial.

I sat down on the edge of the chair and primly folded my hands in front of me. It took a few seconds, but I managed to manipulate my facial muscles into a chilly smile. I was already outlining in my mind the procedure we needed to work on the data leaks, but I wanted to feel him out first before I made suggestions on how he should do his job.

"What exactly is your objective here?" I asked in my steadiest, don't-screw-with-me voice.

Paoli leaned his chair back on two legs. "Oh, I'm just a hang-loose kinda guy. Thought I might like a trip to Silicon Valley and spend some time with you madcap, crazy corporate types. You're such a kick."

"I'm not in the mood for jokes," I said.

Paoli cocked a finger and shot a rubber band against the wall. "I suspected that as soon as you walked in the door. Still, I wouldn't feel right if I didn't advise you that I have a repertoire of jokes that could keep you in stitches. But I can guess by your face that you're not interested."

"You guessed correctly."

"Too bad. Okay, let's get serious." Paoli brought all four legs of his chair back to the floor, picked up a stack of files, and slapped them on the desk with a noise that made me wince. "I'm an information systems security analyst from the National Security Agency. My badge." He held up a badge with his photograph. "The picture's not the best. I've lost a little weight since then. Great diet. One day all I ate was hard-boiled eggs, the next day only bananas, then only ballpark wieners—"

"I'm not interested in your diet."

He wiggled a finger at me. "One of these days your metabolism will change and you will be. But I've digressed. I've been instructed to put the clamps on your little project and find out who, how, and why someone hacked their way into your computer."

I bristled at the word "hack." "You don't know that someone hacked their way into the computer."

"The data got out, Ms. Blake. How do you think the Soviets came up with identical copies of your molecular designs? A lucky guess?"

"They were identical?" Elkin hadn't told me that. I wondered why.

"The spittin' image. I'm all for *perestroika*, but still, we don't give out this kind of stuff for free."

"It still hasn't been proven that anyone broke into the system, and it's foolish to assume anything until we've analyzed all the data. I would think you would know that, Mr. Paoli."

He smiled again. I crossed and uncrossed my legs. "You have every right to be defensive. It said in this file that you wrote the security system yourself, and I'm sure you don't appreciate an outsider walking in here and taking charge of things."

"No, I don't. But I don't have a choice, do I?"

"None at all. You lucked out, actually. You'll be spending most of your time with me since I'm the technical specialist. A lot of the other folks in your department will be questioned by the FBI. They're real gorillas. No fun at all. Now me, I'm an easy guy to get along with. All I want to do is get inside your system and tinker with your machine, if you'll pardon the expression." He tittered as if he found himself very amusing. I did not find him so.

Another rubber band shot off his finger and bounced off my chest. I looked down at the spot where it had ricocheted, then gave Paoli a frigid stare. "Forgive me for saying so, because I haven't worked with the NSA before, but your demeanor isn't exactly what I expected. Are you part of some experimental program?"

If he noticed the insult, he didn't show it. "I'm not really an actual field agent, you see. I'm a technical specialist so I spend almost all my time in government computer rooms. They don't let me out much."

"I can't fathom why."

"So how about a tour of your computer room?" he asked.

"I have a few questions I'd like to ask you first."

"So ask."

"How did the Defense Department find out that the Soviets had the molecular memory designs?"

"The CIA told us. They have ways of finding out these things. They're sneaky bastards."

"And are we working on the assumption that the Soviets stole the designs directly, or that they're buying them from someone else?"

"For starters we're assuming they're buying the data from someone inside your company. If your security system is any good at all, it would be difficult for someone outside the company to steal your data."

"But you're assuming it's not impossible?" I asked him.

"Few things are impossible. No computer system is impregnable, but the Soviets would never risk doing the dirty work themselves. They pay to have it done."

"If we assume it's an inside person stealing the data, it could be someone from Comtech who was working on Project 6, couldn't it? It doesn't have to be an ICI employee."

"Theoretically, sure," said Paoli. "Now how about that computer room tour?"

I glanced at my watch. "Do I have a choice?"

"None whatsoever." He grinned at me as he stood up.

I looked at him and knew that he was going to be a pain in the ass. I was used to working with men who took one look at me, sized me up as a repressed female executive, then decided they could feel superior to me. I enjoyed showing them how badly they erred.

He grabbed his file, I grabbed my notebook, then he followed me down the hall, up the stairs, and around the corner to the computer room. The closer he got the better he smelled and I tried to keep a distance between him and my olfactory glands. Engaged women shouldn't be smelling other men, I told myself. My nose was promised to another. Besides, this guy was more than a little of a jerk, regardless of his aroma. I wondered if there was any way I could rub garlic all over him when he wasn't looking, or maybe I could catch a cold. I pressed my password into the keypad and Paoli followed me in.

"That's a security weakness right there," he said as we walked through the door.

"What are you talking about?"

"The door. I was able to tailgate right in behind you."

"How can anybody prevent that?"

"Easy. An automatic revolving door. It lets only one person through at a time. It's quite effective. I'm surprised you don't have one. After all, I thought you were state of the art here in Silicon Valley."

I did by best to give him a patronizing smile, then when he wasn't looking I jotted a reminder in my notebook to check out revolving doors.

When we first entered the computer room conversation stopped and all eyes turned on Paoli. We weren't used to strangers in the computer area, and the rumor had apparently spread regarding who Paoli was and why he was there. He seemed oblivious to the attention.

Huddled in front of a terminal sat Alan and Joshua. They stared at Paoli as if he were the Gestapo. Somebody, probably Alan, had taken the long yellow strips that said "Police Line—Do Not Cross" and had draped them over the terminal like Christmas decorations. Joshua looked pale, his eyes red and his shoulders sagging. I watched him slowly rise from his chair, brush nonexistent lint off his clothes, then walk over to me.

"I've been framed," he blurted. "The police kept me there yesterday almost two hours. I'm not going to spend the rest of my life in San Quentin. I didn't kill Gershbein. I told the police that, but did they care? You've got to talk to them. Tell then I'm not a killer. I don't eat red meat. I don't even eat chicken. Maybe I'll do fish occasionally, but only—"

"Joshua, you can stop," I said. With all the turmoil over the data leaks I had forgotten to call the police and try to clear Joshua. "It's okay. I logged on to the security audit log last night and it shows you were using the terminal in the east wing until eleven-twenty. When I show them all the work you did, it should prove that you wouldn't have had time to run over here, kill Gershbein, put him in the computer, and get back. It could clear you."

Joshua threw his arms high over his head and danced around me. "I'm free! Did you hear it, Alan? I'm free!"

Alan gave a grunt of disappointment then returned to his work.

Joshua dropped to his knees and clutched my legs. "Thank you, Julie. Thank you."

With a struggle I managed to unwrap Joshua from my

body. "No need to thank me, Josh. The police would have figured it out sooner or later." Probably later than sooner. "Now get back to work. Everything's going to be all right."

Josh gave my hand a quick wet kiss then pranced back to Alan. I tried to ignore Paoli's smirk.

"You guys have an interesting professional style around here," he said as he followed me across the room. "Kind of a cross between Lee Iacocca and Bambi."

"I'm in a hurry, remember? Let's get this over with."

"Not until you tell me how I can get more of the Bambi from you and less Lee Iacocca."

I stopped and turned toward him. He bumped into me. "You're going to see Conan the Barbarian if you're not careful, Mr. Paoli."

He chuckled. "I'll watch my step."

I led him over to the middle of the room where Larry sat, childishly ignorant of the fact that the NSA wished to paw through his most private parts.

"This is the ICI 9000," I said, patting Larry's metal casing. "Larry has three hundred million bytes of monolithic central storage, two independent dyadic processors, five gigabytes of addressable memory, and four sixty-five K high-speed buffers."

Paoli didn't look impressed. He crossed his arms and leaned against a disk drive. "Interesting, but what it doesn't have is intuition, judgment, or even the slightest sense of humor. It's just wires and electricity, Ms. Blake. That's all."

"These wires and electricity can process eighteen billion floating point instructions per second, Mr. Paoli."

"Yet comparing it to the brain of an infant would be like comparing 'Chopsticks' to a Chopin sonata. You people think these things are gods, and that's where you screw up." Paoli walked around Larry and eyed him as if he were sizing up an opponent. I looked at Paoli as if he were something a dog had left on a sidewalk.

"If you think so little of these machines, perhaps you should find another line of work. Something in used car sales might suit you."

Instead of being offended by my remark, he smiled at me.

"I'm interested in equipment. I just don't worship at the altar. Now why don't you explain to me what Project 6 is all about? I read the project brief from Washington, but I'd like some more background," he said, sitting down in a chair in front of the terminal. I stood a cautious five feet away, as if his vibrations alone could be damaging.

I never fared well with men of his breed. He reminded me of all the dirty-faced, slang-mouthed little boys I had known in grade school, the type who pulled my pony tail, threw mud on my dress, then tried to kiss me behind a tree.

"Okay," I began. "It's hard to describe it all."

"I'll try to keep up."

I sat down on the edge of a desk next to the chair where Paoli sat. I wanted to make sure he was looking up at me. I felt it gave me an advantage.

"The project really started about eight years ago when an ICI scientist, Hans Lauhmann, theorized that artificial intelligence could be created with DNA-like material," I recited like a schoolteacher. "I assume you know what DNA is?" I asked with a smile. Talking about my project was loosening me up.

"It has something to do with where babies come from, doesn't it? But let's not drag this conversation down into the gutter. Please go on. I'm rapt."

"The theory suggested that the same combination of chemicals from which all life came could be used to build computer memory. The advantage is that it would reduce the size of one unit of memory to the size of a single molecule."

I looked at Paoli to see if he was impressed. At least I had his attention.

"It's like a recipe," I continued. "The problem is to find the right combination. The final algorithm has to provide a balance of the three elements. But once we get the right material, molecular memory will make the rest of computer technology seem primitive in comparison. And of course the financial payoff from the project could be significant."

"So how did the feds get so interested?"

"They funded a portion of the project because of the potential for national defense. They think miniaturizing artificial intelligence would eliminate the need for land-based strategic control centers and allow them to use satellite technology for control of defense weapons. Eventually every missile could contain the intelligence to control itself as well as other missiles."

"So you're saying all our weapons would be flying around in space, controlling themselves?" Paoli asked.

"Basically. The advantage would be that in a war, God forbid, U.S. defense couldn't be weakened by the destruction of land-based control centers. They'll all be up in space and every missile could be a control center in itself. It wouldn't be enough to destroy just one. You would have to shoot down all of them, and that would be hard to do. Our defense against nuclear war would be impregnable and therefore would eliminate anyone's desire to wage it, at least in theory."

Paoli leaned back in his chair and eyed me. "You know, you don't look like a person who would devote her life to helping out the military."

"I'm not. One of the reasons this project has survived the Defense Department cuts is its potential advantages for medicine. That's what really interests me and why I chose to work on the project. A cell-size computer could actually be placed in the human body. It could control the flow of insulin or transmit electrical pulses or chemicals to fight cancer cells or even AIDS. Of course, there will be lots of uses that can help save lives once the project is completed."

"Sounds nice," Paoli said. "But where is it? According to the brief I read, this project should be completed by now. It looks to me like you're still in the middle of it."

"You're not the first person to notice. The ICI Executive Committee is asking us the same question. Larry's job, even though he is merely wires and electricity, as you put it, is to sift through algorithms of carbon, hydrogen, and oxygen plus a few other substances to identify the combinations that we can test. Then we decide which is the right one. But we're not even to the testing stage yet."

"So what's gone wrong?"

"We're not sure, although we'll know soon. According to statisticians Larry should have come up with an initial subset by September thirtieth. That was three weeks ago. I'm still analyzing it. It's possible that it's just a statistical error."

"Or it's possible someone has your software siphoning off the algorithms before you can get at them," he said.

"You mean a computer virus?" I stiffened. "Viruses are the result of college pranks."

"Perhaps not this time."

I mulled over the virus idea for a moment. "But the security software is tested monthly. I do the tests myself."

Paoli's face twisted into a smirk. "Spare me the professional pride. Somebody has busted into this thing. I'm not thrilled about being stuck here for weeks, but then it's going to be fun turning this computer upside-down and shaking it like a piggy bank."

There was a devilishly smug look on him. He was trying to get to me and he had succeeded, because I could feel the blood rushing to my face. At that moment I would have paid top dollar for a bucket of horse manure.

I stood up and straightened myself into my full five foot three inches. "All right, Mr. Paoli. I'm anxious to get started on this. Give me an hour and I'll put together an outline of how we should proceed. I've already been thinking about it and—"

He held up his hand to interrupt me. "Whoa, lady. I don't need any of that. This stuff is my specialty. Naturally I'll need some cooperation from you, but I have my own procedure, and I work mostly on my own."

His rebuff surprised me. Because I was the project manager, I had assumed that I would be working directly in the security leak investigation. The idea of Paoli rummaging uncontrolled through my department chafed me like sand in my pantyhose.

"I have to know exactly what you'll be doing," I said more loudly than I should have. "I'm still the manager of this project."

A few people in the computer room were staring at us and wondering why I was so excited. Paoli stood up, grabbed my arm, and pulled me behind Larry.

"Calm down, for chrissakes. The last thing I need is you getting everybody upset. I'm an open book. I'll let you in on everything I'm doing. I'm a computer specialist, not a secret agent. Look, I have an outline here of the procedure I'll be using for the next few weeks. Nothing fancy. All standard stuff to be done strictly by NSA guidelines. This should tell you everything." He took a paper out of the file he carried and handed it to me.

I took it and skimmed it. "This looks okay, but you're missing a few things."

Now he did look offended. He pulled the paper from my hands. "I doubt it. What am I missing?" He looked back at the paper and studied it.

"For starters you need to look at the daily backup program before you do anything else. That would be a logical place to plant a bug in the program." I pointed to the first line item on the document. "And here it says you're going to analyze the security software. That will take days and it's a waste of time. Since I wrote the code you should leave that job to me. I can get through it faster and have a better chance of finding a problem in it."

Paoli gave me a funny look, then put the document back in its folder. "I don't need that type of assistance from you. What I do need is to ask you questions and have you answer them."

"Look, Paoli, I don't want to offend you, but that's dumb. Let's divide up some of the work so we can solve this faster," I said. After all, I only had two weeks. I couldn't wait for the NSA to get its act together.

"I can't let you get that involved," he told me.

"And why not?"

"You're a suspect."

"Me?"

"Don't look so shocked. You wrote the security code that was broken into. You're the perfect suspect."

A sudden plunge into ice water would have been less chilling. It hadn't occurred to me until then. They suspected me. My anger of a few moments before turned into a sickening fear. Was this what everyone was thinking, that I had used my own security system to steal Project 6 data and sell it to the Soviets? That was why they hadn't told me about the leaks until today, and Elkin just didn't want to tell me. Without knowing it, I had covered my mouth with my hand, and I guess I looked on the verge of illness or tears or worse because Paoli suddenly looked concerned.

"Now look, they're not ready to lead you away in handcuffs or anything. But you have to admit that you have the knowledge and the motive."

"I admit I have the knowledge, but what is my motive?"

"Get real, Ms. Blake. I don't know what they pay you here, but I'm sure it's a paltry sum compared to what the Soviets would pay you for Project 6 information."

I sank into a chair and looked up at Paoli. "I'm assuming you won't believe me, but I'm not selling anything to anybody."

"Then you can relax."

"But how do I get cleared? I can't have this suspicion hanging over my head, and the situation is so technical there are very few people who could even begin to understand it."

"Bingo. That's why I'm here. The FBI didn't have anyone with the right background and since the Soviets are involved, the NSA is sharing jurisdiction. They sent me to do the technical work. Believe me, I'm good. I guess you'd have to say your fate rests in my hands."

I could think of nothing more disheartening. "Believe me, Mr. Paoli, you may be good, but I'm better. And I'm not about to leave my career and my reputation in the hands of someone who has 'Celtics' written on his socks."

Then I walked out the door. More than just the aroma in the room had turned sour.

■ □ ■

"Password Not Recognized," the screen warned me.

I took off my glasses, squeezed my eyes shut, and opened them again. For two hours I had been staring at the terminal screen, and all the words were starting to look fuzzy around the edges. The stack of personnel files on my desk lay in disarray and it would take twenty minutes just to get them back in order. I was supposed to meet Charles at my house at eight-thirty, only forty-five minutes away. Knowing I was working more hours than usual, Charles had insisted on bringing over dinner. Maybe I could make the date if I hurried.

Perhaps Paoli had time to go through my security software starting from scratch, but I didn't. I had two weeks to solve the data leaks and I couldn't wait for Paoli to plod through his standard procedure. I guess it made sense that I was a prime suspect, and I couldn't blame him for examining the possibility of my involvement. But I had control over so many pieces of Project 6, it would take him weeks of precious time to sort it all out. I had the benefit of knowing I was innocent and could focus my attention on more promising aspects of the investigation. For starters I had gone through the personnel files of everyone who had access to Larry's operating system. Sifting through the documents, I had tried each person's birthday, middle names, spouse's name, mother's maiden name, mother's birthday—any word or number that someone could have used as a trapdoor password. I was working on the premise that for their private password people almost always use a word or number that means something to them. Not only does it make the password easier to remember, it also creates your own secret that nobody else knows. Going through the personnel files looking for that secret made me feel as if I were pawing through their underwear drawers, and it made me uncomfortable. But although I didn't like to admit it, any person working for me who had access to Larry's operating system could have programmed a trapdoor into the confidential files. With Larry it would have been much more difficult than with a normal mainframe computer, but it was still a possibility. I had even programmed my own trapdoor into Larry when I wrote the original security software. I had done it then for testing purposes. But at that time it had been easy since the security software wasn't complete. It would have been many times more difficult once Larry was in production. Still, it was the logical starting point.

I typed in the word "Violetta," Joshua's mother's middle name. Nothing. His father's first name was Wilbur. Nobody would use Wilbur. I tried it. Nothing.

I tried the word "hungry," but Larry just spit it back at me. I was starving.

Next I typed in "Who is stealing your data?" just to see if I could speed up some of the process, but Larry only responded with "Syntax Unrecognized. Please refer to Manual No. F305-G."

"You've got to help me, Larry," I said out loud, but he answered only with his droning machine hum, like a meditation mantra, as if he were telling me to look within for the answer.

■ ◻ ■

At ten-thirty that evening Charles and I lay snuggled in my bed, him in his Ralph Lauren pajamas and me in a long T-shirt. Usually by that time things were starting to get amorous, but that night we were too busy looking over my original flowcharts for Larry's internal security system. The flowcharts were nothing more than diagrams of how data flowed through the various levels of security, a general picture of how the system was designed to work. I thought looking at them would trigger some ideas.

During dinner I had already sifted through them to get a handle on where data could have been stolen, but I had come up with a big zero. To me the system looked well planned and impregnable, the way I had designed it four years ago.

The flowcharts were general enough not to be classified project confidential, so I asked Charles to look at them with me to get his impressions, but he seemed more interested in Vic Paoli.

"So what did the CIA agent say to you?" he asked, after perusing the flowchart for only a moment.

"He's not anything as glamorous as a CIA agent. He's just a security specialist, and an obnoxious one. But he must be good at what he does. Elkin told me that Paoli uncovered thirty-eight separate ways of hacking into computers at the Pentagon."

"That's impressive," said Charles.

"His record is impressive. He isn't. He didn't say too much except that he wants me to cooperate with his investigation."

I stopped there, thinking I shouldn't fill in too many details of my conversation with Paoli. Although Charles had some peripheral dealings with my project, I didn't want to divulge details of my disastrous meeting with Paoli, partially for security reasons and partially because the whole exchange was embarrassing. I had lost my cool with Paoli.

Charles sensed my discomfort. He could sense most things about me.

"Forget about it until morning, sweetheart. You know when you get too wrapped up in something you have trouble sleeping," Charles said as he rubbed the back of my neck. The flowchart slid off the bed as if trying to escape.

"Take a look at this piece of the flowchart," I said, reaching over to pick it up. Charles frowned. "Larry doesn't have communication capabilities. Can you think of any way someone could have broken in remotely?"

With a sigh, Charles gave the flowchart a look. "No, those parts are completely deactivated, and I don't see from looking at this how anyone could have circumvented it," he said, then turned to give my neck a nibble. "Can't we call it a night, Julie? It's almost eleven and I have an early meeting tomorrow."

I hesitantly agreed, put the flowchart back in my brief-case, then switched off the light. Charles rolled over toward me and kissed me lightly.

"You want me to be on top tonight?" he whispered.

"Whatever you want," I said, still thinking about the flowchart.

"Are you sure, sweetheart?"

"I'm sure."

"I was on top last time. It's your turn."

"No, really, it's okay."

Charles rolled over on top of me and I tried to concentrate on our lovemaking, but I was too distracted. I felt guilty about my diminished interest and forced myself to participate the same way I forced myself into an occasional aerobics class. (Okay now, Julie, let's flex those muscles, move those hands, pump those hips, and, whatever you do, don't forget to breathe!)

I closed my eyes and tried to focus on Charles, but my mind was filled only with images of flowcharts, security codes, and Vic Paoli.

■ ◻ ■

The next morning I crawled out of bed while Charles was still dozing, showered, dressed, downed my usual instant decaf coffee and granola bar, and drove to the Comtech offices. Hanson had several of his own programmers and engineers working on Project 6, and although none of them had direct access to Larry's confidential files, they had enough information to have assisted someone, perhaps inadvertently, in the data leaks. At least one of them might have noticed if anything unusual had been going on during the past weeks. I was sure that Paoli or the FBI would get around to interviewing them, but I figured Paoli was too busy combing through my security software to have done it yet. Perhaps the FBI already had. Even so, I doubted their ability to get much information out of them. Hanson's programmers were a different species from the rest of the planet, a mutation in our technological world I'm sure Darwin never imagined.

After signing the Comtech visitors' log book and displaying my ICI badge and driver's license, the receptionist phoned a secretary who then led me into the area that held the programmers' cubicles. They say that an entire company can be characterized by its top management. I reflected upon the accuracy of this theory when I approached Eldon Gannoway, one of Hanson's best programmers who had worked on Project 6. Obese and perpetually perspiring, Eldon was wearing a "No Nukes" T-shirt, plaid Bermuda shorts, black wool socks, and Birkenstock sandals. He sat in front of his terminal, rocking back and forth like an autistic child, typing in programming statements with a demonic intensity, strings of black hair slapping against his cheeks as his fingers hit the keys. I looked around Eldon's cubicle and saw the walls were covered with black-and-white photographs of old movie stars—Mitzi Gaynor, Doris Day, Tyrone Power.

"I'd like to talk to you, Eldon. Do you have a few minutes?"

He stopped typing, froze hunched over the keyboard a few seconds, then looked up at me. I could see that the earpieces of his black-framed glasses were attached to the front with twisted paper clips. On his chubby face he wore a slightly dazed expression as if he had just been receiving a telepathic alien transmission.

"Julie, I'm glad it's you. I need a break, and actually there's something important I really, really need to discuss with you. Sit down. This is vital."

I removed a stack of printouts from a chair and sat down. Eldon leaned closer to me, his face serious.

"You're the only person I feel comfortable discussing this with, because I think you can understand it," he said.

I could feel my pulse quicken. What could he know about the data leaks? "Please tell me about it, Eldon. This is what I'm here for."

"Somehow I knew that." Eldon looked around to make certain no one was listening. "It's like this. I've been doing some reading, and there's a possibility that the gravitational pull and angular momentum of rotating black holes can alter the time-space continuum. This would make time travel an actual possibility. I was wondering if you were familiar with Einstein-Rosen bridges."

My heart sank. "Sorry, Eldon, I'm not. The reason I'm here is to ask you some questions about the project."

"Oh. I'm meeting with the FBI guy this afternoon," he said in a brittle voice that expressed his annoyance at having the conversation turn to the everyday banalities of murder and espionage. "It's turned into a nasty business, hasn't it?"

"Yes, it has. Eldon, in the course of your work, did you ever make any programming changes that could have affected Larry's security software?"

Eldon looked over his glasses at me. "Are you accusing me of something?"

"Of course not. I just—"

"Because if you are," he interrupted, "I'm calling my attorney." He reached for the phone.

"There's no need for that. I just want to ask you questions about your programming."

I felt a fat hand squeeze my knee. "That was a bluff anyway," said Eldon. "I don't have an attorney. I do have some information you'll find interesting."

"What is it?"

"I think the Soviets are way ahead of us in exploring the time-space continuum. Let me explain."

I sighed. Eldon was the first of three of Hanson's programmers I wanted to talk to about the data leaks, and of the three, Eldon had his feet planted the most firmly on the ground. It was going to be a long and difficult day.

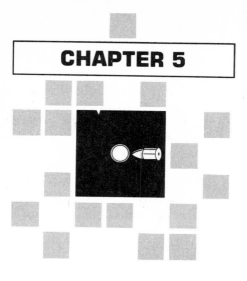

CHAPTER 5

I was in a nightclub once where they had a magician who went from table to table doing magic tricks, like making cigarettes disappear in a napkin and making the Queen of Spades rise from a deck of cards. I remembered the guy pulling little orange balls from out of nowhere and having them pop up in his hand, and we all laughed and applauded. That was how the FBI guy pulled out his badge, all in one fluid movement; it just appearing suddenly in his fingers as if he had pulled it out of his sleeve. I did not applaud.

"We just want to ask you a few questions," said Mr. Coleman of the FBI. He was a big man, probably in his early fifties, with heavy-lidded eyes, graying black hair, a fleshy face, and the type of spreading midriff peculiar to men who used to be athletes in college. Coleman slung around the pronoun "we" a lot although he was the only one in the room with me. Paoli was right, the FBI didn't seem to be a lot of fun. And after spending the first hour of the morning trying to communicate with Eldon and two of his coworkers I wasn't in the mood for another difficult conversation. I sank in my chair and thought of all the things I would rather be doing, like having a root canal. Coleman sat down behind a desk.

"Let me ask one thing first," I said, always preferring to take the offensive posture. "I've been questioned by the police, the NSA person, and now you. Who's in charge here? I'm just asking out of curiosity."

Coleman's eyes looked at me from under his three-pound eyelids. I looked back at him and thought that he was one of those people who I could never picture having sex.

"This is a cooperative investigation," he said. I wondered how cooperative he would be if he knew Paoli had referred to him as a gorilla. "We're involved because there has been government fraud. The NSA is involved because of the Soviet connection and because they have the computer specialist with the right background to investigate the computer leak."

"So why do you need the police?"

"They're handling the murder investigation. We don't normally handle murders. I haven't had a murder in my jurisdiction for over three years."

"At least things are picking up for you," I said. He didn't laugh at my joke.

"We're assisting the local police by conducting the interviews for which security clearance is required. That's why we're here today."

"So you're assuming that Gershbein's murder and the data leaks are connected?"

"We don't assume anything. We're trying to find out if there's a connection."

"Any leads yet?" I asked him, but he ignored my question.

"I have a few things I'd like to ask you, Ms. Blake."

"And I have a few things I'd like to ask you. First I'd like to know if once Vic Paoli goes through my security program and it comes up clean, which it will, will I still be a suspect?"

"I can't answer that."

"Because I can help you find the answer to the data leaks. If we could agree on a plan and divide up the work, we can move a lot faster on this thing. Vic Paoli wasn't too warm on the idea, but I'm sure you'll agree with my approach once I've outlined it for you. I've put together a one-page list of some of the items we need to be looking into. I brought it with me." I took the document out of a thin leather folder and pushed it across the desk at him. Coleman's eyes never left my face. "You see, I think Paoli is attacking this all wrong," I added, but my voice weakened. Coleman staring at me was giving me the creeps.

"You like to be in control of things, to manage situations, don't you, Ms. Blake?"

His question surprised me. "I suppose so, when it's appropriate. I'm a manager. Managers manage things."

"And you're smart. You're the type of person who likes to show people how smart you are. Sometimes you think you're smarter than everyone around you."

"Are you going to show me ink blots next? Yes, I think I'm smart. I'm smarter than some people and not as smart as others. And sometimes I'm really very dumb. Like right now I have no idea what you're getting at."

"Do you frequently work late, Ms. Blake?"

"What?"

"Do you ever work late?"

"Sure."

"How late?"

"Seven, eight o'clock. Sometimes ten. It depends on what I'm working on. Why do you ask?"

"Were you working late on October sixteenth?"

I stiffened. That was the night Gershbein was killed. "No, I wasn't working late that night."

"We looked at the computer access log. It showed you logged on from ten oh-five until ten-seventeen P.M."

I jumped halfway out of my chair. "That's not true. I worked until around eight-thirty, then I went to dinner."

"With someone?"

"No. I went alone. I like to do paperwork while I eat. The log isn't correct. Where did you get it?"

"Vic Paoli," he told me. Of course, the nice jolly guy who wanted my cooperation.

"The log is wrong. I'd like the chance to prove it. Can I have that?"

"Leave the work of proving things to us. You think it over. We can talk tomorrow."

"I don't need to think it over. I didn't log on to the computer the night Gershbein was killed."

"Calm yourself," Coleman said, his voice turning all nice-nice. "No one is accusing you of anything."

"Sure they aren't," I replied. Coleman got up, walked around the desk, and sat on its edge. I could tell it was time for a father-daughter chat.

"I'm going to tell you something for your own good, Ms. Blake. Keep your efforts focused on your work and off this investigation."

"What are you talking about?"

"I know you've been going through the personnel files."

"Who told you that?"

"Your secretary. We've been asking her some questions."

"Well, yes, I asked her for the files. So what's wrong with my going through the files of my own employees?"

"Just stay away from them. Stay away from the computer log."

"But the log is read-only access. I couldn't change it if I wanted to."

"Do your job, nothing more. Do you understand what I'm telling you?"

I understood. I didn't like it. I didn't agree with it. I wasn't going to do it. But I understood.

I answered a few more questions about the inner workings of Project 6, then walked back to my office. So much for the comment from Vic Paoli about him being an open book. Without telling me he had given information, erroneous information, to the FBI that could help convict me of fraud, murder, and espionage. I did not call that being an open book.

When I reached my office Mrs. Dabney was fussing with some papers on my desk. She jumped when she saw me. "Good God, you scared me." Both of her hands were clutching her pearl necklace as if she were afraid someone would rip it off her. Ever since Barbara Bush moved into the White House Mrs. Dabney sported daily a three-strand pearl choker. Come to think of it, Mrs. Dabney looked a little like Babs Bush. She was close to the same age and had similar hair, only she was about fifty pounds lighter.

I started to ask her what went on during her conversation with the FBI and how the issue of the personnel files came up, but then I thought my questions might intimidate her. She had every right to tell the truth about my actions to anyone, especially the FBI.

"I need you to find Vic Paoli for me," I told her. "He's got a temporary office somewhere in the building. Could you tell him I need to talk to him?"

Her hands finally moved away from her throat. "I'm smack in the middle of some letters. I was looking for the address of that Boston company," she said, now apparently peeved at my interrupting the Zen of her work flow.

"The address is on the business card stapled to the rough draft. But please get Paoli first. It's urgent."

"So what isn't urgent these days?" she said, then strutted out of my office. After closing the door I sat down in front of my terminal and logged on to Larry, first by entering my i.d. and password, then by using a small handheld remote-control device to enter another password consisting of eight characters. The password was the date of Frank

Sinatra's birth. After Larry accepted my passwords, I brought up the listing of who had accessed him on October 16, three days ago. The listing was the same one I had looked at Wednesday when I checked Joshua's i.d. The i.d.s are just combinations of letters and numbers. They all look alike unless you know what you're looking for, and even my own i.d. didn't jump out at me that night because I wasn't looking for it. But there it was. It showed I had logged on to Larry at 10:05 P.M. and remained logged on until 10:17. It also identified the terminal used as one just outside the computer room. But that was absurd. At ten that night I was finishing up the Number Three Szechuan special at Fung Lo's, about four blocks from my house. My ulcer and I remembered it well. Being a regular customer, I was certain the owner, Nicky, would remember me and confirm for Coleman that I was there, but that didn't answer the question of who used my i.d., how they did it, and why.

The list of my department's computer i.d.'s was located in my computer disk storage space. Only I had access to it, and I never wrote my passwords down, not ever. I always used combinations of letters or numbers for my passwords, so it was statistically impossible for anyone to guess them. Besides, Larry was programmed to shut off an i.d.'s access after three passwords were tried unsuccessfully. Only Elkin and I had authority to reset the i.d.'s after three failed password attempts.

I logged off Larry and skimmed once more through my procedure log.

"Your highness wishes a word with me?"

I looked up and saw Paoli in the doorway. He was wearing that same rumpled suit with red Adidas on his feet.

"Sorry to disappoint you and your FBI buddies, but I wasn't in the computer room the night Gershbein was killed," I said to him.

"The FBI guys are not my buddies. We barely tolerate each other, and the access log indicates you were there. When I saw it in the log today I had to turn the information over. It's my job."

"But I wasn't there and I can prove it."

"Then who logged on with your i.d.?"

"That's what I'm trying to find out."

Paoli pulled a chair next to mine so we were both sitting in front of the terminal. "So what are you doing?"

I eyed him. "I thought you had your own procedure and you weren't interested in mine."

"Okay, so you were right about the security software. It took me a full day to go through it and I didn't find a thing. Feel superior? Now tell me what you're doing."

"I'm logging on to Larry again, going through my password sequence. I just want to focus on it and try to understand how anyone could get my two passwords."

I started entering my password using the keyboard.

"How about someone looking over your shoulder, like I'm doing now, and seeing what keys you press?" Paoli said with a sarcastic tone.

"I'm sure you're familiar by now with our security rules. I would never use my password while someone was in the room. You, naturally, are an exception."

"My mom always said I was."

I was about to spit back an incredibly clever and caustic retort when an idea hit me. It was Paoli's remark about someone looking over my shoulder that started it. Since my passwords weren't written anywhere, it was impossible for anyone to find them out. That is, unless he looked over my shoulder.

I got up from my chair, reached under the seat, and adjusted it to make the seat higher. Then I pushed it toward the wall, took off my shoes, stood on the chair seat, and began reaching for the acoustical tiles with my fingers. I was too short. I tried jumping but the chair rolled precariously. I noticed Paoli watching me with amusement.

"Ms. Blake, are you having some sort of seizure?"

"I'm trying to see if there was someone or something looking over my shoulder. I'm too short to reach the ceiling. Get up here and look around."

"For what?"

"A camera. There's a fire sprinkler missing over here. Take a look at it."

"I think we should let the FBI do this. I'll go call Coleman."

"We'll call him later. I want to find this now."

"I really think we should wait."

"Do you need Coleman to hold your hand, Paoli?"

You can get a man to do just about anything by questioning his masculinity. I learned that from my mother. I got down from the chair and Paoli grudgingly took my place while I held the chair for him. He still couldn't reach the ceiling so we put the San Francisco and Santa Clara phone books on the chair seat. Paoli was playing with the fire sprinklers when I noticed the air-conditioning vent over my desk. I grabbed a letter opener, got on top of the desk, and pried the grate from the vent. Behind it sat a small video recorder.

"Get over here and look at this."

He jumped down from the chair and came over to me. I pointed to the camera.

"If I had known this was here I would have spent more time on my makeup," I told him.

"Sorry, but I don't think it was your face they were interested in. Don't touch it. The FBI will want to dust it for prints."

I untied my scarf from around my neck, wrapped it around my fingers, and flipped the switch on the camera. I heard a barely audible *whirr*ing sound.

"Smile, you're on *Candid Camera*," I said to Paoli. He crossed his arms and frowned.

"Who has a key to your office?"

"Just me and Mrs. Dabney. Mrs. Dabney keeps the extra key in her desk."

"Is her desk always locked?"

"I guess it's not locked during the day, at least not all the time. She doesn't lock it if she's just leaving her desk for a minute or two. So you think someone stole the key from her desk and used it to get inside my office to install the camera?"

"It's possible."

"But whoever it was had to get behind the camera to focus it and make sure it was aimed properly. Look at the air-conditioning vent. It's only about a foot and a half wide. Who would be small enough to squeeze down it?"

"Don't they make some sort of telescopic equipment to aim camera lenses without looking through the eyepiece? Then you wouldn't have to focus it from behind."

I thought for a moment. "Maybe they do, but if so, it's got to be much less common equipment than a video recorder. The buyer would be too easy to trace. If it were me, I would crawl in and focus the camera from behind."

"We'll have Coleman's folks check out the air ducts and see where they go," said Paoli.

"We don't need to," I said as I put on my shoes. "The manager next door had some kind of foot operation and he's out for a couple of weeks. I'm going to use his office to try something. I'll need your help."

"What are you doing?" asked Paoli, but even though I didn't answer, he followed me out of my office and down the hall. I took my letter opener with me. Mrs. Dabney looked at us a moment, then returned to her typing. We stepped inside the empty office and I shut the door behind us.

"This door doesn't lock, so we'll just have to risk someone coming in," I said as I took off my suit jacket and kicked off my shoes.

Paoli looked confused, but not at all displeased. "There's a motel a few miles away with hourly rates, Ms. Blake. Wouldn't that be more comfortable?"

"Put a lid on it. Move that chair over here next to the wall."

Paoli rolled a chair to the spot I pointed to. I put a phone book and a thick database manual on the seat.

"Now get on the chair and remove the grill from the vent. You can use this." I handed him my letter opener.

"What for?"

"Because I want to see for myself what size person could fit in that duct. It will narrow the field of suspects considerably. Now get up there. You can get at it easier than I can."

Paoli grudgingly stepped up on the chair, almost falling when it swiveled, but I held it steady for him. Using the opener, he pried off the grill. I took the grill from him and put it on the floor.

"You can get down now," I said.

"Thanks ever so. Now, can you tell me what we do next?"

I paused and took a deep breath. "I'm going to be honest with you, because I think everybody deserves honesty. There are many things about you that I find repulsive, but events have thrown us together."

"A lot of people would be offended by that remark, Ms. Blake, but I'll let it pass."

"And I'm going to ask you to do something now that I hope you'll deal with in an adult and professional manner."

"Like what?"

"Kneel down."

"What in the hell for?"

"I'm going to get on your shoulders, then you can boost me into the air duct."

Paoli laughed. "You, Ms. Blake, are a very unpredictable woman. You could hurt yourself and I don't think workman's comp is going to understand. Besides, this isn't our job. Let the FBI shove themselves into air ducts. That's what they're here for. You and I are more cerebral types."

"Why do you keep trying to push everything off on the FBI? Don't you have the backbone to take action yourself, Paoli?"

"Jeezus Christ," he muttered, then knelt on the floor. I hiked up my skirt and put my legs around his shoulders, then he slowly stood up.

"I usually prefer a woman whispering 'oh, baby' when I do this sort of thing. Just out of curiosity, since these office doors don't lock from the inside, just what are you going to say if someone walks in here?"

"I'll come up with something. Now get me closer to the vent opening. Okay, right here. Now hold me steady until I'm standing on your shoulders."

Slowly I raised myself on his shoulders to a standing position.

"This is craziness," said Paoli.

"Don't worry, I took gymnastics in high school."

"How much do you weigh?"

"One hundred and five."

"It feels like five hundred and five."

By this time I had my head stuck in the vent. The opening looked tight, but at least large enough for me to squeeze through, although it was much dirtier and darker than I expected. I knocked on the side of the duct with my fist. It sounded like sheet metal. By using my hands to brace myself I was able to get the upper half of my body into the vent, but I couldn't go farther on my own.

"You'll have to shove me in the rest of the way, Paoli."

"Are you sure it will hold you?"

"It seems solid."

"And once I get you in there, where are you going to go?"

"There's got to be a main air duct up here connecting to this one. Once I get to it I'm going to crawl to the left toward my office." The dust was getting in my lungs and I began to cough.

"I don't like this. Why don't you let me get in there?" said Paoli.

"Because you won't fit. Now shove me in."

With a grunt, he pushed me farther into the duct. The dust had formed webs that clung to my face and hair, and I had to wipe them away from my mouth. There wasn't room enough to get on my knees and crawl, so I managed to drag myself through the opening using my hands and feet.

It occurred to me at that moment that maybe dragging myself through an air-conditioning duct was not a smart thing to do. It was dark and filthy and how did I know it wouldn't collapse under my weight and drop me into who-knows-where? But it was too late for regrets. As I moved, I tested each section of the duct with my hand before I put my weight on it to make certain it seemed sturdy.

Behind me I could hear Paoli trying to say something, but I couldn't make out the words. I calculated that my office should be about thirty feet west of the opening through which I had entered. Slowly, carefully, I inched my way along until I saw a light beaming through an opening and could barely hear the sound of the camera. Then I moved faster, trying my best not to make any noise, because I didn't want to be found wandering inside the air duct regardless of how good my excuse. When I reached the camera, I noticed a timer attached to it. I took a deep breath of clean air, then looked through the lens. It was a closeup lens aimed directly at my keyboard, the camera turned at an angle where my hands could be viewed without being blocked by my body. And me with never the time for a decent manicure. Sometimes the view had to have been obscured if I moved my chair around, but if they filmed every day, whoever had done it must have eventually gotten a good picture of me typing in my passwords. I knew one thing for certain: The camera had been arranged by a smallish person. Although I could maneuver through the air duct, a person much larger than me would have had difficulty. A person the size of Paoli could not have fit.

Since there was no room to turn, I backed out the way I had come in. It seemed to take longer. I finally got my legs out of the opening.

"Paoli, are you there?"

"Naturally."

"Then pull me out."

"Let me pause for a moment," I heard him say, "and describe this image for you since you are obviously unable to see it yourself. A woman's legs, nice legs, shapely appendages, are dangling out of an air-conditioning vent situated high on a wall. Her skirt is pushed up around her hips, exposing—"

"I want out of here, Paoli. Now," I said as loudly as I dared. I felt Paoli grab my calves and he pulled me out. He had pushed the desk close to the vent and was standing on it.

"You're filthy," he said after he had helped me back on the ground.

"It's only dust. Help me brush off. We were right. The camera was pointed at my keyboard. And whoever did it couldn't have been much larger than me," I said as we both brushed my skirt until it was presentable. The remaining dust spots I removed with Scotch tape, and when I put my jacket on I looked almost clean. Paoli put the grill back on the vent, replaced the chair and desk, then we both went back to my office.

"At least this explains how someone got my i.d. and password and how I got logged on to Larry the night Gershbein was killed. I can't wait to see Coleman's face when I tell him," I said, standing in front of my terminal and looking at the camera that was still running.

"I hate to spoil things for you, but finding the camera doesn't get you off the hook. You could have planted it there yourself. You have proven that you can squeeze through the air duct."

A few days later they developed the film and I got to see it. There was no sound, of course, but the camera caught my hand over the keyboard making an obscene gesture where Paoli couldn't see it but the camera could. It was the only time I ever heard Agent Coleman laugh.

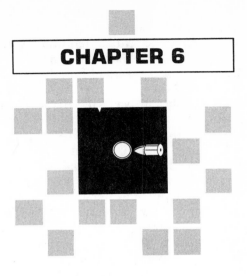

CHAPTER 6

So what do you do when what you thought was terra firma turns to slush beneath your feet? I, Julie Blake, president of her high school graduating class, student of MIT and Stanford, and vocal proponent of women's place in business management, felt like stepping into a nice hot bubble bath and staying there for a couple of years. And then, if I didn't die from terminal pruning, I figured I could get a good job selling lingerie at Macy's. I envisioned myself making tough engineering decisions like whether or not a customer should go for full underwire support. It sounded so nice and nonstressful.

But you have to remain goal-directed and forge straight ahead, chin held high, I told myself. I started Friday afternoon by showing Agent Coleman the nifty little camera I found in my office. If he was impressed, he didn't show it. His cool attitude made me realize that Paoli was right. Coleman figured I could have planted the camera there just to make myself look innocent. I had him talk to Nicky at Fung Lo's and Nicky told him I was at the restaurant until ten-thirty the night Gershbein was killed. That seemed to appease Coleman. After Paoli pronounced my security program 100 percent pure, I wondered if I was off the official suspect list. Coleman took a look at the air-conditioning vent and announced that someone had to have planted the camera from within the duct. When I told him that I had already crawled through the duct to test it, Coleman was not pleased. But since I had done it with Paoli's assistance, there wasn't much he could say about it. To be on the safe side, they searched my office for any other electronic devices, but the rest of my office came up clean. Next I gave the police and Agent Coleman the computer log from October 16. I explained that given Joshua's location and the number of transactions he entered, he never would have had time to kill Gershbein. They seemed to accept my theory, so poor Joshua was off the hook, but my real work had just begun.

I guess everyone at ICI suspected there was a connection between Gershbein's murder and the data leaks. It was too much of a coincidence that both events happened so close together. But for everyone else it was mere conjecture. I had more solid proof. The copy of the security code given to me by Dorothy Gershbein sat locked in my desk, and I battled with myself over whether I should give it to Brad Elkin, to Vic Paoli, or to the FBI. On one hand I knew I should, my duty as a citizen and all that. But I also knew that it would be construed as evidence that Gershbein had been involved in the data leaks. Everyone would assume that he had sold Project 6 data to the Soviets, and in my gut I knew it wasn't true. Gershbein had been my best employee as well as my friend. When he had tried to talk to me the day he had been murdered, I hadn't listened. I figured I owed him one, and the least I could do was not let his name be muddied until I had proven for myself his innocence or guilt. I knew withholding information from the FBI and Paoli was probably illegal or worse, but it wasn't like I was keeping it from them completely. I would happily hand it over to them after I had a chance to go over it.

The worst-case situation would be if Dorothy Gershbein told them she had given me the printout. But even then I could just say I hadn't looked at it closely, that I assumed it was something unimportant. Would they buy that? Probably not, but at this point I was willing to take the risk. I was already a suspect anyway. Besides, it wasn't only Gershbein's reputation that was at stake. It was mine as well.

I don't like to think of myself as egotistical, but in this situation I knew I was the only qualified person for the investigation. I knew more about Project 6 and its technology than everyone else in the NSA, FBI, and ICI combined, and certainly more than Vic Paoli, whether he admitted it or not. All the project data was at my fingertips, and I needed only to analyze it and come up with the right answer. Analysis was, after all, my forte. The first logical question was: Who would want to steal Project 6 data? The answer: everyone in Silicon Valley.

Silicon Valley brims with hungry high-tech companies ruthless enough to steal another company's designs. The law of the jungle rules and corporate espionage is a fact of life, which was the reason security was so tight at ICI. But although I had a certain amount of respect for the general level of technical expertise in the Valley, I didn't respect it as much as I respected my own. Maybe someone could have gained access to the computer room, but I doubted that any of them would be able to break into Larry's security system. I was very thorough when I designed it. But let's say that I'm not as clever as I think I am, and someone did manage to steal the molecular memory designs. Wouldn't they complete the designs themselves and sell them on the open market rather than pawn them off to the Soviets in an incomplete state that made them worth less money?

I sat in my office pondering this puzzle when I heard the intercom buzzer.

"There's a Ruskie to see you. A Mr. Petrovsky," Mrs. Dabney pronounced dryly.

I winced. "Send him in."

John Garrett had called me late the previous day to tell me that the technical exchange with the Russian university would be delayed indefinitely, emphasis on the term "indefinitely." I guess it seemed like a slap in the face for the Russians to have paid for stolen molecular memory designs and then expect us to go through with the public relations campaign. Someone was supposed to have contacted the Soviet representative the night before, but apparently there had been a screw-up. That was all I needed. I wondered if this was the sort of snafu that started wars. As I flipped madly through all my phone messages to see if I had been contacted regarding Petrovsky's appointment, I sensed someone in the doorway. I looked up. A short, roundish, red-faced man dressed in a black suit, a green bow tie, and dark wool overcoat grinned at me. He had one of those faces where his chubby cheeks lifted up when he smiled, making his cheeks look like ripe apples. His hair was slicked back with gel and his cologne wafted through the air. I imagined him dousing himself that morning with Siberian Spice.

"Miz Blake?" he said with the anticipated thick accent.

"Mr. Petrovsky, welcome." I greeted him with my best executive Girl Scout demeanor—warm smile and firm, brisk handshake.

Petrovsky grinned gratefully and waddled over to a chair.

"I am so happy to be in your country. I saw the Golden Gate Bridge yesterday. I rode the cable car and it went *cling, cling, cling*. Magnificent," he announced, then plopped backward into the chair opposite my desk.

"How nice. Mr. Petrovsky, I'm afraid I have some bad news for you."

"What news could be bad coming from such a lovely woman?"

This I didn't need. "You see, Mr. Petrovsky—"

"Call me Rudolph."

"Yes, well, Rudolph, the arrangement between ICI and your university has been delayed because of security problems we're having here."

He slapped his forehead with his palm and shook his head, but his smile remained. "Problems, always problems."

"So, you see, I have no information to give you today, and the tour of the plant has been canceled. I know this is inconvenient, but someone was supposed to have informed you of the delay last night."

"Yes, a person called."

"They did?"

"A man, he called and told me of this delay, but I think to myself, Rudolph, this is America. The situation changes from minute to minute. So I showed up this afternoon to, as you say, check it out."

"I'm sorry you wasted your time."

"Waste my time? Contrarily, Miz Blake. I so enjoy your country. Especially the women. They are so independent." He leaned forward, his hands pressed against his plump knees. "You American women have fire," he said hoarsely with a lascivious raising of his bushy black eyebrows.

I didn't like the tone of the conversation, so I walked to the door to give him the hint that it was time to leave. He got up and walked toward me.

"Well, we must say our good-byes. Would you care to drive to Carmel this afternoon? I hear it's lovely," he asked.

Was I wearing my hair differently? Had I changed my deodorant? I've gone years without being asked out on a date, and suddenly I was being viewed as a ripe tomato, first by Lieutenant Dalton and now Petrovsky. Was I improving with age or were men just lowering their standards? "I don't think so," I told him. "I have a great deal of work to do."

Petrovsky patted me on the behind.

I jumped, then glared at him. "Do that again, buddy, and you'll be singing soprano in the Vienna Boys Choir."

He grinned.

"You American women have such fire," he replied with a twinkle in his eye, then he waddled down the hall. I followed him out because it was security procedure that any visitor be escorted out of the building, but I kept myself carefully out of patting range. Outside his car and driver awaited him. The driver didn't look Russian. He was blond and thin with a punkish haircut and very American clothes, more like a performer in a rock video than a chauffeur. He leaned against the black sedan as if he were bored. Petrovsky and I exchanged good-byes.

I waited until they drove away before I returned to my office, but when I arrived at my door expecting welcome solitude, I was surprised by another visitor. Wayne Hanson paced frantically about my office, running his fingers through his bushy red hair until part of it stood on end. When Hanson got nervous he crackled like a hot wire. I braced myself.

"Hi, Wayne. What's the problem?" I asked, not in the mood for idle pleasantries. Hanson didn't know how to handle idle pleasantries anyway.

"You're the problem!"

He knew how to get my attention. I walked to my desk and dropped into my chair. "How am I a problem?"

"You've been messing with my programmers. You've been asking them questions, snooping around, interrogating them! I won't have it!" His pacing was interspersed with a bouncing movement that reminded me of one of those round, plastic things that bob on a fishing line.

"I didn't interrogate anyone. I only asked a few questions and got fewer answers. And I don't see why that should upset you. I'm sure the FBI and NSA will be doing the same thing."

"They already have. They've practically accused me of murder. They've been all over me, asking me questions, making crude insinuations. I was supposed to go to the chip conference in Boston but they 'suggested' I stay in town! What's happening here?"

"Why do they suspect you?" I asked. I could envision Hanson driving someone to suicide, but murder seemed farfetched.

"Someone saw my car in the ICI parking lot the night Gershbein was killed."

"Is it true? Were you there?"

Hanson looked sheepish. "I was sitting in my car listening to the stereo. New CD player. Latest technology. Very expensive."

I gave him a quizzical look. "That doesn't sound like much of an alibi."

Hanson got frisky again. "What do you mean? What is this 'alibi' talk? You're as bad as the cops. I can't believe this! I, Wayne Hanson, one of the greatest minds in this industry, a technological leader, suddenly reduced to something out of an episode of *Columbo*!"

He snatched a half-eaten Snickers bar out of his ink-stained shirt pocket and furiously bit off a chunk. "I swear I was just sitting there in the parking lot listening to some jazz," he garbled through some chocolate. He saw my dubious look. "I get lonely sometimes. What of it? I don't exactly have a peer group, you know." He paused and swallowed. "Naturally I'm in therapy. Lucky for me I basically enjoy being alone, so sometimes I just park my car somewhere and listen to music."

I believed him. Hanson was twenty-eight years old and by one newspaper account had made at least ten million dollars off Comtech. It probably was hard for him to find friends he could relate to. I made the mistake of feeling sorry for him.

"Did you see anyone around the building that night who could vouch for you?" I asked, trying to be helpful.

"Good grief, you should be a detective. You sound just like one!" he shouted, throwing up his hands. "No, I didn't see a soul. Now I've got you, the police, the FBI, and the NSA interrogating my technical staff, digging into files, your minds just hungering for some dirt. Well, you're not going to get it. My programmers are creative, you know. Technical artistes. They're high strung, delicately balanced. I can't afford to have them pissed off. One of my analysts threatened to quit," he barked, waving his Snickers menacingly in my face.

I nodded sympathetically, but my sympathy was starting to wane. I didn't like being yelled at, and the last thing I needed right now was Hanson throwing one of his tantrums, one of his typically childish tizzy fits where he rudely complained to upper management.

"Of course, you can make all this up to me, Julie. I could forget about your snooping, not talk to Elkin about it if you would help me a little."

"What are you talking about?"

"Well, all of this is really the fault of that secret agent guy, Dick Ravioli, or whatever his name is," muttered Hanson. He shoved the rest of his Snickers in his mouth.

"Vic Paoli."

"Right. He put them up to it," he said, jabbing his finger into my desk with each syllable. "The FBI never would have known I was in that parking lot if Paoli hadn't sneaked around and found out.

"He told them about my being in that damn parking lot and now they're crucifying me. I'm a martyr. Julie, you've got to help me," he said through a mouth still stuffed with candy. Hadn't his mother taught him any manners? Maybe he thought everyday manners didn't apply to him.

"Me? How can I help you?" I silently prayed he would swallow. A tiny wet sliver of projectile Snickers landed on my face.

"You could talk to them. Tell them there's no way I, Wayne Hanson, could be involved in murder. I told them, I said 'Hey, guys, why would I, Wayne Hanson, kill a programmer who was working to advance a project that's gonna make me millions?' The very concept is illogical, but they won't listen. They're too stupid or too in awe of me or something. They're incapable of rising to my intellectual level. They'll listen to you, though. You're the solid, dependable type. You're a woman. You can relate to people and they relate to you. You've got to talk to the police and that Paoli guy. You've just got to."

"Wayne, you know I'd love to help you, but I can't. I have no credibility with the police, the FBI, or Paoli. I'm a suspect too. I'm busy trying to keep myself out of jail."

Hanson froze for a second, his face turned hard, then he leaned over my desk and looked at me. The little-boy demeanor was gone, replaced by something more intense, more brutal. At that moment I thought maybe he could kill somebody.

"If I were you I'd play ball with me," he said, his voice tight and low. "I have a lot of pull around here and I warn you, nobody is going to foul up my finishing molecular memory—not the police, not some lousy Russians, not Paoli, not you, not anybody!"

I got up from my desk, walked past Hanson, and shut the door because I could see Mrs. Dabney listening to our conversation. I turned back to Hanson. His fingers trembled as he fumbled with the wrapper of a fresh Mars bar. I noticed his nails bitten to the flesh.

"Wayne, did you see anyone in the parking lot the night Gershbein was murdered?"

"No, no one. I told the FBI and the police all this already."

"How long were you there?"

"I don't know. I never wear a watch. I think I might have gotten there around nine-thirty. Maybe I was there an hour, I'm not sure. What difference does it make? I didn't see anything."

"But, Wayne, why the ICI parking lot? Why not park at Comtech?"

"Because you guys leave the lights on all night. Otherwise it gets weird. I don't like the dark. I could get attacked. I'm leaving now. I think I have an appointment."

"I have one more question."

"I'm not answering any more questions."

"Why do you care so much about molecular memory? Do you need the money? I thought you were rolling in it."

He gave a high-pitched gasp that sounded like an animal in pain. I had seen a rabbit caught in a trap once that had made the same noise.

"Money? I don't need any more money. What did money ever do for me?"

It could have bought you a better wardrobe, I thought as I looked over his sweatshirt and worn running shorts.

He continued. "What I want, what I will have, is to be the person responsible for the successful development of molecular memory. It's been six years since I came up with something really new. I've been making money off equipment I designed six years ago. *Six years ago*. Do you know how long that is?"

I nodded to make sure he knew that I knew that six years was a pretty long time.

"I have to go now, Julie, but we'll be talking later." Hanson turned on the heels of his red high-top tennis shoes and exited, most likely toward Garrett's office to complain about me. I sat back down in my company-issue leatherette swivel chair, swiveled a little, and thought about whether Hanson was small enough to fit inside the air-conditioning duct. It was tight, but still a possibility. Then I got on the phone and reached Max after coaxing her secretary into pulling her out of a weekly staff meeting.

"So where's the fire?" Max asked when she got to the phone.

"In Wayne Hanson's shorts. He was just here and raked me over the coals about me, Vic Paoli, and the FBI disrupting the delicate psychological balance of his technical artistes. God, he annoys me. He also made several threats about what would happen to me if I don't get everyone off his back."

"So get everyone off his back."

"It's not that easy, but I'm going to start working on it. In the meantime, I need you to keep an eye on him. Let me know if he goes to Elkin or Garrett or anybody over my head. I already have enough problems."

"No trouble at all. Corporate espionage is my forte. I

guess that's not something to joke about anymore, is it? I'll take Hanson to dinner, give him one drink, and he'll spill his guts. You know the effect I have on men."

Yes, I knew it well, well enough to know that some of them went running. Max was not exactly what you would call the demure, retiring type, and her overwhelming personality could send nice boys scrambling home to their mommies. Wayne Hanson was one guy who didn't. He may have been her boss, but she was the one who pulled the strings in their relationship, personal or professional. Max had her typically brief affair with Hanson two years earlier when she was going through one of her younger-men phases. Hanson was twenty-six then, slightly wacko, but not unattractive, especially with the millions he earned when his laser chromosome scanning equipment skyrocketed. Suddenly he was touted as a boy genius as well as a major force in computer technology, but he didn't quite know what to do with it all. Max fixed that problem for him briefly, but she soon tired of him and his eccentricities. With her usual finesse she managed to break off with Hanson and end up with a promotion, a sizable chunk of stock, and Hanson still in love with her. If anyone could handle Hanson, Max could.

"By the way, how much do you think Hanson weighs?" I asked her.

There was a moment of silence on the other end of the phone. "What, are you thinking of wrestling him? How in the hell would I know how much he weighs?"

"You slept with him, didn't you?" I whispered into the receiver.

"But I was always on top, sweetheart. Have you been sniffing copier fluid or something? You sound funny."

"I'm fine. Forget I asked the question. I would still appreciate your help in keeping an eye on Hanson," I said. "I don't think I can have any effect on the FBI, but I can at least take care of Paoli."

"I'd like to take care of Paoli," she said in a voice close to a purr. "I need to drop by your building this afternoon. I'll stop in and see you."

I told her to wait at least an hour. I hung up the phone feeling better about Hanson. Now all I had to do was face Paoli.

■ ◻ ■

By this time it was three in the afternoon and I hadn't had time for lunch. I grabbed a vending machine sandwich of pimento cheese on soggy whole wheat and ate it as I scoured the halls for Paoli. Finally I asked a secretary if she had seen him. She rolled her eyes and pointed to the computer room. His popularity was spreading. I hated the idea of Paoli prowling around the computer area. Only the employees absolutely necessary to data processing operations were allowed inside, and there was no real reason for Paoli to be in there. He could have looked at Larry's programs from one of the terminals connected by cable outside the computer room. I steeled myself for a confrontation and marched toward the room. Before I could get there a hand grabbed my arm.

"Juliet?"

I turned, annoyed at the delay, and faced Albert Wu, a Project 6 manager who worked for me. Wu was a brilliant man, one of a handful of people who knew computers as well as chemistry in the depth the project required. Wu's skills had been essential to the project, and he was a tireless worker. Yet there was something about Wu that bothered me. I could never quite put my finger on it. He was Asian, with eyes that looked like shiny black Junior Mints against a face of baby-smooth, pale skin. The lines around his eyes and a sprinkling of gray in his hair indicated a man in his fifties, yet there was a childlike flatness, an androgynous quality to his face, a constant slight smile that seemed to me a veneer hiding a soul devoid of warmth and feeling. Like an evil, smiling doll, I thought. I didn't trust him.

"Juliet, I understand you're having some difficulty. If I can assist you in any way, I would be delighted to be of service to you. The details of the data leaks are quite interesting to me." He smiled that smile, and I cringed. I just bet you find the details interesting, I thought. Even though Wu had spoken to me about a transfer to the East Coast, I suspected from the way he sucked up to Elkin in staff meetings that he was lusting after my job. I imagined his complex, logical mind calculating ways to oust me, but I wasn't going to give him the chance.

"Thank you. I would appreciate your insights, Albert. We'll set up a meeting soon," I said, but I knew he could tell by my eyes it was no dice. He smiled that smile again and nodded politely. As I walked away I could feel his eyes on my back. God, it had been one bitch of a day. I went back to my office, had a Maalox cocktail, and started out again for my original destination.

I pressed my security code into the keypad. A light flashed green and the door to the computer room clicked open. When I entered I felt the chilled air, and I relived the moment I first saw Gershbein dead inside Larry. How long would it take before I stopped thinking about it every day, every time I stepped into the room? I cleared my mind of the image and looked around for Paoli, but didn't see him. What I did see was most of my staff sitting around a desk playing some sort of group chess match.

"Are you all on strike?"

Their heads turned in unison toward me.

"He's taking a core dump, so Larry's down for at least fifteen minutes," said Alan. The mention of a core dump disturbed me. A core dump meant a listing of everything inside Larry's main memory. It was like slicing open Larry's brain and digging around his cerebrum.

"Who's taking a core dump?" I asked.

Peggy, one of the operations people, pointed her finger to the corner. There sat Paoli behind a desk surrounded by reams of computer printouts. I walked over.

"I'd like to speak with you," I said. I knew he heard me, but he kept on reading, following each set of numbers with the tip of a mechanical pencil. "Mr. Paoli, I know you have work to do, but my people are operating under deadlines and it would help things if you could take your core dumps after normal working hours."

Paoli paused a moment before looking at me, as if there were no urgency to respond. "Oh, hello there. If you're looking for another piggyback ride, forget it. My shoulders are still sore from the last one. Are you sure you only weigh a hundred and five?"

His eyes crinkled at the corners as he smiled. I made the mistake of breathing, thus allowing his musky, slightly spicy aroma to filter into places it didn't belong.

"If it makes you feel better, I'm authorized to do this," he added.

"By whom?"

"John Garrett. You can check if you like, or you can save yourself a long walk in those sensible shoes of yours and just trust me."

The sensible shoes line was a low blow. "My people still have work to do here."

"I'm the good guy, remember? I shove you into air ducts upon command. I pull you back out of them. I could have left you in there, you know." He grinned and looked me up and down with that testosterone-induced glint that comes so naturally to men like him. I could just see him fantasizing that I was a stuffy, sexually inhibited librarian type, and that if the right man walked in, just like in an old Bogart movie, I would take off my glasses, shake loose my hair, and pounce on him like a cat in heat. Naturally I resented this, but what I resented more was the possibility that if I did take my glasses off and shake down my hair I might still be a stuffy, inhibited librarian type. I looked down at my sensible shoes just for a second before I looked back at Paoli. It had been a mistake to have ever gotten on his shoulders.

"Have you found anything in the core dump?" I asked him.

"Nothing yet. I didn't really expect to. It would be too obvious. We're dealing here with something more subtle. By the way, I hear you bribed some Chinese guy to give you an alibi for the night Gershbein was killed. Nice going. I think they bought it."

I could feel my face turn hot. "I didn't bribe anyone. How dare you—"

"Okay, okay, I was just kidding. It was a joke. Ha-ha."

"It was a bad joke."

"Mea culpa. Listen, I'm your pal. I've decided you're innocent."

"How kind of you. What brought you to that conclusion?"

"Call me sentimental, but you shove somebody inside an air duct, you look up their dress, and you feel like you know them. Besides, the NSA ran another check on you at my request and there's nothing in your background that could connect you to anything like this—no money problems, no extravagant tastes, no little messy personal problems or bad habits. Your life's too boring for you to have done anything as daring as selling secrets to the Soviets. And I said so to Coleman."

"Thanks for the vote of confidence."

"Anytime. But the FBI is still interested in you. They give you more credit for ingenuity than I do."

"If I'm still under suspicion, how come I haven't been fired?"

"Corporate image, of course. Innocent until proven guilty, respect for the individual, and all that. But mainly it's because if you go down the tubes then you'll probably take Elkin and Garrett with you. They hired you in the first place. They're scrambling to protect you, at least for now. So you're fine unless they decide to cut bait. All you have to do is cooperate with me. We'll solve this thing and we'll both be heroes."

"I thought you liked to operate on your own."

"I've reanalyzed the situation and I've decided I need your help."

I glared at Paoli and tried to figure out what he was up to. Although Paoli was probably right about Garrett, I knew Elkin was protecting me for reasons other than just to save his own skin. He and I had a lot of history together. Still, I thought, maybe I had been too hard on Paoli. After all, he was just doing his job, and I needed all the help I could get. I decided to tell him about the printout Dorothy Gershbein had given me, but I was interrupted before I got out the first word.

"Well, don't you two look cozy? Strategizing on the takeover of ICI already?"

It was Max, looking very Ava Gardner in a deep-blue silk dress with a high neck and narrow skirt with a slit halfway up the thigh. You didn't have to be psychic to know what she was up to. Her black hair fell to her shoulders, one side of it behind her ear and the other side spilling provocatively about her face. She gave her head a slight toss and it made me think of an expensive Thoroughbred filly. What was it that made me wish she'd trot into someone else's pasture?

"How did you get in here?" I asked. Only two technicians from Comtech were allowed in the ICI computer room and then only under my supervision. Max was a Marketing V.P., and no one with any sense let the marketing people near the actual equipment they marketed.

"Easy. I just walked in behind somebody else," she said with a dismissing wave of her hand. Paoli looked smug.

"See? Tailgating," he said. I shot him a look to let him know that any truce between us was tenuous.

Max leaned silkily against a tape drive and raised one crimson-tipped finger until it barely touched her lower lip. She reeked of perfume. "So, Mr. Paoli, how is your sleuthing going? Find anything interesting yet?"

He smiled. "Quite a few things."

I stared at him trying to see if he was bluffing. Was it possible that he had uncovered something already? If he had, I needed to know what it was. But I had a feeling Paoli didn't give out much free information. I watched Max give him a look that spoke of velvety darkness, French perfume, and cool, crumpled white satin sheets. If they could bottle it I'd buy a basement full.

"If I were you, I'd investigate me quite thoroughly, Mr. Paoli. I'm capable of anything, you know," Max told him.

"Wanna be frisked?" asked Paoli. Max's lips curled upward at the edges.

I found the whole scene disgusting, and I surprised myself with a small pang of jealousy. Paoli had looked at Max as if she were a cream-filled French pastry. Compared to that, he had looked at me as if I were stale bread.

"Well, time for coffee," Max said, and pulled me by the hand toward the door. I made a mental note to send her a security violation memo for entering the computer room, which I felt confident she would throw in the trash. But I had to follow the rules, especially when I was the one who had made them up in the first place.

Before we reached the door I turned and saw Paoli watching us with his cockeyed smile. I gave him a hard look that said I wasn't through with him. He flashed me a white-toothed smile that said he wasn't through with me either. Not by a long shot.

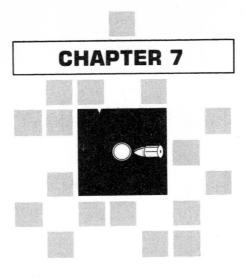

CHAPTER 7

"You're in trouble, toots," Max said as she sipped hot tea. "Hanson was gnashing his teeth on the phone to Garrett after lunch today when I walked in his office. When he saw me he looked real guilty and stopped talking, but I had already heard a lot of the conversation outside the door. Let's just say your name came up several times and the references were less than flattering."

I stopped stirring the artificial creamer into my coffee and tapped my spoon against the table, creating an apparently annoying staccato, because Max finally pulled the spoon from my hand and put it back on the table.

"I knew he would go crying to Garrett," I told her. "He's so spineless." I peered down at my coffee. The nondairy creamer had turned my coffee into something that looked like toxic waste. I usually didn't take coffee breaks, but Max, with her promises of information, had lured me into taking ten minutes.

"So what type of person is most likely to be a corporate spy?" she asked between sips.

"First thing is that he or she has to be an ICI employee," I answered. "Even if someone outside the company, including Comtech, is in on it, there has to be an inside person involved."

"Why?"

"Because that person had to have access to Larry's Project 6 software."

"Someone couldn't tap in from outside ICI?"

I shook my head. "I've studied it and I'm convinced that no one could. Larry's communications facilities were never activated. You have to have access to a computer terminal directly connected to Larry to get at his data."

Max raised an eyebrow. "Well, that makes it interesting. So who has access to Larry?"

"Only a handful of people can access Larry without supervision—Joshua, Alan, Gershbein, Albert Wu, and Elkin. And me, of course."

"Yes, of course, you. So now it gets easy. Who needed money the most?"

"Everybody and nobody. Any one of them could have benefited from a large sum of money. Who wouldn't? But none of them seems the type to do such a thing."

"Jules, what's the matter? That look on your face."

"Max, do you think Wayne could possibly be having any financial problems?"

"Wayne Hanson? He's richer than God. You must be kidding."

"Sometimes even rich people overextend themselves. Hanson has to have been pouring a lot of money into Comtech's research and development the past few years. We're talking very big dollars here. It's possible he could be financially strapped."

"Wait a second, you couldn't possibly, by any vast stretch of the imagination, think that Wayne was working with an ICI person and stole the molecular memory designs?"

"Why not?"

"Because Wayne may be a neurotic, obnoxious geek, but he's not a criminal. Besides, he'll end up making a lot of money off his share of the memory design patent. What's his motivation?"

"We've had to revise our schedule three times in the past two years. The whole project is taking a lot longer than we anticipated. Maybe he needed money fast. And he could have assumed that the fact that the Soviets were getting the designs would never come out. That way he would get paid twice."

"Wayne doesn't have the balls to do something like that. Next thing you'll be accusing him of killing Gershbein, and I know he definitely doesn't have the balls for that."

"Max, he was in the parking lot the night Gershbein was killed."

"So what? He goes there a lot to listen to his car stereo. He's lonely. We all know that."

"But he's in our building almost every day. He could have hidden until most people were gone and waited until Gershbein left the computer room for coffee or a sandwich. Then he could have told Gershbein some excuse why he needed to get into the computer room, then killed him. And he's a likely person to have gotten the idea of hiding the body inside Larry."

"Julie, you're giving me chills. It just isn't possible."

"Anything is possible, Max."

"Look, I've had sex with the man, and I know he's not a murderer."

"How can you know that?"

"He would have screwed better."

I thought a moment. "There's also the size issue," I said, talking to myself out loud.

"Oh, no, Jules, he's like this." Max held up her index finger.

"That's not what I meant. Whoever hid that camera in my office had to have been a smallish man or a female, otherwise he or she never would have fit in the air-conditioning duct."

"You're saying that whoever killed Gershbein definitely is the same person who put the camera in your office?"

"Maybe it wasn't the same person, but there's got to be a connection, and it's possible that if we could identify one of them, he would lead us to the other."

"This makes it simple. It had to have been Joshua, or maybe that girl in operations."

"You mean Peggy?"

"Yes, Peggy. She or Joshua would have fit. Have you asked our dashing Mr. Paoli what he thinks?"

I raised an eyebrow. "I would hardly describe him as dashing. Besides, shouldn't that be your department, Mata Hari? I'm sure you could get much more information from him than I could."

"Don't sell yourself short. You're beautiful, at least you would be if you could just get your hair out of that pony tail and wear a little makeup. On the other hand, stay the way you are because I really don't need the competition. As far as Paoli is concerned, he's anybody's game. I'm really not interested in him."

"Then what was all the slinking and cooing in the computer room just now?"

"Practice, my dear. Practice. I have much bigger plans." Max winked and looked coy, knowing I would pursue the conversation. I was embarrassed to let her know how much I relished the detailed descriptions of her love affairs, so I showed amazing self-control and took two sips of coffee before I asked for more information.

"Okay, so what are your bigger plans?"

Max smiled slyly. "Do you ever have fantasies, Jules? Sexual fantasies?" she asked.

I was fascinated by this unexpected change of subject, but didn't answer.

"You know you do, but you're the type of person who suppresses them, feels guilty about them."

"I most certainly do not."

"Good, then tell me one." Max waited, but I didn't say anything. "See, you are repressed. Fortunately, I'm not. I have lots of fantasies and I revel in them. I imagine being raped by Apaches, seduced by French radicals, handcuffed by William Hurt. But I have this special one that I love the most," Max said in a husky whisper.

If I had leaned over any farther in my chair I would have fallen on my face.

"I'm in an elevator," she began. "It's dimly lighted with music playing softly. It's after working hours, no one is around and I'm alone. Then the doors part. A stranger steps in." Max closed her eyes to savor the image. Why did I have this feeling the stranger was not a washwoman from Des Moines? Max continued. "He's tall, good-looking. He stares right through me, you know, sort of fondles me with his eyes. He presses me against the wall and puts his lips against mine. At first I think I want to get away, but then I don't even try. He makes me feel all hot and liquid, and I push myself against him and we slide to the floor. Then he lifts up my skirt and moves his hand along my thigh. He tears down my panties with one flick of the wrist, and then we make love, right there in the elevator."

There were a few moments of provocative silence during which I envisioned the erotic scene. I felt a warmth all over and I squirmed in my chair.

"So what does this have to do with anything?" I asked in a forced matter-of-fact tone.

Max leaned forward until her face was just a few inches from my own. "Because it happened, Jules. It actually happened last night."

I stared at her, wide-eyed. "Where?" Did I ask so I could ride the same elevator?

"At Comtech. It was around nine o'clock and everyone

had gone home. Almost everyone. I was in the elevator going home when . . ." She didn't finish the sentence. "The only part that didn't correspond to my fantasy was that it wasn't a stranger," Max added with nonchalance.

"You knew him?"

She nodded.

"Who was it?"

"Can't tell you."

"Do I know him?"

"You'll meet him soon enough."

"Will you see him again?"

"Yes," Max said dreamily. "I'm sure of it."

"Max, we're best friends. You can tell me anything. I won't breathe a word." After all, I wasn't made of steel.

"I'd like to, really, but I can't. I don't want to jinx things. This guy is different from the rest. He's stronger, and I don't mean physically. He's powerful, powerful in an intellectual sense. He makes me feel soft and vulnerable in a way I've never felt before." She laughed. "Imagine me feeling vulnerable."

Max's gaze drifted off and I knew it was useless to press her.

"Gotta run," I told her as I stood up to leave, but I knew she barely heard me.

■ ◻ ■

After the coffee break I went to my office, returned some phone calls, and attended a meeting with the personnel department. The topic was employee morale. Seems they were concerned with the negative effect the murder and data leak investigation were having on employees. It wasn't exactly boosting my spirits either. When it was over I checked my messages again, then headed for the computer room. Joshua and Alan were sitting in front of a terminal, their faces leaning so close to the screen their noses almost touched it. I looked at the terminal. On the high-resolution graphics screen was a 3-D photo-quality image of a blonde in a businesslike blue suit.

"How come lately whenever I walk in here you guys are doing everything but working?"

They both turned and looked startled.

"It's just a little program we've written in our spare time. It's five-thirty so it's officially after working hours," said Joshua. "Why are you looking at me funny?"

I had been staring at him, sizing him up to see if he would fit in an air-conditioning duct.

"I'm sorry, Josh. What were you saying?"

"It's a memorial program for Gershbein," said Alan. "We've all contributed to it. The program produces a rather startlingly lifelike image of Meryl Streep. She was Gershbein's favorite."

Joshua nodded. "He kept a picture of her in his MVS utilities manual."

I looked closer at the screen. The image of Streep was excellent.

"We were going to bring in a personal computer and run it at his funeral, but some people thought the function four key portion was inappropriate," Joshua added.

"The function four key?" I asked.

Alan smiled. "Try it."

I pressed the key on the terminal keyboard. Meryl Streep's clothes slipped off and she stood there naked.

"Impressive use of graphic parameters, don't you agree? Hit the space bar and she bends over and waves," said Alan.

"Alan, I think it would be impressive if you and Josh would bend over your terminals and do some work."

Joshua hit a key and Streep vanished from the screen.

"Sorry about that," he said, his face turning pink.

"It's okay. You can make it up to me. I want you to get me a listing of Larry's backup program."

"The whole thing? The one we run at night? I think we keep a hardcopy of it somewhere."

"I want a fresh one. Can you print it off now?"

Alan sat up in his chair. "I know what you're doing. You think the data leak could be a bug planted in Larry's backup program, don't you? How fiendishly clever."

"I get it," said Josh. "The backup program steals the data, puts it on tape, and somebody could walk right out with it!" Joshua was bouncing in his chair. He just didn't look like a criminal to me.

"Could you print it off for me now, please? I think Larry is probably finished with the summary program by now," I said. I wanted to be in the room when he printed it so I would be sure it was the real thing. At this point I didn't trust anyone completely.

While I waited for the printout I called Mrs. Dabney. She had left for the day so I left her a phone-mail message asking for a list of every field engineering person who performed maintenance on Larry. They could be suspects as well.

Joshua trotted over with the printout and put it on the desk in front of me.

"Thanks, Josh. I'm going to use the empty office to go over this. Why don't you come with me? I'd like to talk to you a minute."

He hesitated at first, then followed me to the small office I had used with Lieutenant Dalton the day we had found Gershbein. I sat on the edge of the desk. Joshua sat in a chair. He looked at me with a worried expression and pulled at his lower lip with his fingers.

"You're offended by the Meryl Streep program, right? Okay, okay, but you've got to believe me, we're not into a sexist thing here. Of course, I understand your feelings and I promise you that I'll walk right out of here and program some underwear on her." He started to get up. I gently pushed him back into his chair.

"That's not what I wanted to talk to you about, Josh."

"It's not?"

"No, I just wanted to chat with you a minute."

Josh gave me a suspicious look. He knew that lately I hadn't been in the mood for chats.

"So how's morale around here?" I asked him.

"You mean, like, in general?"

"I mean since we found Gershbein."

Josh thought a moment. "It's okay, I guess. Some people are still real upset. Some don't seem bothered. The field engineering guy who cleaned the blood off the circuits got jittery and asked to be transferred to the marketing office in San Francisco. All the regular field engineering guys are slow with weekly maintenance. I think they're spooked."

"I didn't know that, Joshua. I think there are probably a lot of things, things that may seem small, that go on around here that I don't know about."

"You mean like the Meryl Streep program?"

"I was thinking more along the lines of our work here. Tell me, did you notice anything wrong with Gershbein the few days before he was killed? Was he behaving differently or acting upset?"

"The FBI man asked me the same thing. He asked everybody. So did the police, but I told them there wasn't anything that I noticed. But Gershbein always kept to himself."

"Did you notice him working on anything unusual, anything different from our normal routine?"

Josh shrugged. "He was staying late a lot. But I guess that wasn't so strange, not for him. He left Dorothy home alone too much, I know that."

"So you know Dorothy Gershbein?"

"Not really. I just met her at the family picnic. That's all. But I felt sorry for her being alone at night so much with the baby and everything."

"Joshua, I want you to think about this. Have you noticed any operating system messages coming from Larry that seemed strange to you?"

He shook his head.

"Has anyone in our department been asking questions about the security software, questions you wouldn't expect them to ask?"

"No, not that I remember."

"Has anyone been programming operating system changes lately?"

Josh looked uncomfortable now and had begun pulling on his lower lip again.

"Only Albert," he answered. "But Albert always made the operating system changes."

So Albert Wu had been working with Larry's operating system. I didn't know if I should find it suspicious or not, but I would look into it.

"That's all, Joshua. Thanks. You've helped me."

Joshua stood up to leave. "You think someone in our department is the spy, don't you?"

"I don't think anything. I'm just trying to get as much information as I can."

"You do think it. You think someone we work with is a spy and a murderer. Maybe you think it's me. Is that it? Jeezus Christ." Joshua began to tremble and he grabbed the back of the chair to steady himself. "The FBI probably found out I went to that socialist rally back when I was at Berkeley. That's it, and they told you about it. It meant nothing. It was years ago. I vote Republican, I swear it!"

"Joshua, please, I don't think you did anything. I'm just trying to find out what's going on in the office. That's why I wanted to talk to you. If anything it's a sign that I trust you."

That seemed to placate him. He sighed and his whole body shuddered.

"Will you let me know if you find anything in the backup software?" he asked.

"Sure. And, Josh, I want you to program a swimsuit on Meryl," I told him as he walked out the door. "And make it a one-piece."

I decided to take the backup program to my office. On the way there I looked for Albert Wu but he had left for the day, so I left a message for Mrs. Dabney to make an appointment for me with Albert for Monday afternoon. If he had been making operating system changes, maybe he noticed if anything funny was going on with Larry.

I spent the next half hour in my office going over the backup program, but I needed more time to check it thoroughly. Glancing at my watch, I noticed it was six-thirty. A look out into the hall told me that everyone had gone for the weekend. Seeing the empty halls gave me a strange feeling, as if I had been abandoned by everyone. I shook the feeling off. This was no time for paranoia. There was too much work to do. It had been three days since we found Gershbein, two days since the data leak was announced, and I was no closer to the answers.

■ □ ■

Saturday I went to Gershbein's funeral. Every pew in the church was filled with Gershbein's family, friends and coworkers. He would have been impressed at the turnout. Afterward I felt sad and empty inside, so I did what I usually do when I experience any negative emotion—I buried myself in work. I was back in the office by early afternoon and spent the rest of the day and most of the evening combing the backup program line by line. But it looked like it was functioning okay. That was the problem. I kept probing into things, sifting through the facts, but it all seemed to be functioning fine, except that one person had died and government secrets were being spoon-fed to the Russians. There was venom running beneath the clean corporate surface at ICI, venom that killed, but I had no clues as to its source. And I had this feeling that there was more ahead of me.

I tried to remain upbeat in front of Charles. Although he was interested in the data leaks and asked me a lot of questions, he was happy and energetic all weekend, a sharp contrast to my own brooding state.

"So do you want to do it?" Charles whispered in my ear Sunday night as I leafed through a listing of security access records dating back three years. I had been so immersed in work I had forgotten that Charles was even there. He was very understanding about my bringing work home.

I looked up at him and noticed he was wearing his baby-blue Ralph Lauren Polo pajamas with a tiny horse and rider prancing across the pocket just above his initials.

"What time is it?" I asked wearily.

"Almost midnight."

I closed the file and left it on the nightstand. Charles got in bed and read *The Wall Street Journal* while I washed my face and brushed my teeth. After putting on my best nightgown and a dab of Opium, I crawled into bed next to Charles and switched off the light.

Charles began to whisper something but before he could I rolled on top of him and began to stroke his skin. We shared our lovemaking the same way we shared our evening meals—affectionately, politely, neither partner extending over the boundaries of immpeccably good taste. But that night was different because while I made love to my fiancé I wasn't in my bed in my home. I was in that elevator at Comtech making love to a stranger, imagining a passion I feared I would never experience in real life.

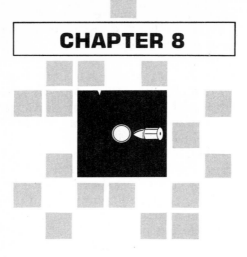

CHAPTER 8

When I left my house the next morning Charles still lay snuggled and asleep in my bed, the covers pulled up to his chin like a baby. Unlike children and small animals, men don't usually look cute when they sleep. Charles did. I kissed him and he smiled and groaned in reply. Trying not to disturb him, I quietly picked up the security software printout off the nightstand where I had left it the night before. I placed it inside my briefcase and slipped out of the house, munching my breakfast granola bar as I got in the car and drove to the office.

At seven the ICI offices were empty except for Larry's operations staff, who started first shift at six-thirty. I indulged myself with a fresh pot of coffee, then sat down at my desk and turned on the computer terminal. Sipping coffee from a Styrofoam cup, I thought once again that I should really get a ceramic coffee mug for the office. Joshua had given me one with a Cathy cartoon on it for Christmas the previous year, but I kept forgetting to wash it, and after a while the fungus inside looked permanent, so I tossed it and reverted back to the sanitary impermanence of Styrofoam. It seemed that most of my food and drink came out of Styrofoam containers or plastic wrappings, but I didn't have time for leisurely homecooked meals. I envisioned that changing once Charles and I were married. I was going to manage my time better, slow down my pace, and I saw Charles and me cooking dinners that we would eat off actual china placed on an actual dining table. Maybe I would even get a cat.

I stopped my daydreaming and turned my attention to the screen in front of me. Still gnawed by questions about the security printout Dorothy Gershbein had given me, I wanted another look at it while no one was around. I pulled it out of my briefcase, placed it on my desk, then entered my i.d. and password into the terminal. Larry responded with a cheerful, preprogrammed "Good morning."

"Good morning, Larry," I said out loud. Does having a computer as one of your best friends mean you don't get out enough? I asked myself. I typed commands onto the screen, requested a listing of Larry's internal software, and went through it line by line, comparing it again to the copy given to me by Dorothy to see if there were any differences between the two. This time I did find something. I leaned closer to the screen, checked it again, and quickly scribbled some notes on the paper copy. The discrepancy was there.

By nine-thirty when I finished my comparison, the office buzzed with activity. I started to take a look at Gershbein's online employee records, but when I tried to get into the personnel files a message stating "Access Denied" flashed on the screen.

"Well, at least one part of your security system functions correctly."

I swiveled my chair and saw Paoli peering over my shoulder. I turned my back to him.

"Good morning," I said.

Paoli didn't wait for an invitation to sit down. I guess with his personality he couldn't afford to. "It is a good morning, isn't it? By the way, I have access to those personnel records, and if you're nice to me I might let you look at them. You, my friend, have been locked out."

Now I turned and looked at him. "Why?"

"Coleman found out you had been pawing through the hardcopy personnel files. That's considered a no-no for espionage suspects. So he had Garrett lock up the hardcopies and lock you out of the online records."

"What could I possibly do with personnel files?"

"To begin with you could remove incriminating evidence from your own personnel records, maybe add incriminating evidence to others."

"All I did was look for names or dates that could have been used as trapdoor passwords. I'm trying to help."

"Well, don't. Not unless you're working directly with me. Coleman doesn't appreciate it. I understand the way your mind works because you and I have similiar technical backgrounds, but Coleman doesn't see it the way I do. You're just going to get yourself in more trouble. Besides, we're duplicating effort. I went through the personnel files myself looking for the same thing."

I eyed Paoli and sipped my coffee. Paoli had brought in his coffee too, but his was in a ceramic mug with a picture of Garfield on the side. I wondered if we would throw coffee on each other before our meeting was over. Part of me hoped so.

"What did you come up with from the personnel files?" I asked him.

"No passwords I tried worked, but I did come up with quite a lot of information. Some of it was pretty interesting, especially when combined with NSA data from headquarters. By the way, what was that science project you won the ribbon for in high school?"

He wasn't kidding when he said the NSA records were complete. Paoli waited for my reply, but he didn't get one.

"Let me guess. You studied the effects of graduated electrical shocks on kittens. No? Sex transplants on guppies? No, not your style."

I gave him a cool look.

"Okay, I'm sorry. It was just a joke. I was only trying to lighten things up a little," he said. "You know, just because I work for the NSA everyone around here treats me like I'm diseased. No one seems to like me and I can't understand it. I'm such a nice guy," he said, flipping through some papers on my desk.

"No kidding."

"No kidding. I've even been described as cuddly."

"Like a tarantula." I grabbed my papers out of his hand. "Is there a purpose to this visit? I certainly wouldn't want you to think that I didn't like you, or that I didn't find you a cuddly teddy bear, Mr. Paoli, but I have a very busy day ahead of me and no time to discuss your personal problems."

"You wouldn't talk to me that way if you knew I had just saved your corporate behind."

"What are you talking about?"

"Coleman interviewed Alan Brewster first thing this morning. He found out you've been tinkering with the computer backup program. Coleman didn't like that. He was going to his boss with it, possibly to discuss pressing charges against you for tampering with evidence, but I told him I'd handle it. That peeved him to no end, but when the NSA talks, the FBI listens."

"I have a right to look at the backup program used by my own department."

"You don't have a right to play around with evidence. You're tampering with information before Coleman and I get it. It doesn't look good."

"Listen, I'm sick of all this game playing. If they think I did something illegal, let them arrest me. And I didn't tamper with anything. I looked at the backup program to see if it could have been used to get data from Larry. As for getting information before you and Coleman, I can't wait around for you guys to solve this. I only have a week and a half left to find the data leak or they're shutting me down."

"Did you find anything in the backup program?"

"No. That was a disappointment."

"A week and a half isn't a very long time, Ms. Blake. Seems to me we should start getting together and maybe swap information. You know, a little mutual back scratching?" Paoli wiggled his index finger to let me know just how much fun mutual back scratching could be. "The sooner we solve this thing the sooner you get rid of me," he added.

"You have my rapt attention."

"Good. Now, I've already gone through those personnel records and I think I have the info you're looking for. No sense in duplicating effort."

"What did you find?"

"What information do you have to give me in return?"

"Quite a bit," I said.

He took the bait. "You tell me yours first."

"Not until you tell me yours."

Paoli studied me a moment to decide if I would cheat him. "Okay. There is a programmer in this building with a history of hacking into large computer systems. There is also one person on your staff who visited Russia five years ago."

"Old news," I told him, although some of it wasn't. "I'm well aware that Joshua McCormack was charged with a misdemeanor during college for dialing into the telephone company's computer and erasing his bills, but the phone company dropped all charges in return for him telling them how he did it. That was one of the reasons I hired him."

"Do you trust him?" asked Paoli.

"Completely."

"Enough to stake your job on it? Because that's what you're doing."

"Joshua is in the clear as far as Gershbein's murder goes and you know that. The computer log proved that

Gershbein was murdered while Joshua was logged onto a terminal in the other wing of the building."

"That sounds nice, but it won't hold up. Someone with Joshua's technical skills could have altered the clocking device so the computer log would show the wrong time," said Paoli. He stood up and leaned against the wall, pushing the picture of ICI's founding father out of place. I could see Harold T. Gordon's stolid expression peeking reprimandingly at me over Paoli's shoulder.

"It's possible, but unlikely. An alteration like that would be noticed by the morning operator. Everything that went through the computer would have the wrong time on it. Somebody would have noticed it, and as far as I know, no one reported any such alteration."

"As far as you know," Paoli said.

"It's a long shot and you know it."

"Okay, it's a long shot, but it has to be looked at."

"Why do you care who murdered Gershbein? Your job is to find out who stole the data."

"Right, except the person who killed Gershbein and the person who stole the data are one and the same."

I stiffened and looked down at some papers so he couldn't see my face.

"And how do you know that?" I asked.

He walked closer to my desk and leaned toward me. "Work with me today, help me with this thing, and I'll tell you. I have free time from three to five. How about it?"

I leaned back in my chair to increase the distance between us. I detested bargaining, but I had to find out how he had made the connection between Gershbein's murder and the data leaks. "Okay, I'll meet with you, but I'm due at a meeting now and I'm booked solid the rest of the day. I should finish up my paperwork about seven. We can talk then."

"Until then," Paoli said as he walked out the door, tipping an imaginary hat.

As soon as he was out of earshot I picked up the phone and dialed Lieutenant Dalton.

"Do you have any news about the Gershbein murder?" I asked him quickly.

He hesitated. "Well, you see, the ICI 3000 has been down all week and it has hung us up a little. All of our fingerprint files have been fed into the computer, so we can't get at them. Your field engineering people are out here now and I'm sure it will be up any time."

I thanked him for his efforts and hung up. No offense to Larry, but computers were rapidly becoming more of a pain than a pleasure.

■ ◻ ■

I pushed my chair into a corner opposite from Paoli, unconsciously squaring us off like boxers before a bout. I looked him over, tried to size him up, to dissect his strengths and frailties so I could tuck him away in a category where he would no longer require consideration. But the man resisted definition. He came across as brash and obnoxious, but I sensed he was quietly calculating. He projected this image of silly boyishness, but his résumé proved he was intelligent and experienced in his field. I wanted to find him my intellectual inferior, but I knew that he was my equal. And there was an intensity behind his *poco loco* façade that told me he had to be taken seriously.

I watched him as he sat across from me flipping through the pages of a file. His jacket was off and I could see the outline of muscular arms beneath his shirt. I wondered if his chest was smooth or whether it was covered with dark fur, and I caught myself with the thought like a child caught with a forbidden cookie. Feeling guilty, I forced it out of my mind. I looked out the window and gazed at the lighted parking lot that was empty except for a few cars. It was seven-thirty and already dark outside.

"So tell me," I said, turning back to Paoli. "Tell me how you've connected the murder and the data leaks."

He closed the large file and held it in his lap. "I checked

the audit logs. Gershbein accessed the Project 6 security software the night he was killed."

"So?"

"I checked those audit logs going back three years. The security software was accessed normally about once a month for maintenance. In the last month it's been accessed fifteen times, always by Gershbein. Then the last night he accessed it he got shot in the chest. Doesn't that seem like a remarkable coincidence?"

"Gershbein wasn't involved in stealing the designs," I said.

"You can't know that."

"I know Gershbein. He never would have done it. I think he noticed there was something wrong with the security software and he was trying to correct it. That would be just like him, to notice the problem and keep at it until he fixed it."

"So the murderer killed him because he was tampering with the security software?"

"And destroying the means of stealing the data. That has to be it," I said.

Paoli shook his head. "Only I've checked that software backward and forward, including all coding changes. It looks solid. There was nothing for Gershbein to fix."

Apparently he hadn't noticed what I had about that software, but I didn't want to tell him what I knew. Not yet.

"You told me earlier that you had important information from the personnel files. What is it?" I asked, changing the subject. I didn't notice that I was nervously tapping a pencil against the desk. I guess the sound was annoying him because he grabbed it from my hand.

"Why are you so jittery?" he asked.

"I'm like this when I haven't eaten." I caught myself twisting my hair with my fingers, so I clasped my hands in front of me.

"I have potato chips in my briefcase. Want some?"

"No, thanks. Let's go on."

"Well, I have a few things you might be interested in."

He took a heavy folder out of his briefcase and opened it. "Alan Brewster visited Russia in 1975 during a summer when he was attending Cal Tech. He's currently a registered Democrat, visits his mother once a week, and belongs to a bridge club. I've checked him out and he doesn't look too promising, but he's worth keeping an eye on," said Paoli, spreading the files across my desk. "There are a few other people worth tagging. For instance, Peggy Thompson worked ten years for an ICI competitor."

"You don't have to worry about Peggy. I hired her away from that other company and it took a lot of convincing. She's very smart and very loyal. She also doesn't have direct access to any confidential data."

"Still, I don't want to rule her out. Okay, I've given you my information. Now you give me yours," he said. "Or was it all just a bluff to lure me to your office at night so you could be alone with me?" He followed the remark with a laugh. I didn't find it funny.

"Gershbein had a printout of Larry's security code that he kept at home. His wife gave it to me last week."

Paoli looked puzzled. "But Gershbein had authorization to the code anyway. We've already connected him to the data leaks because we know he kept accessing the security software. What's so interesting about him taking a software printout home with him?"

"Because the printout was classified confidential. Gershbein shouldn't have taken it off the premises. I just can't figure out why would he do it."

Paoli emitted an exasperated sigh. "Come on, let's talk reality here. People are always breaking rules, committing little office crimes, stealing supplies, cheating on an expense report. So he took a printout home that he wasn't supposed to. What's the big deal?"

"You don't understand. Confidentiality is the crux of our work here. People just don't break those rules. If you steal a pencil sharpener you get your hand slapped. If you violate a security rule you get fired immediately. Gershbein loved his job. Something important must have motivated him to take such a risk."

"Maybe he was going to give it to some nice little Russian," said Paoli. "Maybe he had been selling information to the Soviets all along, and when they didn't need him any more they killed him."

"But if that's true, they wouldn't have killed him. Why kill off a good source of information?"

"Maybe they didn't trust him. If he was selling stuff to them, obviously his ethics were less than impeccable."

"Then why would they kill him *before* he had turned over the security software? Why not wait until after they received it?"

"Because they didn't know they were going to get it. It was the molecular memory data they wanted, not your security system. Gershbein could have been throwing it in as a freebie, like when department stores give you one of those little samples of free aftershave when you buy a shirt."

"My security software would not be given away as a freebie."

"They probably would have preferred the aftershave." Paoli chuckled at his poor little joke. "The point is, Gershbein was in the middle of this thing."

"But only because he knew the security system so well. He noticed a problem and he looked into it."

"I think you're wrong."

"I'm right and eventually I'll prove it to you. Now listen to this," I continued. "I compared Gershbein's copy to the code actually running inside Larry, and there are some differences you missed."

"What differences?"

"Some minor reorganization of coding statements. Nothing that would affect how Larry processed data. Gershbein could have done it just to experiment with ways to improve Larry's processing efficiency. Gershbein did things like that. He loved to tinker. But there was one change that was odd." I could tell by Paoli's expression that I had him, at least temporarily, under my control. It felt good. "It was a nonsense line of code, an execution statement that didn't do anything. I've been comparing different copies of the security code, and as far as I can tell, Gershbein entered this execution statement the night he was murdered. Here it is." I grabbed an envelope and wrote on the back.

"EXEC 11,14," Paoli read.

"EXEC is an execution statement in assembler language, but Larry's security code was written in Fortran. 'EXEC' means nothing. I also checked back to statements eleven and fourteen, and those were simple lines of job entry code. The whole thing just doesn't make sense."

"Could Gershbein have started to make code changes and just not have been able to finish?" asked Paoli.

"If the changes had been on the printout he kept at home I might have thought that, but he never would have put experimental coding changes actually inside Larry. It's too risky."

"Why are you so intent on protecting Gershbein? Can't you believe that one of your precious employees could betray the hallowed halls of ICI?"

I looked at Paoli with narrowed eyes. If I had been a cat I would have hissed and scratched him. "You know what your problem is, Paoli? Your problem is that you don't know these people, you don't really know or care about them or the project. You fly in from out of town, sift through some paper, and then because you're from a government agency think you can start making judgments about people and situations that a week ago you had never heard of."

"And your problem, Ms. Blake, is that you're so stuck in the middle of it that you've lost all objectivity. You're too close to the situation to see it realistically."

"I'm handling this situation quite well."

"You need my help to figure out this mess and you know it."

"Don't flatter yourself. What I do know is that I'm not interested in arguing with you. Are we finished here?"

"Not yet. I want to take a look at that security code."

"We can look at it some other time."

"We'll look at it now. You're supposed to be cooperating with me, remember?"

"That's right, you're in charge of things around here, aren't you, Paoli?" I snarled, then flipped the switch on my terminal. After two seconds the ICI logo screen flashed brightly. I keyed in my passwords then requested access to the Project 6 program. The words "Project 6" printed across the screen. I began to key in a command when suddenly the screen went blank.

"What happened?" Paoli asked.

"Damn," I said, and hit a few more keys, but the messages on the screen were garbled. "I got a message from Peggy earlier today saying that there was a problem with some of the terminals. I guess they haven't had time to fix it. Gershbein's murder has field engineering spooked about touching the equipment. Their response time has really slowed down lately."

"Must be a terminal problem," Paoli said as he pressed a few keys.

"ICI terminals have the best performance record of any hardware on the market. I'm sure it's just a loose cable."

Paoli sighed. "It's a terminal problem."

"It's the cable."

Paoli grabbed the cable into the back of the terminal and jiggled it, but it was snug.

"See? I told you, it's a terminal problem."

"The cabling is obviously loose at the control unit," I said.

"Ten bucks says it's a terminal problem."

"You're on. The control unit is upstairs in the computer room. You can see for yourself."

We both stood up then Paoli followed me down the empty hallway and up the stairs. Everyone else in the building had already gone home. I pressed another code into the keypad outside the computer room door and we walked in. The second-shift operations person was at his desk. When he saw me he asked if I would watch things while he went to the cafeteria for a vending machine sandwich, and I said okay.

"This is the control unit." I pointed to a large metal box the size of a picnic ice chest sitting in a long line of identical units, all humming, their lights blinking happily. There were at least eight cables coming out of the unit I was interested in and all were securely fastened. I needed to find out which cable connected to my terminal. I studied them, narrowed it down to three, but I needed to follow the cables along the flooring several yards to make a final determination of which one was loose.

"So what do we do now?" Paoli asked.

"We need to take up the flooring," I replied. Every computer room has flooring raised two feet off the base to make room for the thousands of black rubber-encased cables that connects the equipment. The floor is set in removable twenty-inch squares of metal-framed soft tile. I walked over a few feet and lifted up a segment, exposing a mass of wires.

"This isn't it. The one I'm looking for has a blue identifier along the side. Let's try over there." I crawled to the left a few feet. Paoli squatted beside me, obviously amused at seeing me crawling around on my hands and knees.

"I suppose you're enjoying this," I told him as I tried to pry up another piece of flooring. He grinned at me and I wanted to spit at him.

"Can I at least help you with that?"

"I can handle this myself." Using all my strength, I pulled on the flooring, but it wouldn't budge. It looked buckled, as if someone had stomped on it. "Do you have a knife or anything I could get this up with?" I asked. Paoli shook his head. "Then go back to my office and get my purse. I have a nail file that might do the trick."

Paoli scooted off and came back holding my purse as if he had a dead rat by the tail. Why are pseudomacho guys always so afraid to hold women's purses? Makes you wonder. I grabbed it and scrounged inside until I found my nail file. I slid it into the space between two flooring squares and applied pressure, but the file snapped in two. I cursed, throwing the broken file to the floor. It slid under a chair and I noticed a woman's hair comb lying behind one of the chair's legs. The comb was black lacquer set with pearls, the kind women wear to decorate their hair. After seeing that the comb's teeth were metal, I grabbed it, then jammed it into the flooring, and pressed hard, but the flooring still wouldn't move.

"This is definitely stuck. I guess I'm ready to see how strong you are," I said to Paoli, backing off to let him give it a try.

He smiled a cocky smile, got down on his knees, wedged the comb into the rim of the flooring, and popped the square out easily. Then he let out a terrified yell.

I leaped down to see the source of his fear and my eyes widened.

What had popped out along with the flooring was a human hand.

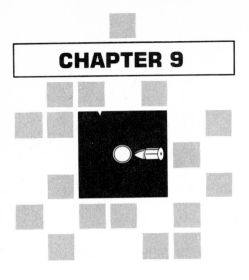

CHAPTER 9

I turned my head in revulsion, but something compelled me to look again at that gnarled flesh that had once been a human hand. It reached out through the gap in the flooring as if in anger, its flesh a putrid gray, its fingers curled into an angry claw. Paoli jumped forward quickly, ripping out squares of flooring until the body was exposed. I crouched behind him, afraid to come any closer.

"Get over here. See if you can identify this guy," Paoli instructed. I was frozen for a moment, caught between horror and macabre curiosity. I looked at Paoli, then slowly crawled toward the gap in the flooring and peered down. I saw an ashen face, its features contorted, the black eyes dull, the mouth slightly open revealing a bluish tongue. The body lay tangled in a web of black cables, but I clearly recognized the man who had offered me his assistance only a few days before. One thin black cable was coiled around his neck.

"I know him. It's Albert Wu." We were both still crouched by the body and I grabbed Paoli's shoulder for support. "He's dead."

Paoli gave me a sour look. "No, he's just taking a little nap here under the flooring. Of course he's dead."

I detected a wavering in Paoli's voice, and sensing his fear made me feel stronger.

"One of us needs to frisk him," I said.

Paoli looked at me with his mouth open. "Great idea. He could be armed and dangerous."

"Look, we've got to call the police, but first we should check his clothing and see if there's anything, any evidence that could lead us to whoever killed him. If the police get it first they'll tie it up for weeks, and we've got to work faster than that. But we have to be quick about it, because the second-shift operator will be back any minute."

"You're suggesting we withhold evidence from the police?"

"No, I'm only suggesting we take a look at it before they do. What harm could it possibly do?"

Paoli mulled over the idea a moment.

"Okay," he answered. "Go ahead and frisk him while I call the police."

I stood up. "Wait a minute. I'll call the police and you frisk him."

Now Paoli was standing too, and we glared at each other.

"Why do I have to frisk him?" he asked.

"Because you're the NSA person."

"So what does that make me, James Bond? I'm a computer specialist, not a secret agent. Body frisking is not in my job description.

I scowled at him, hoping to shame him.

"Okay, okay, I'll frisk him," he said. "But you stay here

with me and let me know when the operator comes back in the room.

I gave him an atta-boy pat on the back, then took my scarf from around my neck.

"Use this to cover your hands so you don't leave fingerprints," I said.

"It scares me the way you use those things." He took the scarf from me and got down on his knees by Wu's body. His face puckered and his eyes clenched shut as he gingerly put one hand inside Wu's coat pocket.

"Don't be a wimp," I said. "He won't bite."

Paoli looked up at me with an expression that was less than pleasant. "You know, that's a pretty sexist remark coming from Ms. Liberated Female Executive. I don't see you jumping in here to shake hands with him. Why should I like doing it any more than you just because I'm a man?"

He had a point. "You're right. I'm sorry. Here, let me help." I got down on my knees beside Paoli and tried not to look at Wu's face.

"Okay, you take his pants, and I'll take his shirt and coat pockets," Paoli instructed.

I hesitated but then I took a tissue out of my pocket, put it over my hand, and slowly reached for Wu's pants pocket. I turned my head to the side so I wouldn't have to look at the repulsive thing I was doing and my fingers accidentally slipped underneath the waistband of his pants. The tissue slid away and my fingers touched cold rubbery flesh. I jerked my hand out. An icy shudder moved through me. The feel of Wu's body reminded me of when I was a kid and my mother would make chicken and I would open the refrigerator and grab a cold piece. By now I was definitely feeling sick. More than ready to give up my frisking idea, I was desperate to get out of there. But I looked at Paoli who was busily patting around Wu's torso and I knew I couldn't give him the satisfaction. Okay, Julie, I told myself, this is no big deal. Death is part of the cycle of life. Death is natural, although the cable wrapped around Wu's neck made me pretty sure he hadn't died of old age. I stuck one finger inside Wu's pants pocket. Except for some loose change and his ICI badge, it was empty. I tried the other pocket.

"I think I've got something," I said, then pulled out a worn brown leather wallet and handed it to Paoli.

"You go through this and I'll call the police," I told him, feeling I had done my duty, then left to make the call. The officer I spoke to sounded pleasantly surprised when I told him another corpse had been found at ICI. After I hung up I saw the operator returning with his sandwich. I led him inside one of the offices and told him to stay put, then I raced back to Paoli and the late Albert Wu.

Paoli had his hand in Wu's shirt pocket. He removed a piece of paper and examined it.

"What is it?" I asked.

"An address, I think." He folded it and put it in his wallet. It was then I noticed how pale he was turning. He sat down on the floor, closed his eyes, and took several deep breaths.

"What's wrong?"

"This is giving me the creeps. I think I'm gonna pass out," he said, his face turning whiter and his breathing heavier.

"Don't faint on me now, Paoli. Here, put your head down, like this." I pressed his head toward his knees. He stayed that way a moment, then he lifted his head and looked at me.

"I feel like an ass," he said.

"You look like one, but at least a little color is coming back to your face. I'll get you some water."

I fetched a paper cup of water for him and by the time I returned the police had arrived, led by a befuddled ICI security guard. I took the security guard aside, told him to call information for Elkin's phone number and get Elkin to the office right away.

"Where is it?" a stocky, bushy-haired policeman asked

Paoli. I resented a member of ICI's scientific research team being referred to as an "it," but looking at Wu, the term did seem to apply.

Lieutenant Dalton showed up and he gave me a cheery wave. Paoli pointed to Wu's temporary grave in the flooring and the three policemen walked over to take a look and stared for several minutes. One of them returned his attention to Paoli and me and asked us the expected questions. The police photographer had started snapping pictures when I heard a commotion outside the computer room.

"Get off me, you dweebs!" screamed Wayne Hanson as he forged his way into the room, flanked by two policemen. "Julie, tell them who I am!" Hanson was wearing dirty shorts and a stained T-shirt and looked more like a street derelict than the president of Comtech. Even in the midst of the current tragedy I enjoyed watching Hanson play fisticuffs with the police. I allowed the scene to continue a moment before I explained to the police that Hanson had every right to be there, which, of course, he hadn't.

"How did you know what had happened here?" I asked him, once the police had unhanded him and were out of earshot.

Hanson looked at me with disbelief, as if I had asked if the sky was blue or the Pope Catholic.

"After the meeting about the data leaks I paid the security guard to call me if anything happened here. I have to protect my investment, you know," Hanson said as he walked over to take a look at the body.

"Yeach," he said, making a face as he stared at Wu. "This is really disturbing." Hanson crooked his finger to summon me. I didn't move so he walked over to me instead. "Julie, we can't have this sort of thing going on here."

I guess I didn't realize how frayed my nerves were, because my reaction to Hanson surprised me.

"What do you want from me?" I said to him. "You talk like this is due to some sort of mismanagement on my part, like I didn't read the management guidelines regarding the proper storage of bodies!" By now I was shaking and Hanson was babbling something, but when I saw Brad Elkin walk in, I dropped the conversation. I had other priorities. Elkin looked at me, then went over and took the obligatory look at the body. Soon the police, Hanson, and Paoli were huddled around Elkin, and I decided it would be advantageous to join the pow-wow.

"We can't be sure until they run tests, but he could have been dead for up to twelve hours," a detective explained to Elkin.

"You mean Wu was killed during working hours?" I asked, interrupting the conversation. They all turned to look at me.

"What are you going to do, dock his pay?" the detective asked.

"I had a meeting with him this afternoon and he didn't show," I told him.

"He had a great excuse," said Paoli.

"But how did the killer get the body under the flooring during the day without being noticed?"

"Easy," said Paoli, Mr. I Think I'm Going to Pass Out, now suddenly sounding cool and calm. "Whoever did it didn't get him under the flooring until after hours. In the meantime they could have hidden him anywhere."

"But there are always operators in the computer room," said Elkin.

"Not in this area. This section is mostly for tape archiving, and it's blocked from view by those tall tape racks. I would imagine that the glass wall between the two rooms is soundproofed to muffle equipment noise," Paoli said, looking to me for approval. "It proves that the killer works for ICI."

"How?" asked Elkin.

"Because although it's possible that someone outside the company could have gotten in after working hours and killed Gershbein, it's highly unlikely that a non-ICI person could be wandering around the computer room during the day."

Elkin looked distressed and I couldn't blame him.

"We appreciate your help, Vic, but I think we have it under control here," Elkin said.

"You have it under control?" he responded. "Two people in the same department have been murdered within one week. They're dropping like flies around here and nobody has a clue."

I saw Elkin stiffen. "I hope you don't let the murder investigation interfere with your work on the data leaks," he said.

"On the contrary, this is part of my work on the data leaks."

A pall settled over the group. We were quiet for a moment until Hanson broke the silence.

"Well then, does this mean that Wu and Gershbein were responsible for stealing the data?"

"Of course," I answered. "Wu stole the data, killed Gershbein, then in a fit of guilt strangled himself with a cable and hid himself under the flooring." I was still angry with Hanson for his previous impoliteness.

Hanson looked at me. "I wouldn't be so sarcastic, Julie. This is all your fault. If the project data had been totally secure in the first place, the data wouldn't have been leaked and no one would be dead because of it, would they?"

Before I could reply, Elkin came to my rescue.

"I wouldn't make accusations like that, Wayne. Julie is in no way responsible for what is going on here now. And I would be careful about spreading malicious rumors," he said in a commanding tone.

Hanson stiffened his puny physique to as forceful a posture as possible. "No rumors, malicious or otherwise, had better spread anywhere, Brad. Comtech is going public soon. If the news gets out that Comtech is involved in an ICI project in which corpses are coming out of the floorboards, it might shake the market's confidence, if you know what I mean. You've got a problem here and you better fix it." He spun around in Dalton's direction. "And by the way, I've been in my Comtech office since early this morning and

I can prove it, so don't try to pin this one on me!" he snarled, pointing a finger at Dalton, then he turned and stomped out.

Elkin put his hand on my arm as we watched Hanson walk away. "I apologize for his rudeness. There's no excuse for that."

"It's not a problem," I told him.

"Julie, I was going to tell you this tomorrow, but I might as well let you know now. We're asking everyone in your department to take a lie detector test. It's voluntary, of course, but it would set a good example if you would take the test first."

I wondered if setting a good example for the troops was the real reason he wanted me to be the first one to take it.

"Of course."

"And I think it might be best for you if you were taken off the project. I know we've discussed this before, but things have changed. The situation here is going to be increasingly difficult, and a management change might be a good idea from everyone's perspective. You understand."

My stomach felt as if it had dropped out of my body. After the evening's events I shouldn't have been surprised by anything, but Elkin's statement floored me. I wasn't sure if he had said it for my benefit or to cover his ass in front of everyone.

"We had an agreement, Brad. Only five days have passed since our meeting. We agreed that the best thing for the project is for me to be doing exactly what I was hired to do, and that's to make sure it succeeds. What we need now is stability and a strong front. If you move me out it's going to look like we're floundering," I said to Elkin. He didn't look convinced. I was about to make my second pass over the target when Paoli jumped in.

"I need Ms. Blake involved in order to continue my investigation. No one has her knowledge of the project's technical workings. If you change management now it will take months longer to get this cleared up. I think it would be a big mistake to take her off. I'm sure my management in Washington will agree," said Paoli.

Elkin looked at me for what seemed a long time. "All right. You'll stay on the project at least for another week."

I nodded.

"Now go get some sleep, Julie. You look like you need it."

Elkin walked away. They had removed Wu's body, and there were only two policemen and Dalton left in the room doing fingerprint dusting. The policemen had tried to talk to me, but after answering the initial questions I had asked them to continue the interview the next day. They didn't seem happy about it, but they agreed, mainly because Dalton okayed it. I looked at my watch. It was 11:00 P.M.

"Guess I'll see you tomorrow," Paoli said.

"Thanks for helping me out with Elkin."

"I didn't help you out. I helped myself out because I need you. You're not the only one with your tail on the line."

I would have smiled at him if I had had the energy, which I didn't.

"You could do one thing for me," he asked.

"What?"

"Let's not use last names anymore. I think I read in Miss Manners that finding a body together puts people on a first-name basis. You can call me Vic."

I nodded. "Okay, and I guess anyone who has looked up my dress can call me Julie. Good night, Vic."

"And by the way, I owe you ten bucks. It was a cabling problem after all. Good night, Julie." He smiled and walked out.

It wasn't until then that I realized how exhausted I was. I felt limp and empty, and if I had been anything other than a stiff upper-lipped masochist I would have cried. Instead I walked toward the door to go to my office and got my briefcase. I heard my name called. Turning, I saw Dalton walking toward me.

"Two murders in one week. Pretty wild, isn't it?" he said casually, as if he were describing the latest dance craze.

"Yes, it is," I answered, then turned to leave.

"ICI has asked the police department to do the polygraph tests. Brad Elkin just told me in the hall that you've agreed to go first." Dalton tossed the words at me quickly, as if they were an embarrassment.

I stopped, then turned to face him. "Sure, why not?"

"It's not a bad experience. You'll probably find it interesting," said Dalton. "Call the station tomorrow and make an appointment. Here's the name of the person you'll need to see." He handed me a slip of paper, then hurriedly said good night.

That capped off the evening for me. I was now definitely and formally a murder suspect. I tried to imagine for a moment what it would take for one human to kill another. It was something I couldn't fathom, and what scared me was that there was someone near me who could fathom it, could plan it, execute it, then walk around calmly. The idea made me nauseous.

When everyone had left I walked outside to my car. The California night air hung with a lonely blackness as I finally headed down Highway 101 toward home. I would have liked to roll down the windows, to allow the cold night air to cool my face, but I kept the windows up, the doors locked tight as if that could keep away the evil that seemed to surround me. The highway is a lonely place in the dead of night. It allowed the fear I had been suppressing to swell up inside me, to expose itself on the surface until I hid it away again the next morning.

CHAPTER 10

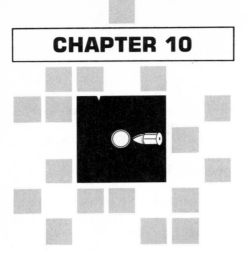

That night I dreamed of Albert Wu. In my dream he knocked on my door. I opened it and saw him standing there, staring at me with his waxy face, his eyes bulging, his mouth opened into a hideous gape, and the black cord wrapped around his neck until the skin pinched and swelled. I tried to scream, but no sound came. I slammed the door, but Wu kept pounding and pounding on it until the awful sound throbbed inside my head and I thought my brain would burst. Finally I awoke, drenched in sweat and fear.

At first I thought I was still dreaming, but then I realized the pounding was real and coming from my front door. Taking a second to steady myself, I rolled over and read the clock: 7:00 A.M. I had managed only three hours of fitful sleep, having spent most of the night lying in my bed wide-eyed, staring into the darkness. It was like when I was a child and every shape and every shadow seemed like a monster lurking. Only now the monsters were real.

The knocking grew louder. I dragged myself out of bed and threw on my flannel robe. Opening the door a crack, I saw Charles. My heart soared for a moment, I was so glad to see him, but then he held up the front page of the *Chronicle*, which had SILICON SLAYER STRIKES AGAIN emblazoned across the front, and my heart did a crash landing, no survivors. I snapped off the chain, opened the door, and grabbed the paper out of Charles's hands.

"Julie, tell me what the hell happened last night," Charles demanded as he followed me, my face glued to the paper, back to the kitchen. The news story described in inaccurate detail the discovery of Wu's body under the flooring as well as a recounting of Gershbein's murder one week earlier. It also said that the coroner estimated that Wu's body had been put under the flooring very early that morning, sometime between 7:00 and 9:00 A.M. The police theorized that the killer planned to retrieve the body later that night and dispose of it elsewhere. I found that part especially interesting since Paoli and I had probably foiled the murderer's plan. The story quoted the ICI security guard and the police and speculated that the murders were connected. All ICI staffers had refused to comment.

The article mentioned ICI frequently, but there was no reference to a confidential project or any data leaks. That at least was a blessing, but my name sprang up in the second paragraph, along with Paoli's, as the discoverers of the body.

"Are you listening to me, Julie?"

"Yes, Charles, what is it?" I mumbled, still absorbed in the story.

"For God sakes, tell me what went on last night!"

I looked up at Charles and saw he was getting rosy around the ears. "It's all in the newspaper article, which you obviously read. Wu was murdered and I found him. What else is there to say? God, I need coffee." I walked to the counter, Charles at my heels, and rattled around the cabinet for a clean mug. I filled it with water, a little milk, and a teaspoon of instant decaf coffee and stuck it in the microwave. My name in the paper could only worsen my problems.

"What were you doing there so late with Paoli, anyway?"

I slammed a spoon down on the counter. It didn't make much of a noise, but I guess it got my point across. "Don't pull a jealous act on me this morning, Charles. I can't stand it, not now. Paoli and I were working on the data leaks."

"And just how did you find Wu?"

"We were having sex and we happened to roll over on top of him," I snapped. Charles didn't look amused. "My terminal wasn't working right. I was checking the cables under the floor in the computer room and I found him. Poor Albert. And now it's all over the papers and my name smack in the middle of it. Garrett will have my head for this."

I pulled my coffee out of the microwave and stirred it. With a frown Charles looked at my cup. I didn't offer Charles any because he never drank coffee unless it was made from freshly ground beans taken recently off the back of some mule in a South American country. If my coffee didn't come from freeze-dried crystals I didn't recognize it. My ulcer didn't allow me to have the real stuff, so I had to settle for decaffeinated. I sipped my instant brew and tried to stop my hands from shaking.

Charles took off his jacket, put it on the back of a chair, and loosened his tie. "I warned you to stay out of this investigation, Julie. I knew it would only dig the hole deeper for you, but you wouldn't listen to me."

"Paoli said he needed my help."

"So you're taking advice from Paoli now, is that it? He doesn't care about your future or what damage could be done to your career. He's using you."

"He's not using me, Charles. We were going over the personnel records. He was giving me background information on some people, the terminal malfunctioned, we were checking the cables, and then suddenly Wu turned up under the floor."

"That's it? That's all you have to say? Wu just turned up under the floor sort of nonchalantly? Aren't you even upset about it?"

I set my coffee cup down with a little too much emphasis and it splashed on the table. "Of course I'm upset. Look at me. Do you know what it's like to find someone you know murdered? I'm more than upset, Charles. I'm panicked. I can't sleep anymore. I keep thinking about Albert and how he looked lying there. I think about Gershbein with blood all over him and I feel so helpless because I think of who might be next." I reached for my coffee but when I lifted it my hands were shaking so badly the coffee sloshed over the sides. There was now more coffee on the table than there was in my cup.

Charles saw me staring at the puddle and walked over and put his arms around me. Turning toward him, I buried my face in his chest and he stroked my hair. It felt good just to be held.

"It's all right, darling. I'm sorry I brought all this up right now. It's just that I'm very worried about you. How could I not be? There's a killer loose and you always seem to turn up in the middle of the whole mess. Julie?"

I looked up at him.

"I think you should leave the project, for your own safety," he said.

"You sound like Brad Elkin."

"You should listen to him."

"I'm not leaving the project. I won't do it. I've devoted five years to it and we're close to being finished. If I did leave and they replaced me, the project would never be successfully completed. I'm the only one who can do it."

"Now really, you think you're the only person who is capable of doing the job?"

"I know how it sounds, but I'm the only person who knows the molecular memory work from the beginning."

"What about Elkin?"

"He sees it from a much higher level. He doesn't have the technical grasp of it that I do. You know that."

"Listen, Julie, you have to think about yourself. If you don't want to think about your safety, then think about your career. Staying in the middle of this can't be helping you professionally."

"That's precisely it. If I'm going to continue with my career then the source of the data leaks has to be uncovered. If I give up and let Elkin transfer me off they'll shut down the project. I'm sure they'll continue to investigate the murders, but the data leaks might not ever be solved if I'm not there."

"Whether the data leak issue is solved or not isn't your problem."

"Yes, it is. I don't want it hanging over my head. I'll always imagine people thinking that I was stealing the data myself or that I was incompetent enough to let it happen and never figure out why. I couldn't live with that."

Charles looked down at me, studying my face, then he kissed me on the forehead.

"Promise me one thing, and that is you'll stay completely out of the murder investigation. Let the police and the FBI handle it. Will you promise me?" he asked softly.

"I can't promise anything, Charles. I'm sorry, but I just can't promise anything."

■ □ ■

"It's been hell's kitchen in here. The shit is flying. I've got fourteen phone messages for you already," Mrs. Dabney said with irritation in her voice. A ballpoint pen stuck out of her bouffant hairdo. The phone buzzed and she pulled the pen out of her hair like a sword from a scabbard and used it to punch the blinking button angrily.

She then placed it back in its original over-the-ear position. I noticed purple lipstick had traveled up the fine lines surrounding her mouth and I wondered if I should tell her.

I decided against it, sensing that at the moment she would not be receptive to helpful criticism. The ICI clock over her desk read 9:25. It had been three years since I'd arrived this late for work, but I had purposely waited, reasoning that it would take at least an hour for the general hysteria over the newspaper article to die down so the phone wouldn't be ringing incessantly. I was wrong. Mrs. Dabney slammed down the receiver and sighed.

"Three calls from John Garrett, two calls from newspapers, one from Channel Four news, one from Channel Eight, some assorted calls from around the building, and, oh, yes, here's one from your mother in Sacramento." Mrs. Dabney handed me the stack of white paper slips. The mention of my mother made my neck and shoulders tighten and I could feel my mountain-grown Folgers eating its way through my stomach lining. I wondered how my mother had found out so quickly. Did she have radar?

"Should I hold your calls?" Mrs. Dabney asked as I started to close my office door behind me.

"I'll take all calls except from newspapers or TV stations. You can tell them I'm not available for comment." I paused. "And please call Lieutenant Dalton's office and schedule a lie detector test for me this Friday. Tell him that's as soon as I can make it."

Mrs. Dabney's head spun toward me. "A lie detector test?"

"Yes. It's just a formality. Please schedule it," I said calmly, then retreated back into the safe haven of my office. Don't let them think you're scared, Julie. Meet it head on. I sat down and was unlocking my desk drawer when I got the first buzz.

"It's John Garrett," announced Mrs. Dabney.

"I'll take it," I said, as if I had a choice. Mrs. Dabney connected us.

"Julie, John here. Seems like we've got a little problem."

No kidding, John.

"Meet me in my office at ten," he instructed.

"I'll be there."

Garrett hung up without saying good-bye. He sounded upset, but I knew I could always handle Garrett. The phone buzzed again.

"Your mother." Mrs. Dabney said the words slowly and haughtily as if announcing the queen. My mind raced. Can you tell your own mother that you're not available for comment? I wondered. I could handle Garrett, Brad Elkin, the press, and the police, but the prospect of dealing with my mother left me quaking.

"Put her on." I heard the *click* that connected our phone line and I gripped the edge of my desk. "Hi, Mom," I said too cheerfully.

"Baby, you pack some things and come home. Now."

"Who told you, Mom?"

"Chuck called this morning." Mom loved to call Charles Chuck. "He asked me to talk some sense into you. He says you're in danger. I will not have my only child in danger."

I took my Maalox out of the desk drawer and began shaking it. I liked to think of it as the Acid Stomach Marimba.

"Mom, Charles is overreacting."

"People are popping up dead in your office and you say Charles is overreacting?"

"He shouldn't have called you."

"Somebody's got to tell me what's going on. You never do. He called me because the man loves you. When are the two of you getting married?"

"I don't know."

"Your ovaries aren't DieHard batteries, you know. If you want children you'd better get started."

I opened the Maalox and took a swallow that stuck in my throat.

"I've gotta go, Mom," I said, choking on the thick liquid.

"Juliet, I want you to come home."

"I can't and that's final."

"Final is when you're dead, Juliet."

"Our building has security. I'm perfectly safe."

"Your security hasn't stopped two murders. I could come get you."

"Bye, Mom. I love you."

"Don't hang up on me, Juliet."

"I have to go. Believe me, I'm perfectly safe."

"Call me tonight?"

"Okay, I will. Now good-bye. And I love you."

"Love you too."

We hung up, disconnecting the umbilical cord between us, and I sighed with relief. After Mom, handling John Garrett would be a snap. I rang Mrs. Dabney and told her to hold all calls except for Elkin or Paoli, then I turned to my terminal and entered my i.d. and password. Apparently once they removed Wu from the wires the terminal worked fine. I requested access to Larry's security data, the screen paused, then responded with "Access Denied. Consult Your Security Coordinator." It had to be a mistake. I was the security coordinator. I tried logging on again, but the same message appeared. I picked up the phone and dialed Brad.

"Good morning, Julie," he said.

"Hi. Got a problem. I tried to log on to Larry just now but there's been some foul-up and I can't get into the internal files. Could you authorize an i.d. change for me?"

"I'm sorry, but there's no mistake. I got a call from the executive committee in New York this morning. Everybody is frozen out of the Project 6 files until this situation is cleared up."

"Brad, I have to get in every day to check algorithm results."

"Sorry. This came down from headquarters. There's nothing I can do, but I'll check the results and keep you updated."

"Hold on a minute. I'm the one who wrote that code, but you get to look at it and I don't? To lock me out of it is ridiculous, not to mention an irrational reaction to the facts. We can't stop progress on the project. That's what the killer probably wants."

"Have you read the papers?" he asked.

"Yes, I have. The news coverage is unfortunate."

"It's a disaster. A friend of mine at the *Chronicle* said they're doing a feature tomorrow on computer sabotage. Reporters are trying to get in here, Coleman has brought in a pack of FBI people, and Jennings from headquarters is breathing down my neck. There's been some formal discussion about tabling the project."

"You and I had an agreement. I have over a week left."

"Decisions from headquarters supercede any agreements between us. There's not much we can do to stop it."

"Yes, there is. We can find the killer."

Elkin reflected on that statement for a second. "I think you're getting carried away. The police have the job of finding the killer. Both the NSA and the FBI are consulting with them. I'm sure they'll come up with something soon."

"Not soon enough. It will take them months to find out anything. We can do it much faster if we work together."

I heard Elkin take a deep breath.

"Julie, I want you to try to relax for a few days. I know this has all been a terrific strain on you. Nobody would think less of you if you took a week off. If you give yourself a chance to rest, I think when you take a fresh look at this whole thing you'll see it in a different perspective. I'm flying to the East Coast tomorrow to talk to Jennings. I'll do my best to stall them a few days. I've got to go now. Drop by my office this afternoon and we'll talk, okay?"

"Okay," I answered. I put down the phone. My stomach churned and gurgled uncomfortably. To be denied access to Larry's project files was a slap in my corporate face, but what really bothered me is that now I couldn't look at the security code Gershbein had been working on. My intuition told me that program was the key to both the data leaks and the murders, if only I could find out how. I would find out. I had to.

I ran my fingers through my hair and closed my eyes. When I originally wrote the security code I had put in a trapdoor password, one that no one knew but me, as a safety precaution when we were doing the original testing. I had intended to cancel it, but just never got around to it because I was so busy and it had never seemed that important. Maybe deep inside I knew one day I would need it.

You're thinking crazy thoughts, Julie, I warned myself. If I got caught using it I could be fired. Maybe Charles and Brad were right. Perhaps I should relax a little, take a few days off, let Paoli and Coleman uncover the data leaks and the police work on the murder. Getting involved was only going to cause me trouble. But then, whether to get involved wasn't the issue, since I was already involved up to my eyebrows. I could tell from Elkin that the executive committee was ready to shelve the project in order to avoid more bad publicity, but I still had some time. The next scheduled executive committee meeting would be in one week on the first of the month. Even if they did decide to do it, they wouldn't make a final decision until then. The only way to stop them would be to solve the data leaks and the murder before the meeting. I needed to look at that security code, but I had never been the type of person to break rules. I never got speeding tickets, cheated on my taxes, or took more than nine items into the supermarket express line.

But then, that was before somebody started murdering my employees.

■ □ ■

Garrett's secretary ushered me into his office. He sat behind a large, contemporary oak desk, the surface neatly arranged with only a few stacked papers, indicating an efficient man in the middle of an efficient work day. Garrett was on the phone. He acknowledged my presence with a nod and motioned for me to sit. I sat. Garrett had a corner office with two adjoining glass walls, and I looked out and saw Silicon Valley spread out in front of me. We were only five floors up, but I was still impressed by the view. Silicon Valley didn't have any skyscrapers because of a fear of earthquakes and the constant knowledge that one properly centered 8.0 on the Richter scale could send all our castles tumbling to the ground.

Garrett stayed on the phone long enough to let me know I wasn't too important, then hung up.

"Good to see you, Julie," he said, leaning back in his leather chair and smiling a casually condescending smile he must have practiced for years. "I guess you know what our topic of discussion is today."

"The spawning season of the humpback whale?" I asked in a tone too sarcastic for my own good. The corners of Garrett's mouth turned downward.

"Do you see that plaque on the wall to your left?" asked Garrett, pointing to a small oak-and-brass square on an uncluttered wall. "Do you know what it says?"

My insides clenched into the scowl I dared not show on my face.

"Opportunities for individuals," he said. I lip-synched as he uttered the words.

"That's the ICI motto," he explained reverently, although he didn't need to. We all had the motto drilled into us during our ICI training days.

"What exactly is your point?" I asked, getting bored with whatever song and dance he was doing. I didn't like business meetings in which the participants spoke Corportese, a demilanguage filled with corporate cliché and innuendo. He eyed me with irritation.

"The point is that we at ICI can't be upholding our motto of opportunity for individuals if individuals are being murdered on ICI premises. Being murdered is not an opportunity, wouldn't you agree? And it doesn't do much for the corporate image." He paused. "What do you think we sell here at ICI, Julie?"

"Computers?" I answered, although I knew it was a trick question.

"Wrong. We sell an image, an image of solidity, confidence, and trust in the American capitalist system. When

ICI employees get shot and strangled right here in the office, what do you think it does to our image?"

I assumed there was no need for me to answer.

"It turns it to horseshit," he said gravely. "Do you have any idea how bad these murders look to the boys in New York?"

"The boys" were the executive committee and a term I resented since there was at least one woman among their ranks.

"We'll find the murderer," I said.

Garrett gave me a cockeyed look, as if he couldn't fathom my obvious inability to grasp simple concepts. "Have you seen this?" He held up the "Silicon Slayer" headline. "I've been hip deep in horse manure because of this," he said, raising his voice nastily. He slammed the paper on his desk. Then he paused and took a breath. "Look, Julie," he said, in a voice turned softer. "I want the director's job that's opening up in New York when Jennings retires this year. I want it bad, and I'm not going to get it unless this mess gets cleaned up."

"I'm trying to clean it up now, John."

"I don't want you trying to do anything! I want to find this killer as much as you do, but you keep your nose out of it for your own safety. That FBI person is hopping mad about you digging around. For ICI management to get stuck in the middle of it makes us all look worse. We've got to keep our distance from the thing. Let outsiders do the investigating. That's their job and I have complete confidence in their ability to do it." I started to speak, but he held up his hand to stop me. "I know what the score is here, Julie. You're young. You're the type of person who likes to take a problem by the horns and wrestle it to the ground, and I like that. But I'll tell you something you won't read in management books. In a company like ICI, if you see a mess on the floor as big as this one, you hold your nose and tiptoe around it. You let other people get dirty and you keep yourself clean, and for me to keep clean on this, you have to keep clean. I don't want you playing Nancy Drew around here anymore. Just do your job, no more, no less. No finding any more dead bodies. Leave that to the janitors. Until this mess is over I don't even want you on the premises after six. It doesn't look right. Do you understand what I'm saying?"

"Yes, sir."

"Because if you don't, you're going to get your butt and your fancy résumé kicked right out on the street. Are you with me?"

I nodded.

Garrett walked around the desk and patted my shoulder, once again turning calm and paternal.

"You know, I've always liked you, Julie. I usually don't take to recruits from high-priced graduate schools. I've always believed you don't learn business in a classroom. You learn from experience. But you're different from the rest. You're a bulldog and I like that. We'll get through this little snafu and once I'm a director you know I'll have a job for you at headquarters. Are you with me, Julie?"

"Yes, sir."

"Can I count on you?"

I forced a smile.

"Good girl."

Garrett opened the door to let me know our little chat was over. I stood up, we shook hands, and I walked out the door. After heading directly to my office, I called Charles and canceled our dinner date for that evening.

I figured I better not try the trapdoor password during working hours. It was too risky. It would be better for me to come back late that night.

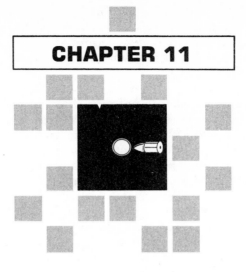

CHAPTER 11

The words glowed a liquid green against a background of fathomless black. If I stared long enough I could see my own reflection in the glass of the terminal like some shadowy character lurking behind the message on the screen.

"EXEC 11,14." I looked at the statement over and over again, feeling that it held some answer, at least a small piece of this puzzle of death that surrounded me, but its meaning remained elusive.

I rubbed my eyes and yawned. It was 10:00 P.M., the only time I dared come into the office and try the trapdoor password. I had to go past the security guard when I came in, but I distracted him with gossip about the murders so he didn't notice that I hadn't signed my name to the front-desk control log. After our chat I made my way through side corridors where there was less chance of my being seen. There was a small windowless room with a terminal on the second floor and I did my work there, but my effort had yielded nothing.

Why had I ever gotten into this business anyway? Deep inside I had always thought of myself as an artistic type, so how had I become so fascinated with these mammoth machines, these soulless, hulking information crunchers that performed their duties without compassion or caring? Maybe that was what attracted me. Machines were cold and powerful, the ultimate machismo that stirred all those subliminal primitive desires that I was certain lurked behind my outwardly feminist psyche. Yes, Juliet Blake, wunderkind of International Computers, Inc., had sexual longings for an ICI 9000, nocturnal yearnings to comingle her data, to have its powerful commands inserted forcefully into her disk space, to climax in ecstasy with simultaneous output.

"Do you have fantasies, Larry?" I typed playfully on the screen.

"Syntax unrecognized," Larry responded innocently. But I felt in my bones that Larry wasn't telling all he knew.

■ □ ■

"Half the people here look like they've been embalmed. The only way to recognize Wu is to find the guy lying down," Max said as she, Charles, and I entered the funeral chapel.

"You're a very crude person," Charles said, and clutched my arm more tightly as if to pull me away from Max's influence.

"Oh, get that broomstick out of your ass, Chuckie," she replied. "What is this anyway, a funeral?"

Charles grimaced and I gave Max a look that warned her not to get in one of her usual squabbles with Charles. The morning promised to be difficult enough.

"Okay, I'm sorry," said Max. "Funerals make me think

of death, and thinking of death makes me nervous, and when I'm nervous, I'm crude. It's a defense mechanism."

I wasn't feeling exactly light and giddy myself. I steered Max and Charles toward seats near the back.

"Are we the only people here from the company?" Charles whispered as we sat down on a hard oaken pew.

"No, look over there. That's Pete Morrison, Sandra Lacey, and some other ICI people." There were about twenty company people in the room, but by normal standards the ICI turnout was small. A quiet and aloof man, Wu had not made many friends in the office. In comparison, the turnout for Gershbein's funeral had been huge. People from every department had shown up.

Max elbowed me. "I know you were his first line manager, so you're the one who should be here, but couldn't one of the all-powerfuls have gotten off their duffs and shown up here too? I mean, the man was murdered on ICI premises. You'd think there would be a bigger ICI management turnout to pay their respects."

"The management guidelines say that only one manager must attend an employee funeral. Anyone after that is strictly optional. But I guess at Comtech you don't have management guidelines," said Charles. Max opened her mouth to retort, but I interrupted.

"It's the end of the quarter and the division review is coming up. Everyone is buried," I said. I saw Max raise an eyebrow. "Okay, bad choice of words. But we're here and that's what's important."

I looked over the room and noticed a small group of Asians I assumed to be Wu's relatives. I saw his wife, whom I had met a year before at an ICI party. I didn't remember her first name, but recognized her as she spoke with someone near the front of the room. Most of his family lived in Hong Kong and New York. Wu had been moved by ICI to the Santa Clara facility six years earlier. He had told me that he was interested in moving back to New York to be with his family, but so far I had been unable to obtain the necessary transfer, although I had tried several times.

The service began. Charles entwined his hand with mine and we listened to the anticipated oration about Wu's devotion to his family, to his friends, and to ICI. The company had been such a large part of Wu's life, as it was for all of us. Most people worked for companies from nine to five, managing to forget their jobs when they walked out the office door. But ICI was different. The company was a paternal figure that filtered into all parts of our lives. We depended on it, believed in it, respected it, even feared it sometimes. I guess that's why it bothered me that more ICI people weren't at the funeral. In a sense, we were his family too. But I knew the murders had everybody spooked, and people wanted to block it out of their minds. What I remembered most vividly of Wu was that he always seemed to be in the office. He was there when I arrived in the morning and there when I left in the evening. It was sadly appropriate that Wu should die there.

I didn't like funerals. I'm sure nobody does. I watched Max and Charles listening to the minister, both of them wearing looks of appropriate solemnity, but I knew this event didn't really touch them and I longed for their sense of distance. I felt a rawness inside me, a surrounding malevolence outside me—feelings that were becoming disturbingly familiar.

As I scanned the room for persons I recognized, my eyes fixed upon one face in particular. It belonged to Vic Paoli. He looked at me and when my eye caught his, he winked. What was he doing there? And why did I feel guilty just looking at him? I quickly turned my head back toward the minister and squeezed Charles's hand more tightly.

The eulogy was thankfully short. Everyone rose to view the body, including Max and Charles, but I hung back. I had already seen Wu as a corpse and didn't need to relive the experience.

"Come here often?" a voice whispered from behind me. I turned and found Paoli.

"What are you doing here?"

"Just looking around, checking the room for suspects," he said.

"Collared anyone yet, Dick Tracy?"

"Nope. Everyone looks appropriately bereaved and totally guiltless. Too bad. But it's not a total loss. I need to talk to you."

"About what?"

"The address I found in Wu's pocket."

I pulled him out of the chapel and into the foyer.

"Women usually want to be alone with me, but this is a little sick, don't you think?" he said as I led him behind a large potted palm. I ignored the remark.

"So tell me, what is it?" I asked him when I was certain we were alone.

"We can't talk here. Dump Troy Donahue and meet me in the parking lot in fifteen minutes. We'll take a drive and talk."

"I can't do that. Meet me in my office this afternoon."

"No, not in your office. How about the bar in my hotel, the Marriott, at seven?"

I nodded. Paoli grinned and cast his eyes over my shoulder. Then I felt fingers curl around my arm.

"Julie, darling, what is he doing here?" Charles asked, looking at Paoli with disdain. Charles slipped his arm around my waist and pulled me close to him.

Paoli smiled. "To pay my respects. I don't believe we've met. I'm Vic Paoli."

"I've heard of you."

"Well, see you later," Paoli said quickly, then he moved to another part of the room.

"I think it was incredibly inappropriate for him to be here," said Charles, looking stiff. He waited for my agreement but didn't get it. His display of possessiveness in front of Paoli had bugged me. What was I, some motorcycle gang member's Big Mama? I was ready and willing to express my displeasure, but we were, after all, at a funeral. I figured our fight could wait.

"I think we should pay our respects to Mrs. Wu," Charles said. He led me to the end of a line of people expressing their condolences to Mrs. Wu and a few other family members. She looked about forty, was petite with a fragile pale face and dark eyes that looked like they had worn their saddened expression long before the death of her husband. Clasping everyone's hand and muttering her thank yous as they passed, she wore a slight, sad smile as people expressed their regrets. But when her eyes reached mine the smile fell from her face like breaking glass from a window.

"You," she muttered hoarsely, as if it were a curse. "You killed my husband."

Her voice was loud and bitter enough that Charles and several other people turned their heads in surprise, but no one's surprise could match my own. I pulled my hand that dangled out to shake hers quickly back. Looking at Mrs. Wu, I saw a hostility I didn't understand. The hate in her eyes sent a chill through me.

"All you ever cared about was the company. Oh yes, the company." She spat the last word like an obscenity. Her body was stiff and her shoulders were thrown back. Her small fingers were curled as if ready to tear into my flesh.

"You pushed and pushed and pushed him and never cared for anything but squeezing all you could out of him. If he hadn't been working late that night, working because you forced him to, he would still be alive."

I felt her hands grasping my shoulders. She shook me as she spoke the words, her face contorted with anger, tears streaming down her cheeks. I couldn't tell you how long she held me there. I felt suspended in time with this woman's fingernails digging into my shoulders as everyone watched, horrified. But they all froze in place. No one spoke or moved to my defense. They were too shocked to move. I know I was. I heard the words she spoke, but they only confused me.

It was Paoli who finally broke in and removed Mrs. Wu's clenched fingers from my shoulders. She fell back as if she would collapse, but Paoli supported her with his arm and led her to a chair where relatives quickly surrounded her. Paoli motioned to Max, who took my hand and hurried me out of the funeral home.

We stood on the steps. Max kept her hand on my arm and said soothing words I didn't hear as we waited for Charles to bring the car.

CHAPTER 12

"She was a crazy woman," Paoli told me as he waved down the waitress to order more drinks. "Don't dwell on it."

"I can't help it. I never asked Wu to work late, not once, at least that I can remember. And the way she looked at me, with all that hate in her eyes."

He caught the waitress's attention and pointed to our empty glasses. "But that hate wasn't for you. It was for what you represent. To her you represent ICI, and she hates ICI because she lost her husband to it, and obviously in more ways than one."

"It has to be more than that. I want to understand what she's got against me."

Paoli spit the ice cube he was sucking back in his glass.

"Is it so important that everybody love you? Isn't that over-achieving a bit?"

"I don't need everybody loving me. I don't need everybody even liking me. But that woman hates my insides. I'd like to know why."

Paoli picked up his glass, tossed a few ice cubes in his mouth, and began crunching them. When I was in high school people said crunching ice was a sign of sexual frustration. I pondered that for a moment.

"If it makes you feel any better," said Paoli, "Coleman found out what happened at the funeral and he called Mrs. Wu."

"How did Coleman find out?"

"There were some other ICI people at the funeral. Apparently Wu's wife trying to squeeze out your tonsils made lively office gossip this afternoon. Coleman heard it, so he checked it out."

"But why call her? That probably upset her even more."

"Because Coleman's job is to figure out what's going on around ICI, not to soothe the feelings of widows. He got curious so he called her."

"So what did she say?"

"Coleman could be holding back on me, but he said she told him that you had asked her husband to work a lot of nights."

"But that's not true!"

"Don't get excited. Just because she said it doesn't mean we believe it."

"Coleman could believe it. He probably thinks I've been luring Wu into the office every night and then finally killed him."

"The coroner's report estimated the time of death between two and four A.M. Tough time to come up with an alibi."

"As a matter of fact, I was with Charles."

I detected the faintest scowl on Paoli's face.

"I doubt that the word of your fiancé would hold up

with Coleman," he said. "I mean, Charles would do anything to protect you."

"I'm sure you're right."

"You're off the hook anyway. Coleman and the police are looking for a man as the killer."

"This is one case of sex discrimination I'm happy about. But why a man?"

"Because Wu was strangled, and strangling is a very physical process. He could have fought off a woman, at least a woman of your size."

"So we're looking for a man or a rather hefty broad. Maybe I could help by going to the drugstore down the street and hanging out by the queen-size pantyhose."

"You're cute, Blake."

"That's what my mother says."

The waitress brought our drinks, a scotch for Paoli and a gin and tonic for me. I usually didn't have more than one drink, but I was still shaken from the scene at the funeral home. I had belted enough Maalox that afternoon to coat the Cow Palace, and it hadn't helped much. Maybe the gin would. I smiled at Paoli in gratitude for his information on the morning's trauma. Max and Charles had made gallant attempts to calm me, but I wouldn't let myself be calmed. I preferred facts to soothing words. I took a sip of my drink and looked around the bar crowded with happy-hour patrons. The room was dark, warm, and smelled of beer and mildewed bar rags. The decorating scheme was tacky faux-Polynesian with fake palms in the corners and fishing nets hanging on the walls. Over the bar hung a painting of a tawny-skinned girl standing on a beach and wearing a lei and a grass skirt. Looking around the room, I could hear bits of other tables' conversations. They all seemed to be discussing computers or software or microchips or some subject too new to even recognize. For the first time I could remember I wished I could get away from it, just for a while. I imagined myself with the Polynesian girl in the picture. I bet she didn't know anything technical. I visualized the two of us walking down some beach in Tahiti and talking about shells and high tide and what kind of fish goes best with guava juice.

"I've checked into Wu," Paoli continued. "He got passed up for a big promotion several months ago."

"I know that. I was his manager, remember? It was a promotion that would have sent him back east, which was where he wanted to be. It fell through because headquarters decided at the last minute that they needed someone with a stronger marketing background. But I was pushing for him from the beginning. I was the one who recommended him for the job in the first place."

"Did he know that?"

I took a sip of my drink and thought a moment. "I can't say. I knew he wanted to go back east to be with his family, and I thought the position would be a good one for him. I put his name in and made sure his chances were good before I told him about it. But I guess I never directly said to him that I was the one who recommended him."

"Maybe he thought you were the one who killed his chances."

"Why would I do that?"

"To keep him on Project 6 where you need him. And he might have told as much to his wife."

"That's absurd. Surely he knew I would never stand between him and a promotion he deserved."

"Well, maybe he didn't know it. And maybe he was mad enough to tell his wife that you had cut him out of that promotion. Maybe he was mad enough to want revenge, mad enough to sell confidential project data to the Soviets."

I put down my drink and looked hard at Paoli. "So you think Wu was responsible?"

"It's just a hunch. He was working late every night, telling his wife you were making him do it. What was he doing all those nights? Anyway, I'm going to start checking it out. That's why I wanted to talk with you."

I watched Paoli as he took a contemplative sip of his scotch, and it crossed my mind that some women probably found him a very attractive man. It crossed my mind that I was one of them. It crossed my mind that I should slow down on the gin.

"So let's get down to business," I said quickly, pushing my half-finished drink away from me. "What about the address in Wu's pocket?"

Paoli leaned across the table. "The slip of paper I found in Wu's pocket wasn't only an address. There was some Chinese writing as well as two dates—yesterday's date and tomorrow's. There was also a time of one-thirty P.M. I checked out the address yesterday. It's an apartment building in San Francisco on Powell Street, a pretty ordinary building with average-looking people coming in and out. I watched it from across the street all day, but I didn't notice anything unusual. But then, I didn't know what or who to look for."

"So what was the Chinese writing?"

"It was sort of strange. I showed it to a guy in a ginseng store in Chinatown and he said the words mean 'pork,' 'pearl,' and some Chinese phrase that translated closest to 'two-faced' or 'two faces.' "

"Pork, pearl, and two-faced? It sounds like a country singing group," I said.

"I think it's much more than that."

"So what are we going to do about it?"

"That's what I wanted to see you about. I have a favor to ask of you." He leaned closer to me and I leaned farther back in my chair. "I want you to watch the doorway of the building with me tomorrow. You'll recognize anyone from ICI or Comtech that goes in or out."

"If you're thinking that Wu was going to meet someone at this address, isn't this person going to know that Wu is dead?"

"I think there were several people meeting Wu at that address."

"You mean 'pork, pearl, and two-faced'? You think they're people?"

"I think they're code names for the people Wu was working with. And just because Wu can't make the meeting doesn't mean the rest of them won't show. In fact, I think Wu turning up dead will provide an interesting addition to their agenda."

I pushed back my chair, trying to put a little more distance between us. "Listen, Paoli, you could be right about this, but right now I'm loaded with work. The project's at a critical point."

"I think you're at a critical point, Julie. We need to watch that building tomorrow because it will help uncover who is leaking project data and possibly who murdered Gershbein and Wu. I need your help. I'm not familiar with the people at ICI. You are. Besides," Paoli said, watching my face carefully, "you've got the jitters because Wu's wife accused you and ICI of being insensitive to her husband. Don't you owe it to her to do something that might help find her husband's murderer?"

That one caught me off guard. I reached for my gin and tonic. "Don't try to manipulate me, Paoli."

"Too late. You're manipulated. I can see it in your face. And you're supposed to call me Vic, remember?" He smiled.

I sighed. "What time tomorrow?"

"Nine in the morning. Meet me in front of my hotel."

"But why go so early? I thought you said the time on the paper was one-thirty."

"But there were two dates written and I can't be sure which day the one-thirty time is connected to. It's best if we watch the building all day, at least until it gets too dark to see anything."

I agreed. We sat without talking a few moments, sipping our drinks and listening to the soft music drifting through the dim bar. My hands lay on the small table, and when I felt my fingers accidentally brush against Paoli's, I jerked them quickly away.

■ ◻ ■

When I announced to Mrs. Dabney that I would be out all day, she stopped typing, her red lacquered fingertips hovered over the keys, and she eyed me suspiciously through her rhinestone glasses. I would be at an off-site meeting, I explained, and would call in for messages. I could see the gears turning in her mind, telling her that it was very unlike me to be away from the office during the fourth-quarter review, and with all the strange things going on at ICI, it just seemed that much odder to her.

But then suspicions were running rampant through the office. A secretary down the hall had quit because of the murders, but Mrs. Dabney was too tough a bird for that. Since Gershbein's death she kept a steel meat pounder in her desk drawer for protection. Some of the systems analysts had started a betting pool on who would be arrested for the murders, and I wasn't too pleased when I saw that several people had bet on me. One of the salient features of ICI was its calm, competent atmosphere. The company had a reputation for hiring well-educated, work-oriented professionals, but seeing their coworkers turn up dead at the office was enough to unsettle even the most diligent employees, so I didn't mind a little gallows humor. I put five bucks on the night janitor, just to show I was a good sport.

A cloud of gloom had settled over the office. Headquarters had beefed up the number of security guards in the building. People had begun referring to the computer room as the morgue. Everyone eyed each other with mistrust and no one worked late. Who could blame them? Some of the programmers refused to enter the computer room at all, preferring to work at terminals in outside offices. Those who did enter did their best to cope. Joshua would open the backs of all the large equipment to check for corpses before he started working, and another analyst wore a Mace pen around his neck. I tried to ease the tensions as much as I could, but there was little I could say to reassure them.

I fought off a few pangs of guilt as I waited in front of the Marriott for Paoli. I should have been at the office, but I wanted to investigate the address as much as Paoli did.

And he was right, I would be able to recognize any ICI faces that entered the building. A couple of weeks ago I had been a model employee. Now I was hacking into confidential software, sneaking out of the office, and lying about my whereabouts. It felt good.

A layer of morning fog blanketed the valley, making the scenery look like a segment from an old black-and-white movie. I had started to wear my trench coat but it had seemed too tritely spyish, so I opted for a light jacket over my brown jersey dress and now I was shivering with cold. Paoli pulled in front of the hotel in an inconspicuous white Toyota. He leaned across and pushed open the door for me. He was wearing blue jeans, a gray sweatshirt topped with a leather jacket, and running shoes with no socks. His hair, still wet from his morning shower, fell in shiny haphazard curls around his forehead. I had a girlfriend once who had paid ninety dollars for that same hairdo.

"Can we turn on the heater?" I asked as I got in. Paoli obliged. He was unusually quiet, but then I never really liked a morning person anyway.

"There's a Thermos of coffee and some doughnuts if you want them," he said as he pulled onto Highway 101 toward San Francisco.

"Is it decaffeinated?"

"No, regular."

"I can't have caffeine. My stomach," I said, reaching for a doughnut.

Paoli looked at me. "What's wrong with your stomach?"

"An ulcer."

"You need to relax, Julie, take things easier," Paoli said as he drove onto the freeway.

"You're telling me this on the way to a stakeout to catch a murderer?"

"You don't have to worry about anything today. I'm here."

I couldn't help laughing. "Sure, tough guy. You're the one who faints when he sees a dead person."

"That was different."

"Really? How?"

"I wasn't expecting it."

"But I guess today you're ready for anything."

"I brought coffee and doughnuts, didn't I?"

Paoli grinned and I faked a sneer, then poured myself some coffee to spite my stomach. Paoli rambled on about computers and the NSA and how the Celtics were doing. He sounded energetic and happy, like a kid on a field trip. I envied his lightheartedness, but couldn't share it. I mostly tuned him out, focusing my thoughts on the project and that mysterious line in the security code.

After about forty-five minutes I saw the hills of San Francisco in front of me. Paoli exited the freeway and maneuvered through the traffic to Powell Street. We drove down Powell a few blocks then he pulled to the curb.

"You're parked illegally. This is a loading zone," I told him.

"Relax. I'll pay the ticket." He pointed across the street. "That's the building."

I stared at the white stone building with a wide, arched doorway. It looked disappointingly ordinary. So what did I expect, bloody swastikas painted across it?

"So what do we do now?"

"We're doing it," he replied. "We sit here and we watch the front of the building." Paoli poured himself another cup of coffee and settled more snugly into his seat.

"This doesn't seem very productive," I said after a moment's silence.

"Do you always get bored this quickly? Try to get the Zen of this. Just keep your eyes on the doorway. We don't want to miss anything. It was today's date that was on that slip of paper. Someone is going to show up there today who could be connected with the murders. And if it's someone from ICI or Comtech, we're going to know it."

"But what if Wu was the only person who was supposed to be here today? Maybe the other words on that paper don't represent people. Maybe it was a shopping list or something. This could all be a waste of time," I said, taking off my jacket to get more comfortable.

"You're right, it could be, but this is the only lead we have, so we've got to check it out."

After the first fifteen minutes I began getting restless. I kicked off my shoes and experimented with various sitting positions, counted backward in hexidecimal, tried to remember lyrics from old songs and the names of all my boyfriends from age sixteen. The last one didn't take too long. I could never be a policeman or a CIA operative. I just can't sit still for more than ten minutes, and keeping my eyes fixed on the apartment building was making me sleepy. Paoli, obviously the possessor of a low threshold of amusement, seemed to be having a good time. He had brought along a backpack filled with taco-flavored potato chips, granola bars, and little boxes of fruit juice that come with a straw glued to the side. He just sat there staring at the building and crunching and sipping. Pretty soon I joined him. We didn't talk much. Our mouths were too full. I guess we knew chatting would distract us from our spying duty, although we did manage to take turns running to the grocery at the end of the block to replenish our food when it got low. I traded the store owner a twenty-dollar bill for bathroom rights. I told him we were photographers and we were sitting in the car measuring light levels for a shooting session of San Francisco buildings. Then I had to fake my way through a short conversation with him about what film is best for low light levels.

Powell was a busy street with people continuously walking by the apartment building. A few people even walked inside, but I didn't recognize them. For lunch Paoli bought us deli sandwiches and root beer. By early afternoon I felt fat and bored and was questioning my good sense for being there. Paoli was still disgustingly cheerful, but he must have been getting bored too, because he started talking a lot.

"This is my first stakeout," he said as he gazed out the car window. It was midafternoon. "I joined the NSA so I could work with computers. They have some of the best data processing technology in the world. It's been interesting and I like the research and the technical end of things."

I crossed my arms and slipped farther down into my

seat, not in the mood to hear Paoli's innermost thoughts. He apparently didn't notice my lack of interest.

"Still, I've always wanted to be an agent, to go undercover, to investigate real people instead of machines." He paused, still looking out the window. "Maybe I should transfer to another department, you know, to do something more creative than computers."

"But computers are creative," I argued for lack of anything better to do. "Some people just don't realize it. Technology is one of the most creative arts. What you create is as abstract and conceptual as art, and yet it contributes to people's lives."

Paoli took his eyes off the doorway long enough to glance at me. "I never thought of it that way before."

"So start thinking," I replied. We sat quietly a few more moments, then Paoli again broke the silence.

"How did you get interested in computers?" he asked.

I sighed. It was all starting to remind me of a Girl Scout campout when late at night we would sit around in our tents and spill our guts because there was nothing else to do.

"My mother wanted me to be a ballerina."

Paoli started laughing. I shot him a look and he tried to stifle his mirth.

"What's so funny?"

"It's just that you don't seem the ballerina type."

"I wasn't, but my mother had convinced herself I was, so I started dancing swathed in a pink tutu from the age of five. My mother was obsessed with the notion that I become a dancer."

"So how did you wind up a computer technician and not a prima ballerina?" asked Paoli.

"I was clumsy. Whenever I stumbled at a recital, Mother would fire the ballet teacher and get another one, but it never helped. My heart just wasn't in it. What I really loved was mathematics and physics. I got that from my father. He died when I was little. I guess I also loved it because it was my escape from ballet lessons, and at least it was something I was good at."

"So you gave up art for business. I guess that's what most people do."

"But I didn't give up art. I just found my own way of expressing my creativity. Molecular memory is a work of art."

"I know, I know, you've already told me, but I just can't think of anything associated with a conglomerate like ICI as art."

"What have you got against ICI?"

"It's the bigness, the coldness of it."

"That sounds ridiculous coming from someone who works for the federal government."

"At least the government has few pretensions about itself. It's an inefficient, out-of-control bureaucracy, but it knows it, and people know to get out of its way. Its shortcomings are out on the surface for everyone to see. But ICI is different. It's this massive, finely tuned mechanism, so swift and sleek that it gives no warning. If you don't anticipate it, it crushes you. I have a hard time seeing you as a part of it."

"You make it sound so cruel. There's nothing sinister about ICI. We all just work together and we follow the rules and—"

"Come on now, Julie," he interrupted. "Don't give me that we-just-follow-the-rules routine as if it included you."

"What do you mean?"

"I've done a little homework on you the past few weeks, Julie. You've broken a few rules."

"I don't know what you're talking about."

"I'm talking about the ICI plant in Santa Clara where a family of illegal aliens were working a few years ago. Immigration got wind of it, tried to clamp down on you, but those workers mysteriously turned up with green cards and Immigration got a new ICI computer."

"I did nothing illegal. Mostly I just used the ICI attorneys out of New York. Immigration already had that computer on order. I only got delivery speeded up. Those people were going to be sent back to a poverty-stricken part of Mexico where they wouldn't have enough to eat. I had to do something."

· 165 ·

"But you broke the law as well as ICI rules on illegal aliens and on use of corporate legal facilities."

"I didn't break the rules. I bent them a little. I don't know why you're giving me such a hard time, Paoli. Ever since you came here you've been on my back about everything from my security procedures to my fiancé. Maybe you don't like the way I do things, but—"

At that moment somebody across the street caught my eye. I practically threw myself in Paoli's lap trying to get a better view. "Look! That guy coming around the corner!"

Paoli turned to look across the street, which was difficult with me on top of him. I slid back closer to my side of the car.

"You know him?"

"That's the driver for the Soviet professor I met with, I'm sure of it. They were both at ICI last week, right after the announcement of the data leaks."

I recognized the guy, his blond hair in the punk cut and his baggy black clothes. We watched him as he walked up the steps and looked at the apartment directory by the front door.

Paoli pulled on his jacket.

"Where are you going?"

"I'm going to follow him. You wait here."

He got halfway out of the car then looked back at me. "Don't get out of the car, okay?"

I didn't like him giving me orders, but we didn't have time to argue. "Just hurry up. He's going inside," I told him.

I watched Paoli jog across the street and inside the building, then I sat in the car feeling left out of the excitement. I wasn't the type to sit around feeling useless. I stared at the front of the building. The driver had taken time to read the resident directory outside the door. I had to know what names were on the list. Paoli hadn't stopped to look at it, even though it could have given a clue about whom the driver was visiting.

I pulled on my coat, got out, and dodged traffic to cross the street. I felt nervous and a little frightened, but it was exhilarating. When I got to the doorway I looked through the glass panels but saw no one in the hallway. I turned to the directory and read it, but didn't recognize any of the names.

"You don't belong here, Miz Blake," a deep, familiar voice said behind me. A fearful squeak emerged from the back of my throat, and I spun around to find Mr. Petrovsky. He was dressed in the same dark wool overcoat he had worn the day I met him, but at that moment his face lacked its previous playfulness. He kept his hands deep in his pockets, and it crossed my mind that he could have a gun. My body went rigid.

"The trouble for you could be large. I advise you leave here immediately, Miz Blake," he said in a low voice.

I tried to see his eyes through his thick glasses, but they were fogged from the cold air and the heat of his breath. I didn't say anything. We just looked at each other. I saw his right hand begin to move out of his deep coat pocket. I told myself that even if he had a gun, he wouldn't shoot me on the street. No, he would force me inside first, then kill me. I wondered if Russian professors had diplomatic immunity. My heart raced as my eyes fixed upon his hand, which was almost out of his pocket. If I ran, would he take the chance of shooting me? I remembered seeing Gershbein's body, the way his face had looked, the blood all over his chest.

Then I screamed. Just as Petrovsky's hand emerged I shrieked as loud as I could, a short, shrill yap of a scream. Petrovsky jumped and the cigarettes he had pulled from his pocket fell to the ground. He cursed in Russian, dashed inside the building, then disappeared.

"What happened?" Paoli yelled, running around the corner of the building toward me.

"It was Petrovsky. He was here!"

"Who's Petrovsky?" he asked frantically.

"The professor from the Soviet university. He went inside the building."

"But you screamed. Did he try to hurt you?"

"No. I thought he had a gun, but he didn't. I think he ended up more scared than me." I started laughing when I remembered the look on Petrovsky's face when I yelled.

Paoli's expression turned stern. "I told you to stay in the car."

"Sorry about that. I don't take orders well. I saw you go inside the building, but just now you ran up to me from the outside."

"I went out the back and was checking around outside when I heard you scream. Did this Petrovsky guy say anything to you?"

"Yes. He warned me to stay away, that I would be in trouble if I didn't. Did you find the driver?"

"No, I lost him, but that's okay. At least we know Wu and Petrovsky are connected." Paoli grabbed my hand and tried to lead me back to the car, but I shook my hand loose.

"I've been crossing streets by myself for years, Paoli."

His face turned sheepish. It seemed funny to see him embarrassed when he was usually so cool. We crossed the street and Paoli got in the car. I slid in the other side.

"So I saw Petrovsky at the same address that was written on the paper in Wu's pocket. What does this really prove? That Petrovsky killed Wu and Gershbein? I don't think we have enough evidence to support that conclusion," I said while Paoli pulled into the traffic.

"You're right, but at least we have a start. There's got to be some connection."

"Hold on a second. I just thought of something. If those words Wu had written were really code words, then Petrovsky must be 'pork'?"

"How do you come up with that?" asked Paoli.

"Because he's fat, like a pig. Maybe Wu referred to him as 'pork.'"

"Maybe that's a motive for Petrovsky killing him," he said, then chuckled.

"I'm sure he never called Petrovsky that to his face. Wu was very polite. It was just a private word he used."

"So who are pearl and two-faced? Maybe the driver

person we saw. From his looks he couldn't be a pearl, but he could easily be two-faced," said Paoli.

"So that leaves pearl."

"Sounds like a woman."

"Not necessarily. A pearl is rare and valuable. That could be a man as well as a woman."

"I'm glad you think so. I knew you had a romantic side," Paoli said with a grin.

"Remember what you said after we found Wu's body? You said it had to be someone who worked for ICI because an outsider certainly would have been noticed. Especially an outsider like Petrovsky or his driver. If Petrovsky is involved with this, there had to be someone from ICI working with him."

"I've already come to the same conclusion," Paoli said. "Maybe you and I have been in the wrong business all these years. Maybe what we should do is put our obvious investigative skills to more productive use."

"Maybe you should keep your mind on your driving," I said after another car's horn reprimanded him for a careless lane change. Paoli gave me a look and we didn't do much talking the rest of the drive.

Dusk had settled in and I watched the glow of the passing headlights, my mind filled with thoughts of Wu and Petrovsky and the data leaks. The Wu/Petrovsky connection was fascinating, but it hardly began to put the puzzle together. Still, it was a lead and at this point anything helped.

About half an hour after we left San Francisco the sun had disappeared behind the hills on Highway 280. The heater in Paoli's Toyota was barely functioning, and I reached under the seat for my leather gloves. My hand struck something metallic and hard. I pulled out an odd-looking camera.

"What's this?"

Paoli looked at it. "An infrared camera with a special drive on the shutter. I got it from a guy in our West Coast office. That little contraption on the bottom attaches to the dashboard. It will take a picture every four seconds. You can use it with infrared or regular film. Pretty high tech, huh?"

"If you had this camera, then why did I have to come along? I could have just looked at all the photographs of the apartment building and told you if I recognized anyone."

"That's true, but I've always thought the personal touch is so important, don't you? I mean, you can't tell me you haven't had a good time." By now his face had broken into a full grin. I tossed the camera behind me into the backseat.

"Hey, don't break that. It's borrowed."

"I'd like to break your skull. You just wanted to get me in the car alone with you."

Paoli's grip tightened on the steering wheel. The smile had left his face. "Don't flatter yourself."

"It's true, isn't it? We didn't need to watch the building today at all. This was a game, a game that wasted a lot of my time."

"If you want to think that, go ahead. I could have just taken photographs, but the fact that you confronted Petrovsky in person did us a lot more good than just photographs of him would have. We now know for sure he's involved, because otherwise he wouldn't have warned you to stay away. Jeezus, you're such a prima donna. You think every man around is just dying to jump into your worsted wool panties. Well, count me out."

I bristled at the insult and we drove the rest of the way in frigid silence. Me, a prima donna? Absurd.

Paoli pulled into the parking lot next to my car. I hurriedly put on my coat, pulled on my gloves, and grabbed my purse.

"I'll see you tomorrow," I told him, then started to get out of the car.

Paoli grabbed my hand and pulled me toward him. I thought he was going to kiss me, and I responded by smacking him on the side of the head with my purse. He was still holding his head and looking confused when I leaped out of his car, into mine, then sped off into the darkness.

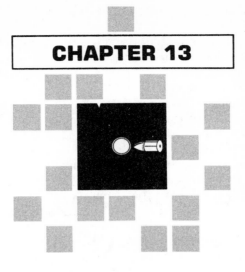

CHAPTER 13

Ms. Faye Oldenburg, police officer and runner-up in the Arnold Schwarzenegger look-alike contest, grimly, silently taped the wires to the skin on my arm. They seemed like tiny electrodes from an old sci-fi movie that would probe into my soul and discover if I was loyal and trustworthy, then transmit the information to some far-off planet. Did I lie, did I steal, did I wrap the black cable around Wu's neck and pull it tightly until the life was strangled out of him?

"What is your name?"

"Juliet Blake."

"What is your address?"

"Fifty-six thirteen Club Drive, Palo Alto."

"What day of the week is this?"

"Saturday."

I saw Officer Oldenburg give me a look that would freeze a flame. I laughed.

"Okay, so it's Friday. I just wanted to make sure your equipment was working."

Ms. Oldenburg looked at her equipment to make certain my simple truths registered correctly, then she referred to a list of questions about Gershbein and Wu. Did I see them alive the nights they died? Did I suspect anyone of killing them? Did I have any information that would be important in finding the murderer? Did I know anything regarding the data leaks that I hadn't told the NSA or FBI?

"Are you withholding any information regarding the deaths of Albert Wu or Ronald Gershbein?"

"No," I answered calmly. I was unafraid of the questions because I knew my answers would pass the test. I, of all people, trusted the capabilities of machines. But what kept running through my mind were all the other questions and answers I couldn't be sure of. I imagined how the machine would react if my interrogator asked me the really tough questions. Do you truly love Charles? Do you want to spend the rest of your life with him? Do you believe that, as Paoli told you, ICI would crush those who stood in its way, Ms. Blake? Have the past years of devoting your nights and days to the company really been worth it? And finally, Ms. Blake, did you fight off Vic Paoli last night because you wanted to get away from him or out of fear that maybe you didn't?

■ □ ■

"Well, hell," Max spat as she slammed her Gucci clutch bag on my desk and her fist onto her cashmere-swathed hip. She gave her sleek black hair an angry toss like a Thoroughbred horse with its bit too tight. "That Wayne Hanson bugs me."

"Hold on a second," I told the engineer on the other end of the phone line, then put my hand over the mouthpiece. "Sit down. I'll be through in a minute." I was glad to see her. I had spent my entire afternoon alternating between answering phone calls, pondering the data leaks, and thinking about Paoli. I needed some friendly diversion, however brief.

Max collapsed huffily into a chair, took a mirror out of her purse, and lovingly examined her face as if it were the only thing on earth she could really count on. I finished with the engineer and hung up the phone.

"Good afternoon, Max."

"I wouldn't pass judgment so quickly if I were you. Wonder Boy Hanson is trying his best to get you canned from the project."

"How do you know?"

"I found memos on his desk this morning summarizing his meetings with Garrett, but then he caught me rummaging through his desk. We had quite a fight. The little slime-sucking geek even threatened to fire me. Can you believe that? Of course, I laughed in his face."

"Would he actually fire you?" I asked.

Max looked at me as if I had just asked something very stupid. "Of course not."

I leaned back in my chair and exhaled with dismay. "How far has it gone?"

"Pretty far. You're still okay. Garrett refused to take you off the project, probably because Wayne dribbled Twinkie crumbs on him again during the meeting, but Wayne is ready to go over Garrett's head, and Garrett can't hold off forever." Max scrunched up her nose. "Finding Albert Wu's body didn't reflect well on you, you know."

I knew. Max settled in her chair and her expression changed suddenly from cat to a cuddly kitten.

"Well, so much for bad news. Would you like to hear the latest on my love life?"

"No time, Max," I replied, shuffling some papers to the side of my desk to make room for a new batch.

"Well, it's going fabulously. Fantastically. My new lover is the most scintillating man I've ever met. Do you want to know where we made love last night?"

"No."

"On his desk. We were in his office. He was finishing up some work and I was waiting for him. Suddenly he flipped off the light, pushed everything off the top of his desk right to the floor with a sweep of his arm, then he lifted up my skirt and he made love to me," she said breathlessly. "It lasted forever. I think I may have a paper clip indentation permanently on my thigh." She paused and took a breath. "Jules, can I tell you something?"

I didn't bother to respond, knowing that at that moment an space alien landing would not prevent her from telling me.

"I think I'm in love with him."

I dropped my pencil. "That *is* news," I said, suddenly fascinated. Max had never expressed more than a passing interest in any man. "Well, Max, I think it's wonderful. It's romantic." I smiled at her and was surprised when her face turned pensive.

"It frightens me a little."

"Why should it frighten you?"

"Because I'm out of control with him. I don't like that feeling."

"Who is this guy?"

She stood up and retrieved her handbag.

"What does it matter?" she said with a sigh. It mattered a lot to me at that moment, but I didn't want to push her. I thanked her for the information about Hanson and we agreed to meet for lunch later in the week. Then I tried to get back to work.

The phone rang. I muttered a curse and picked it up.

"I want to apologize," a voice said quickly. I recognized Paoli. "I was completely out of line. I don't know why I did that last night."

"Forget it. I'm embarrassed about the way I reacted.

The whole scene was very high school and beneath our dignity. It must have been the excitement of our first stakeout," I joked.

"It's more than that, I—"

"Listen, Paoli," I interrupted. "I'm engaged to Charles and I'm not the type to amuse myself with flirtations. So just put a lid on your animal passions and we'll be fine. We've still got work to do."

"I know," said Paoli, sounding relieved. "That's the second reason I called. I had headquarters check Wu's bank statements. He made a thirty-thousand-dollar deposit in cash three months ago in ten-thousand-dollar increments to three separate accounts. I assume it wasn't his monthly ICI pay."

"You assumed right. But maybe he had a rich uncle who died."

"I checked. He didn't. Besides, you don't spread cash over three separate accounts to three separate banks on the same day unless you're hiding something."

"Then we can deduce that Petrovsky was paying Wu for the project data, then after he got it, he killed Wu to keep him quiet," I said. "But then why would Petrovsky kill Wu before he had received the final molecular memory designs? The designs aren't completed yet. So far the Soviets have only gotten preliminaries."

"I don't think Wu was killed by the Soviets. I talked to a friend of mine in Washington. He said they don't usually bump off informers. They're too hard to come by and they like to save them in case they need them later. But like I said before, they would never murder Wu on ICI premises. It's too risky. Especially if they were meeting with Wu on a regular basis. It doesn't make sense. It would be too easy to just bump him off someplace secluded then dump him in the ocean."

"How morbid. Don't forget, there are some other missing pieces. Number one, why was Gershbein killed?"

"That still puzzles me," he replied.

"Number two, how did Wu get the Project 6 data?"

"Also puzzling."

"Number three and number four, who installed the camera in your office and who are the people Wu referred to on that piece of paper?"

"Both puzzlements."

"So we're not much better off now than we were before, right?"

"Wrong. We can be pretty certain that Wu was involved in the data leaks and that Petrovsky was on the receiving end. And we can also be fairly certain that Wu wasn't the main person involved in stealing the data since he was obviously expendable. Now that's more information than we had a day ago. What I want to do now is go over the security access records. We need to check Wu's i.d. and see if there was any way he could have accessed confidential data. You have the records, don't you?"

"Of course."

"Good. Then I'll meet you tomorrow in your office at six. And Julie, don't tell anyone what we've found out. It could be dangerous."

"I can take care of myself."

"I noticed that last night. And by the way, congratulations. I hear you passed your lie detector test."

He hung up.

Going over the security access records was important, and luckily I had printouts so I didn't need the access to Larry that had been so rudely taken away. What I did need access to Larry for was more time to look at the security code. The night I had used the trapdoor password I had logged on to Larry for only five minutes at a time, hoping that an operator looking at the access logs wouldn't notice brief log-on times. They wouldn't stand out against the hundreds of other entries in the log. But an hour-long session would, and that was the amount of time I needed on the system to go through the security code. Not to mention the chance someone would notice my i.d. in the control log and know I was poking around where I wasn't supposed to. I needed a valid i.d. and password so I could log on to Larry and look at the security code uninterrupted, but who had an i.d. and password that hadn't been canceled? I knew I could call Paoli and use his, but after the episode in his car the previous night I didn't want to ask him for any favors. Instead I headed straight for Elkin's office.

His secretary wasn't at her desk, so I walked right in. Elkin was reading a letter. His suit jacket was off and he had tortoiseshell reading glasses perched on the end of his nose. There aren't many men who look good in reading glasses, but Elkin definitely did. He looked like one of those men you see in ads for expensive scotch—all strong boned and elegant looking. He heard me come in, looked up, and smiled.

"Hello, Julie. Have a seat."

I sat.

"What can I do for you?" he asked, smiling a smile of flawless teeth.

"I need a password to get at Larry's security code," I said abruptly.

Elkin's smile dimmed only a little. "You know that's impossible. The passwords have been canceled until the data leaks are fixed. It was a decision out of headquarters."

I stood up so I could be looking down on him. "I'm sure you still have a valid password. It's company policy for at least one person on the premises to have access to any code."

Elkin laughed. "You've always impressed me with your memory for details."

"I need to use your password," I told him, leaning over his desk. His smile turned into an inquisitive frown.

"Why do you need it, Julie?"

"To look at the project security code."

Elkin's eyebrows rose.

"Brad, I think the answer to the data leaks is in there somewhere and I can find it."

"We've already gone over that code. It was naturally the first thing Vic Paoli did, but he didn't find anything."

"He missed it. He's not as familiar with the code as I am. I wrote it."

"He's the finest expert in the country. You're wasting your time, Julie."

"I need to see that code."

"We would be risking both our jobs if I gave you my password."

"Our jobs aren't worth two cents anyway if these data leaks don't get fixed."

Elkin studied me a moment, then turned his gaze briefly to the wall.

I walked around the side of his desk to get in his field of vision. "We can solve this data leak problem, Brad, but not by sitting on our hands and waiting for someone else to do it for us."

Elkin laughed softly. "The first time I met you was when headquarters sent you over to interview for this job. I didn't even want to see you. I assumed you were too young and too green. Do you remember that?"

"Very well. You acted like a grizzly bear defending his lair."

"After I had talked to you only an hour I decided you were the brightest person I had seen come through this company and that you were the right person for this job. I've never regretted that decision."

"So trust me now."

Elkin stared at me a moment then tore a blank sheet off a memo pad, scribbled something on it, and handed it to me.

"You can use it tonight and only tonight. I'll change the password tomorrow morning," he said, and swiveled in his chair so I could only see his profile. "Julie, I don't like this. It's dangerous, and I don't mean for our jobs. I mean for you."

"Don't worry. After all, what can happen in a computer

room?" I said, then walked out the door without waiting for his reaction.

■ ◻ ■

I went home after work for a quick dinner and returned to the office around eight. After signing in with the security guard I went into the main computer room and sat down at a terminal. Jeanene, one of the night operators, was doing routine data backup, but her presence didn't bother me. There was no need for me to be furtive using Elkin's password. I logged on to the system and requested access to the security code. The screen suddenly went blank.

"Hey, what happened?" Jeanene yelled from across the room.

"I don't know." I got up to check the other equipment. All equipment lights were off.

"Looks like we took a power hit," said Jeanene. "It's funny though that no building lights are out. It's like someone just pulled the plug on the computer room."

"What about the backup power?" I asked her.

"Looks like it didn't kick in for some reason."

An uneasy feeling crept over me. Jeanene, on the other hand, seemed grateful for the break in routine.

"I'll call field engineering, but I doubt they'll be able to have this back up until morning," she said.

I doubted it too, and so did the person who sabotaged my attempt to access the security files.

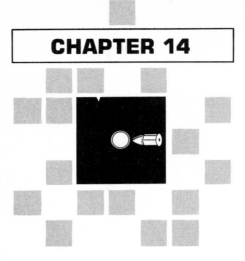

CHAPTER 14

"Somebody must have seen me go in there," I told Paoli as I watched him shoot rubber bands against my office door. They were piling up on the floor.

"Maybe the power just got cut off accidentally. It happens," he said nonchalantly.

"We have three sources of electrical backup. You really think it could have been an accident?"

"No, but it doesn't hurt to lay out all the possibilities, even the benign ones. And why did you go to all the trouble of asking Elkin for his i.d.? You could have used mine."

"If I had you would have insisted on coming to the computer room with me."

"Is my company so terrible?"

"Sometimes, yes."

"You know, you're lucky I'm not the type to get offended," said Paoli, even though his expression claimed otherwise. "Did you tell Elkin what happened last night?"

"No, I didn't have the chance. I was tied up almost all day. I went by his office around six but he was gone. Besides, I'm trying to stay out of his way. I only have less than a week to solve the data leaks, and every time I see Elkin there's a chance he's going to tell me the project has been shot down."

"No one can say you don't put in enough hours. What time is it, anyway? I'm starving."

I checked my Seiko. "It's eight-thirty. I'll go down to the snackroom and get some sandwiches."

Paoli clutched his throat in mock horror. "God, no, not the ones from the machines. I tried them last week. They're inedible. Let's go out."

"I think we should go through the access records one more time," I said.

"Julie, we've gone through them three times already. There's nothing there. Nobody accessed any confidential information. Not Wu, not Gershbein, not anybody. Going over the records another time won't change that."

I knew he was right. I opened my desk drawer, got out my Maalox, and unscrewed the top.

"What is that?" Paoli asked.

"Dinner." I took a soothing swig. Paoli shook his head with disgust.

"You're slowly killing yourself. You've got to ease up," he said, sounding repulsively maternal. I sneered at him as I drank more Maalox. "When was the last time you had fun, Julie?"

I looked at him. "What do you mean by fun?"

Paoli closed his eyes and grimaced. "See what I mean? You've forgotten the definition of the word. Why not loosen up some, get some zest back in your life?" He stood up and made his body do some sort of scaled-down shimmy to give me a visual representation of what loosening up was like. It looked to me more like a joint problem.

"Thank you for the advice, Dr. Feelgood. Can we get back to work now?" I asked.

He pulled the printout from my hand and dropped it on the floor. "It's eight-thirty. Work day's over. Let's go have some fun."

"I don't want to have fun."

"Then let's eat. You do eat, don't you? I know you do. I've seen you eat. You take little dainty bites and chew them like a squirrel. We'll go to a restaurant I know in Palo Alto. It's pizza. Very informal. I promise, we won't have any fun. We'll just satiate hunger. Come on," he said.

I picked the printout off the floor. "Look, Paoli, I'm sorry, but I just don't feel like socializing right now. I want to work. Besides, I'm supposed to meet Charles later."

"So we'll work over dinner and then you can go home to Charles. It will be good for him for you to be a little late. Keeps him guessing. Besides, I have lots of ideas about the data leaks that you and I haven't even discussed yet. We can talk about it over pizza. So get your coat."

I analyzed it. Actually I needed dinner and a few hours off so I could be fresh tomorrow morning. Even though it was Sunday it was the only day I had to catch up on my work. Everything going on with the murders and the data leaks left me with little time for my regular workload. And to be honest, I wanted to avoid Charles. His company hadn't been too relaxing lately. He was intrigued, like everyone else, by the project investigation, and he was always asking questions about it, suggesting solutions, playing Sherlock Holmes. It wasn't what I needed after a full day at work. I knew a person could get too immersed in a technical problem and lose objectivity, so I always suggested to my engineers that they take short breathers from complex technical problems in order to regain a fresh view. It was time I took my own advice. I grabbed my coat.

We drove the few miles to Palo Alto in Paoli's rented

Toyota. There were still candy wrappers on the floor that I recognized from our stakeout. When we walked into the restaurant it turned out to be more elegant than the casual pizza place Paoli had previously described. There was no pizza on the menu. I wished I hadn't come.

The waiter seated us at a small table in the corner. I looked around the room to make sure there wasn't anyone there I knew, not wanting to be seen at a restaurant at night with Paoli.

Paoli ordered two glasses of white wine.

"How do you like the restaurant?" he asked.

I jerked my head back around. "The restaurant? It's fine. I just want to eat and get back to work."

Paoli shook his head. "You're hopeless. You're so tight. Maybe this was a bad idea."

I took a shaky sip of wine. "We have to eat, don't we?" I said, trying to sound casual.

"So why are you so jumpy?"

"I'm not jumpy," I snapped, knocking over my wine with my hand.

Paoli looked offended. "Sure, you're not jumpy. Everything was fine at the office, but now you're acting like I bite," he said with annoyance, then waved down the waiter to clean the mess and replace my wine.

"I'm sorry," I muttered.

"Look, we're just having dinner. Just having dinner won't violate the sanctity of your engagement to Troy Donahue," said Paoli.

"Don't call him Troy Donahue."

"You're right. I apologize. I promised you that we weren't going to have fun, and you see, we're not. I also promised you we would talk business, so let's start with the computer."

The waiter took our order, then Paoli, true to his word, told me some other theories he had about the data leaks, but as he and I discussed each one, we found some reason to rule it out. The wine and the discussion couldn't rid me of my discomfort from being there with him, and I was glad when our food arrived, hoping for a reprieve from conversation. Paoli kept talking. He told me stories about other computer security cases he had worked on for the NSA and how he had solved them. I was impressed with his technical expertise, but I didn't allow myself to compliment him. His ego seemed big enough already. He had that way of using his hands when he spoke and he seemed so passionate about some things, so nonchalant about others. I looked at him through the candlelight, and I was thinking how cute his laugh lines were when I remembered that I had forgotten to call Charles. I excused myself quickly, found a pay phone in the back, and nervously dialed Charles's number.

"I was expecting you here an hour ago. Where are you? I've been worried," he said.

"Well, I'm having to work late again. The security access records, you know," I explained, feeling awkward.

"But I just called your office and you weren't there."

"I've been in the computer room." Was that a lie? I asked myself. After all, I didn't say that I was in the computer room that very minute. I said "I've been in the computer room," which was, strictly speaking, quite accurate, since I had been in the computer room earlier in the day. But it was still a lie. Why the clumsy subterfuge all of a sudden? I had never lied to Charles before.

"Darling, I know how hard you're working, but I've hardly seen you this week. I miss you," he said.

"I miss you too." Lying was getting easier. I had hardly thought about him in days, I had been so busy. Guilt washed over me. "How about dinner tomorrow? I'll cook you a fabulous dinner." Cooking a fabulous dinner meant stopping by the gourmet deli for takeout.

"Great," he replied, sounding consoled. We hung up. I walked back to Paoli.

"Is Charles surviving?"

I gave him a sour look. "We should go," I said to him. Paoli studied me a moment then waved down the waiter. After we both grabbed for the check we finally agreed to split it, left the money on the table, then walked outside.

The night air was cold. I pulled up my coat collar and held it at my throat as we silently walked to the car. Maybe I would go to Charles's apartment after all and surprise him, I told myself, although I didn't really want to. Paoli fumbled with the car keys trying to unlock my door, then he stopped and faced me.

"Julie, there are some things I'd like to say to you."

I tensed. "Let's keep it for tomorrow, okay? I have some time around ten."

"Can't you stop talking about work for five minutes?"

"Work is the only thing you and I have in common, Paoli."

"It's not the only thing we have in common and you know it."

"Okay, we're both mammals composed largely of carbon and hydrogen."

"Sometimes, Blake, you can be a bitch."

He turned and started to walk around to his side of the car. That's when I grabbed his arm and pulled him toward me. I put both of my arms around his neck, pulled his face down to mine, and kissed him good and hard. It threw him off balance for a moment, but he recovered quickly. In the next moment his arms were around me, pressing me against the side of the car.

We kissed for what seemed a long time. My glasses were getting smashed, but I figured I could buy a new pair. When our lips parted I opened my eyes and saw his face looking soft and serious. I lifted my lips to be kissed again. Wrapping my arms more tightly around his neck, I held on to him, for it was one of those kisses that enveloped every ounce of energy and concentration. He pulled me so close and kissed me with an intensity that made my insides feel they would ooze right into my sensible shoes. It was the perfect kiss, an encompassing kiss, reminiscent of some old movie or forgotten teenage passion, a kiss all hot and sweet, and I thought I might come just from our lips touching.

When the kiss ended, he looked at me as if there were something he wanted to say.

"Don't talk," I told him. He didn't.

It was a short ride to his hotel. We exchanged no conversation. I was torn between embarrassment and lust, and lust was winning. I didn't want to talk and Paoli sensed it.

We walked into his hotel room. He didn't turn on the light. I sat down on his bed and tried to think of sophisticated and flippant phrases, but I couldn't. It crossed my mind that I would look sexier if I took off my glasses, but I didn't want my vision blurred as I watched him undress. He was bathed in the half-light coming through the window from the street below. I could see that his body was hard and muscular and beautiful. So much more perfect than my own, I thought. When he came near the bed, I reached for him and pulled him toward me. I buried my face between his neck and shoulder and ran my lips and teeth against his skin because I thought I couldn't stand another second of not touching him. He pulled back and smiled. It wasn't a smile of domination or of mocking but a smile of ironic delight and understanding. Gently he slipped the clip from my hair so that it fell around my face. He removed my glasses, then he made me wait while he unbuttoned all my buttons, carefully and slowly, one by one.

CHAPTER 15

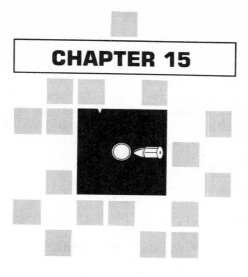

I awakened in a dark hotel room at four-fifteen in the morning feeling confused and ashamed and ready to do it all over again. I had heard stories about women who woke up in strange hotel rooms with men they hardly knew, but I had always figured I wasn't the type. That's what I got for figuring.

Paoli lay next to me sleeping like the dead, his arm sprawled across my waist and his head nestled on my chest. After my eyes adjusted to the dark, I lay there watching his face, listening to him softly snore, studying the outline of his lips and nose. Gently I pressed my face against his hair and breathed in his aroma, and I thought how different he was from the other men I knew.

He was a gentle, tender person, yet there was something exotically male about him. He had a style of movement, a manner of speaking, an eau de testosterone that seemed to ooze out of his pores. For a moment I considered waking him so we could make love again, this time slower, with my eyes open so I wouldn't miss anything. But then I thought of Charles and my rapture gave way to guilt. A dozen horrible thoughts ran through my mind. What if Charles had called me late last night and I hadn't been home? Should I confess to him? Would he forgive me? Never. I wasn't even sure I would want him to.

Quietly, guiltily, I slipped out of bed without disturbing Paoli and groped in the dark for my scattered clothes and shoes. During the previous night's passion my clothes had shot off like the space shuttle, and now they were tossed across the room in the most inconvenient places. Naked, I felt around in the dark and found my blouse hanging over a lamp, my skirt and panties tossed in a corner, my shoes on opposite sides of the room. At the end of the bed I found my panty hose in a condition requiring burial. I searched for my bra but it seemed to have disappeared, perhaps evaporated by the sheer heat the two of us had created the night before. Then I saw it lying under Paoli's shoulder. It looked like he had his arm through one of the straps. I didn't want to leave it behind, but I needed to get out of there. I tried pulling the bra out from under him, but Paoli began to stir and I didn't want to be there when he woke up. After making a managerial decision to sacrifice the bra, I pulled on my shoes and tiptoed out the door. The hotel lobby shined with a fluorescent glare that didn't suit the early hour, making it difficult to stealthily slip past the night clerk. I was embarrassed at leaving a man's hotel room at 4:00 A.M., certain my rumpled appearance broadcasted my indiscretions to the world. There goes your typical Silicon Valley computer slut, techno-tramp, I imagined the hotel clerk muttering under his breath. He probably had a relative who worked at ICI. The clerk looked up at me as I passed the desk and

I looked back to make sure the bedsheet wasn't stuck to my shoe and dragging behind me. Humbly, I bowed my head, found a pay phone, then called a cab.

When I reached home I showered thoroughly as if I could wash away all traces of the previous night, but with the warm water beating against my skin, I thought of how Paoli's body had felt against me, the words he had whispered in the dark. Last night I had felt sexual and sinful; the freedom of those feelings had enveloped me like a drug. I wanted to feel it all again, and at the same time I wanted to forget it ever happened.

A half hour later I was washed clean, at least on the outside, and was ensconced in the paperwork I had brought home with me from the office. That evening Charles came over and I prepared the meal I had promised, complete with wine, candlelight, and several courses that I microwaved with domestic efficiency.

I worked, I cooked, I pampered Charles and did all the things I was supposed to do, but the whole time I kept thinking about Paoli and what it had felt like to be with him in his hotel room the night before. And now what I was doing on the outside no longer jived with what I felt on the inside.

On Monday morning as I led the weekly Project 6 checkpoint meeting I glanced across the conference table at the tense, expectant faces in front of me and for an instant I felt like an imposter, a child playacting in a grown-up world. Yet there I was at the head of the conference table with everyone in the meeting looking to me as their leader. I was suddenly unsure of how and why I had reached that stature and whether I deserved it.

"A few days late is understandable," said Ed, one of my systems engineers. Tall and bony, he leaned back in his chair and gripped the side of the conference table until his knuckles turned white. Ed had given up a promotion to first-line management in another department the previous year because he preferred to work on Project 6. Now I could tell he was questioning that decision. "But five weeks is something else. Let's face it, we've got a major screwup on our hands."

Jim, another project engineer, sat opposite Ed, nervously clicking the button at the top of his mechanical pencil. Jim had transferred from Atlanta six months earlier and his attitude was a bit more optimistic. "Our statisticians were just wrong about the estimate. It's just going to take a little longer."

"Numbers don't lie, Jim," said Lorenzo, a statistician ready to defend his honor.

"But people do. Maybe you were painting a rosy picture for the executives' benefit," said Ed. Lorenzo stood up, his fists clenched at his sides. I had never had a fistfight break out in a staff meeting and I hoped this wouldn't be the first. I could have broken in and quieted them, but I thought it would be better to let them get it out of their systems, at least up to a point.

Always the southern gentleman, Jim came to Lorenzo's defense. "He wouldn't do that. Let's be rational. The mathematic results were checked by several people."

"The bottom line is this," said Ed. "Silicon Valley is in a slump. Both MCP and ANARO are planning to lay off people. That will make six companies this year that have made cuts. And ICI isn't faring much better economically than anyone else. The company needs a success like molecular memory, and it needs it bad. I don't care about defense weapons or medical devices nearly as much as I care about just keeping my job. But if we don't come up with a usable design soon, we're all going to wind up at the unemployment office."

An analyst in the back of the meeting room stood up and moved to a seat at the conference table. "You're all beating around the real issue. This project has been sabotaged. It's obvious. We're never going to get the right memory results and we're all going to be out of work."

I raised a hand to quiet them. "There's no reason for us to be concerned about our jobs. You know I'll stand behind you regardless of what happens. So let's concentrate on the project."

"Julie, I know you would do whatever you could, but what if you lose your job? A month ago I would have bet my salary against that happening, but now, with everything that's going on . . ."

Ed didn't finish his sentence. Instead he let it hang in midair like somebody's dingy laundry. Of course, everybody had been thinking it, but only Ed had the nerve to say it.

"I understand your concern. ICI has a firm contract with the government for molecular memory and there's been no indication that funding won't continue. So let's get down to work, shall we? Ed, I want you to get the algorithm read-outs from the past six months and compare them to the current ones. See if there is anything different in the current formats that would indicate processor error. Jim, I want you to get with Joshua and run a full set of diagnostics on Larry and have the results on my desk tomorrow morning. Unless anyone has something to add, we'll conclude this meeting and meet again at the same time next Monday. Yes, Lorenzo?"

"I received the memo that Larry is to be operated remotely from New York starting tomorrow. What's the purpose of that?"

"We're just trying to keep employees out of the building after normal working hours. I know it's an inconvenience, but we have to live with it. The regular staff will resume at eight in the morning as always."

I paused for other questions, but there were none.

"If any of you need to speak to me privately, you know my door is open. Thanks for your time."

People straggled out. Morale had not improved in the last few days, and a moroseness hung over the group. It was only ten-thirty, but I was already tired. I hadn't gotten much sleep the night before.

I walked out of the conference room, relieved at finally being alone, and went into the rest room to gather my thoughts before returning to my office and the inevitable barrage of calls and messages. Looking at my reflection in the mirror over the sink, I studied my features. They had an evenness that I would have considered attractive if I had seen them on someone else, but when I looked at myself in the mirror all my features seemed to melt together and I saw nothing distinctly, as if I were some fuzzy cartoon character thinly drawn on a page. I had always had little sense of my physical self. I remembered when I was eleven finding a quasi-dirty book under my friend's bed describing the titillating adventures of a blonde in outer space. In the few paragraphs I dared to read, it described the intergalactic heroine's breasts as large, ripe melons that heaved beneath her thin spacesuit. As my own breasts were not even close to the size of melons, I secretly viewed myself from that moment on as deficient in the sensual attractiveness category.

Paoli had whispered the night before how I had excited him from that first day we met. I closed my eyes and let the memory wash over me. Then, watching myself in the mirror, I removed the clip that held my pony tail and watched my hair fall slowly forward around my face. I brushed it, then took a seldom used plum-colored lipstick from my purse and carefully applied it to my lips. I gazed at my reflection and was pleased with the results. There were feelings in me that morning that were different from the day before, and the mirror showed them on my face. I smiled at my reflection, then checked my watch. I had another meeting in five minutes.

■ ◻ ■

"Either you've been fired, you've had a religious experience, or you're pregnant. There couldn't be any other reason compelling enough to drag Juliet Blake away from the office long enough for lunch at a restaurant," Max said as she munched a carrot stick. The restaurant was one of those steak and seafood places with lots of dark oiled wood and potted ivy. The food was average but it was close to the office and the service was fast.

"I spent the night with someone last night, and it wasn't Charles," I told Max. I only had an hour for lunch, so I couldn't waste time with chitchat.

Max stopped crunching her carrot. Her lips curled into a smile. "So, I was right. You had a religious experience and you could be pregnant. Who was the lucky guy?"

"Vic Paoli."

Max's eyes widened. "And you could be fired too. I was right on all three counts. Good work, Jules."

She leaned across the table. "So how was he?" she whispered. "I want details—positions, body description, everything."

"I don't want to discuss details."

"And why the hell not? I tell you all my details. If you're not here to give me details, then what's the purpose of this lunch?"

"I'm not sure. Yes, I am. It's just that I don't know what to do now."

"About what?"

"About Charles."

"What about him?"

"Well, first of all, should I tell him?"

Max laughed. "You're kidding, right? Of course you don't tell him. It's none of his business. You're not married yet."

I took a sip of coffee and wondered if I, or anyone, should ever trust Max's judgment.

"But that's the other issue. After last night I'm not even sure I *can* marry him."

Max flipped her carrot stick over her shoulder and looked at me, her eyes huge. "Wow. One night with the Italian Stallion and you're ready to dump Charles. It must have been some night. I'm creaming my pants just thinking about it. What did he do to you, and do you think he would do it to me? I'll pay him."

"This isn't a joking matter, Max."

"So who's joking?" Max saw my irritation and softened her approach. "Okay, I'm kidding. I'm sorry. It's just that you're usually so solid and straight-laced, and now here you are suddenly quivering like Jell-O on a vibrating bed."

"I'm not quivering."

"Yes you are, and there's no need to. My advice is to not take last night seriously. You've been under a lot of pressure at work and you're probably feeling some premarital jitters. Combine the two and, wham, even Juliet Blake goes in for a one-night stand. It's nothing to be ashamed of. In fact, I'm quite proud of you. Just think of last night as a chance happening, the result of a fluke planetary alignment, something you did for a lark. Believe me, that's how men look at it. Just forget about it. At least until ten years from now when you're having sex with Charles for the three thousandth time in the missionary position and you need some additional erotic stimulus. Think of it then."

I stared down at the limp lettuce the waiter had just brought me. I didn't want to think of the previous night as a one-night stand. It had seemed like more than that, but Max knew more about these situations than I did.

The waiter brought the rest of our lunches and we ate in silence. Max had to be right. I had been under a lot of pressure and it was understandable that I would get carried away by a couple of drinks and some heavy breathing. It was just one hop in the sack to be savored for a moment, then forgotten. I was sure Paoli looked at it that way, especially since I hadn't even heard from him since that night. Not that I expected a dozen red roses, but shouldn't he have called or something? He was probably feeling smug and macho, musing over what a fool I had made of myself. And what if he told anyone we had slept together? The thought made my stomach twist into a knot. I would take Max's advice and forget the whole thing. My night with Paoli was a one-time-only mistake and it would never happen again.

Max threw a twenty on the table. "Well, kiddo, this conversation has been scintillating, but I've got to get back to next quarter's marketing projections," she said as she took out her compact and checked her face. I was looking at her face wondering how she managed to keep her makeup on all day when I noticed the comb that held the left side of her hair. It was black lacquer set with pearls, identical to the comb I had seen on the computer room floor the night Paoli and I found Wu's body. I almost choked on my coffee.

"Max, where did you get that comb?"

She reached up with one hand and touched it as if to remind herself what it was. "This? Saks, of course. But I'm sure that they don't have them anymore. I bought them so long ago."

"Them?"

"Well, they're sold in twos, but I lost the other one somewhere. They don't hold well. But if you like it, I'll give this one to you. It would look good on you, quite sexy, although it sounds like you don't need any extra sex appeal," she said with a wink, slipping the comb from her hair and handing it to me. I stared at it as if it were some evil talisman. I shook my head.

"No, really, you keep it," I said nervously. I looked at Max and thought of Albert Wu's reference to a pearl. Max was exotically lovely with her black hair and pale skin. She had a rare beauty, and it took only one look at her to know she was expensive. Was she the pearl Wu had referred to in his note?

"Aren't you leaving with me?" Max asked.

"No, I'm going to sit here a minute and finish my coffee. You go ahead."

"It's up to you." Max shrugged and put the comb in her handbag. After she left I sat alone at the table a few minutes and wondered how her comb had gotten into the computer room that night. I didn't like what I was thinking.

■ ◻ ■

"So, honey, do you want to be on top tonight?" Charles whispered in my ear as we lay on my bed. I didn't put down the file I was reading.

"It doesn't matter. Whatever you want, honey."

"Maybe we should try something interesting," Charles said, nibbling my neck. I gave him a kiss. The evening had gone well. I had again microwaved a more than adequate dinner, then we crawled into bed where I went over some work and Charles read *The Wall Street Journal*. Everything was so comfortable with him. I needed stability, I reminded myself, and Charles was the one person who could give me a sense of security, of belonging with someone. Obviously the night with Paoli was merely premarital jitters.

"Should we set a wedding date?" I asked, putting down my file and snuggling my head onto Charles's shoulder.

He looked at me with surprise. "I've been trying to get you to set a date for eight months now and I've never been able to pin you down. Why this sudden change of heart?"

"I don't know. It's just been on my mind. I was thinking about June."

"June what?"

"I don't know what day yet. But it will definitely be in June." June was many months away, a nice, comfortable distance. Charles flipped off the light. He began massaging my shoulders and kissing my neck, but something inside me stiffened under his touch. I closed my eyes and thought of Paoli, the passion and the energy, his tenderness after we made love. I imagined his lips on mine, his hands on my body, his low moans.

"So did we decide who was going to be on top?" asked Charles, but I didn't answer. I rolled on top of him and made love to him, but it was Paoli I was making love to that night with every kiss and every caress. When we finished I lay awake in the dark, trying to push Paoli out of my mind.

The next morning I brought Charles his coffee while he was still in bed.

"You were so sexy last night. A volcano," he told me. "I didn't realize I could arouse that in you."

I smiled sweetly and quickly changed the subject.

"What time does your plane leave?" I asked. He was going to Seattle on business.

"About three-thirty, I think. I'll call you tonight."

"I probably won't be here," I replied, then regretted it. I had planned on using the trapdoor password that night, but I wasn't sure I should tell Charles.

"What are you doing at the office every night, Julie? No one is supposed to be there after working hours."

"I'm investigating Larry's internal security code," I said after a long silence.

"But I thought all the passwords were canceled."

I hesitated, then spoke. "I'm using an unauthorized password that I programmed in four years ago."

As soon as I said the words, I regretted it. I didn't know why I had told him. Maybe I wanted to cover myself for that night with Paoli, or maybe out of guilt I needed to share some secret with him to increase the bond between us.

There was an unfamiliar expression on Charles's face, a combination of surprise and anger that I didn't understand. He got up from the bed and threw on a robe.

"Julie, it's unethical for you to do this," he said in a voice more controlled than the look on his face.

I sat on the bed. "It's unethical for me to have my employees murdered and my work destroyed without doing everything I can to stop it."

"If they catch you they'll fire you."

"No one will catch me. I've already used it once before, but I didn't have enough time to study the software in detail. Tonight I will. Charles, there's something wrong with that program, I know it. I just need some time to uncover it."

Charles studied my face a moment. He sat down on the bed next to me and took my hand in his. "Julie, it's dangerous. I can't let you do it."

"No one lets me do anything, Charles. I don't need permission from you or anyone else."

"Then at least promise me that you'll wait until I get back from Seattle, so I can be there with you."

"I can't promise that."

Charles stiffened, but his face turned soft. "Julie, I love you so much. I can't let anything happen to you. At least tell me you'll consider waiting."

"All right, I'll consider it," I told him, though I knew it was a lie.

■ □ ■

As I walked past Mrs. Dabney's desk toward my office she pointed a ringed finger toward the door and scowled.

"He's in there," she warned me.

"Who is?"

"That NSA guy."

My heart did a swan dive and a back flip then topped things off with a triple gainer. My past had left me unprepared for social situations that most single women probably handled nonchalantly. I was embarrassed to face him. But then, why should I be embarrassed? I asked myself. Suddenly I could think of plenty of reasons. He had seen me at my most vulnerable. I hadn't had sexual experiences with many men, and even those hadn't been anything like that night with Paoli. I had come unglued with him. He must have thought I was a crazy woman, the way I had pounced on him, especially once we were alone in bed. Like a woman on Weight Watchers confronted with a four-layer cake, all of my hungers came tumbling out of me and I had my mouth, my hands on every part of his body. I had gasped, moaned, purred like a cat and begged him for more. And now I was supposed to walk into my office and discuss computers with him?

I caught Mrs. Dabney eyeing me with curiosity as I stood frozen before my office door. When I saw her staring I quickly grabbed the doorknob and turned it. I walked in and a rubber band struck my face.

"Ouch!"

"Whoops. Sorry. Well, that's what you get for coming in late. It's eight-fifteen, you know. How unlike you. Mrs. Dabney and I have been here since seven-thirty."

Paoli energetically spewed forth the words, thankfully sparing me the humiliation of risking an opening line. He was wearing a navy sport coat, which, for him, was the equivalent of formal attire. Had he worn it for my benefit? I closed the door behind me, walked over to my desk and flipped through some phone messages, then sat down. I could feel the perspiration under my arms. I wanted to tell him about my lunch with Max, about her comb matching the one I found near Wu's body, but I didn't. He would jump to the same conclusion I had. And that was all it would be—jumping to a conclusion. I wasn't about to implicate my best friend in a murder because of a silly hair comb. I told myself that there had to be a dozen ways the comb could have made its way into the computer room, but good sense insisted there weren't. If my pride had let me I would have poured out the information to Paoli, but my pride stood firm; at least it was firm until Paoli took my pink lace bra out of his pocket, raised it in the air, and let it fall onto the desk in front of me, like some pink bird doing a crash landing.

"I was going to have it bronzed, but then I thought it would look funny under your sweaters," he said.

I gaped at it, flustered, then scooped it up, threw it in a file drawer, and slammed the drawer shut.

"What can I do for you?" I asked. My prim tone of voice threw him for a second, but he recovered quickly.

"What can you do for me? Well, let's see. You can go to dinner with me at a little restaurant I've heard of on Muir Beach, then we can drive to a hilltop and look at the stars, then go back to my place, drink a little champagne while I tell you all my boyhood stories."

"I'm not interested."

"Okay, I'll skip the boyhood stories."

I tried to look cool and aloof. "I have a busy day ahead of me. Is there a business reason for this visit?"

A look of uneasiness appeared on Paoli's face. "I'm sorry. I didn't mean to interrupt you. I just thought you might want to have dinner tonight."

"Well, I don't." I avoided eye contact.

"Later in the week?" he asked, looking like an energetic

· 199 ·

puppy. I tried very hard not to think about how attractive he was. I reminded myself about Charles. I reminded myself about my dignity. I reminded myself that Paoli probably thought of me as a quick lay, a conquest, some casual entertainment for a guy from out of town.

"No," I told him. "And I resent your asking."

Paoli looked befuddled. "You resent my asking? What's going on? I figured—"

"You figured wrong."

Paoli looked at me with a hurt expression that quickly turned to resentment. "I guess I did. Well, we need to talk about something regarding the project. It's important. Do you have time today?"

"No, not today." I checked my calendar. "How about tomorrow morning at eight-thirty?"

"That will be fine. So glad you can fit me in," said Paoli. Then he exited.

I watched the doorway a long time after he had passed through it. I wanted to call him back, to apologize and tell him how awkward I felt about what had happened between us. I wanted to blurt out that maybe my best friend was a murderer. I wanted to let myself relax, to be comforted by him, to tell him that I was falling in love with him.

But I didn't. Instead I got control of myself. What would my father say to me if I asked his advice on this situation, assuming we could have this type of heart-to-heart conversation, which I'm sure, if he were alive, we could? "Get realistic, Julie," he would tell me. "You get starry-eyed, you jump into an office romance, and the next thing you know, your name and phone number are scrawled on the wall in the men's room." It wasn't going to happen to me. I shut my office door, sat down at my desk, and undertook the arduous task of getting Paoli off my mind.

CHAPTER 16

The ICI building appeared strangely ominous in the night, like a dark fortress, imposing and impregnable. A chill ran through me as I approached the side entrance. Don't get rattled, I told myself. There was no need to be afraid. After all, hadn't I been there a thousand times before? But for some reason that night the place felt different. Maybe it was the way I was lurking outside the building like a cat burglar. I was even wearing a black sweat suit so I would be less visible in the dark.

I had parked my car several blocks away and approached the east side of the building on foot. All the managers had received notices about beefed-up security. After asking around earlier in the day I had learned that this included four security guards—two at the front desk, one patrolling the inside of the building, and one patrolling the outside. I hid behind a trash bin and waited for the security guard to pass by a few times so I could get a feel for his patrol pattern. The trash bin held the fragrant remains of the day's ICI cafeteria lunch. ICI cafeteria lunches didn't smell that great at noontime, so by evening the aroma was downright foul, but I stuck it out long enough to figure out that the guard passed by the east entrance about every ten minutes. The third time I saw him walk by, I gave him five minutes to get to the other side of the building, then I dashed on tiptoe to the side entrance door.

By 10:00 P.M. the after-hours cleaning had been completed and only a few strips of light beamed from the windows. I pressed my external security code in the keypad by the door and entered quietly.

The hallway was dark. I could barely see, but I didn't turn on the light. I let my eyes adjust to the darkness then slowly felt my way down the long hall. Cracking open the door that led into the first floor corridor, I saw that a few offices were still lighted. I slipped inside. I thought I heard a sound and stopped. I waited. Everything again was quiet. I peeked around the wall of the lobby and saw two security guards intently focused on a *Twilight Zone* rerun on a miniature TV.

I needed to find a terminal where I had the least chance of being seen. The last thing I needed was Coleman grilling me about what I was doing dressed like Bat Girl and sneaking around ICI at night. My office on the first floor was too close to the men's room for me to feel safe from the eyes of a full-bladdered security guard, so I decided that the computer room was my best bet. It was windowless and soundproofed. Even if the guard decided to stick his head inside, I would hear the door *click* after he entered his password. There was so much equipment in the room it would be easy to duck behind something to hide.

I continued around the corner and up the stairs to the third floor. After waiting until I was certain the hall was empty, I headed toward the computer room. When I reached the door I pressed my password into the keypad. The small green light flashed and the door clicked open. I walked inside and felt the familiar coolness of the room, heard the steady drone of the equipment. Like Christmas tree lights flashing, the equipment lights blinked merrily in the dark. I exhaled with relief and flipped on the lights. No one outside would be able to see or hear anything from inside the computer room.

Sitting in a chair in front of Larry's control terminal, I opened my briefcase and took out Gershbein's copy of the security code. Since seeing that comb in Max's hair, my worries about the murders had intensified. I was a nervous wreck. I thought about it constantly, and it kept pushing work, Charles, and sometimes even Paoli from my mind. But Paoli kept sneaking back into my thoughts even as I dwelled on the security software.

My latest theory was that the "EXEC 11,14" statement was incomplete. Perhaps Gershbein had been in the process of writing the code but was never able to finish it. I entered my i.d. into the terminal. After receiving the initial menu screen, I entered my trapdoor password.

That was when the lights went out. I twisted around. The room was dark, but the equipment was still powered on, and I was bathed in the green glow of the terminal screen.

"Damn," I muttered. Last time the overhead lights had stayed on but the equipment had powered down. This time the equipment was fine but the lights were out. It was certainly feasible since the equipment was on a different power source from the rest of the building, but I still found it an amazing coincidence that I had power problems the only two times in the past few days I had tried to log on to Larry after hours. I thought about what to do. Whom could I go complain to? I had sneaked inside in the first place, and I wasn't about to leave. It was a little spooky there in the dark, but I could easily see the statements lighted on the terminal, so I decided to stick it out.

I continued with my work, then I heard the *click* of the door opening. I froze. Footsteps entered the room. There was a solid *thud* of the door closing, but I couldn't see the visitor. Whoever it was just stood there in the dark. A shudder ran through me as I sat rigid in my chair. It flashed through my mind that it had to be a security guard. Because of the power outage he probably had come into the computer room to check the equipment. Yes, that had to be it. My original intention had been to hide from a guard, but the room was so eerie with the lights off I was glad for the company. But why didn't he move or speak? I had to be plainly visible in the light from the terminal.

The footsteps came toward me.

"Who's there?" I called out in a voice brittle with fear. No answer. I heard the steps coming closer, very slowly, each step carefully measured, the heavy, solid sound of a man's footsteps. My chest tightened and I could feel a tingling in my arms and legs. To cry out for help would have been useless since no one could have heard me through the soundproofed walls. In the darkness I couldn't even see the door. Images of the corpses of Wu and Gershbein flashed in my brain. He was there with me. The killer was there.

I stood up next to the terminal, hoping to draw the intruder to the light so I could see his face. Through the darkness I could make out the outline of his body but could distinguish no features.

He came closer, only a few feet away now. I grabbed the back of the chair to stop the trembling in my hands. Now I could see his face emerging from the shadows. He wore a black ski mask with only his eyes and mouth exposed. He paused and I could tell he knew I was trying to draw him to the light. Before coming nearer he jerked the power cable from the back of the terminal, ripped it loose, and the room plunged into total blackness.

I felt hands wrap around my throat. I couldn't scream or cry for help, but could only gasp for the air that was being squeezed out of me. Clawing at his fingers, I struggled to break his grip, but his hands seemed like steel. I felt as helpless as an animal caught in a trap, but like an animal I fought to save myself. Gagging, I writhed and clawed at him, pulling desperately at his hands, but that only encouraged them to squeeze more tightly. I could feel the air being choked off from me. The pain in my throat intensified until I felt as if my neck would snap in two, and I felt I couldn't fight him anymore. I couldn't get any air. I could hear my own choking gasps, feel my own saliva running down my chin and my body was beginning to go limp. But that was when it happened. At that moment I was flooded with anger that this man was going to take my life from me, and the anger gave me new strength. I twisted beneath him and raised one hand. I reached up underneath his mask and clawed at his face, sinking my fingernails deep into his eye and cheek. He howled and released one hand from my throat to protect himself. The lessening of pressure on my windpipe allowed me a gulp of air. With as much force as I had, I shoved my knee into his groin. He groaned and fell backward against the terminal, and I heard the keyboard slam into something hard. With my hands outstretched in front of me I moved quickly, feeling my way toward the place where I thought the door was, stumbling against the equipment as I moved. A hand grabbed my leg and I fell and hit the floor. With my other leg I kicked violently, putting the heel of my shoe into the attacker's body. The grip on my leg released.

I had one advantage over him. I knew the floor plan of the room and he apparently didn't, or else in his panic he was disoriented. As I heard him knocking into equipment I continued to feel my way toward the door. But he was close behind. If I paused he could be on me. I felt my way behind a large rack of tapes near the rear of the room. The rack was a tall, spindly metal contraption set on rollers, with hundreds of large plastic reels of tape hanging in rows from the top of the metal bars. As I crouched behind it, I heard him breathing. He sounded out of breath from our struggle or maybe from his own anxiety. He had paused to figure out my location. I kicked the tape rack with my shoe to draw him nearer. The footsteps came closer. He was almost upon me.

I jumped from my crouched position and pushed the rack with my hip and shoulder until it tumbled onto him. I heard his grunt and the sound of his body hitting something. Hundreds of tapes crashed down and rolled onto the floor.

Frantically I made my way toward the door, but now, disoriented, I no longer was certain where it was. Running my hands against the wall, I groped for the door. It wasn't there. My heart bounced around the inside of my chest. I heard him getting up, untangling himself from the metal canisters. I would not die in there, I told myself. I would not die.

My hand hit the door handle. I turned it, opened the door. The lights were on in the hallway but there was no guard. I ran, stumbling down the hall. I didn't care what lights were on or who saw me. I wanted out of there.

I ran down the stairwell and when I spotted an exit door I headed for it. I opened it and found myself in the underground parking garage. It was cold and empty but brightly lighted. I ran down a short flight of steps and started running through the garage, then stopped. A black Ferrari sat parked near the garage entrance. Someone was in it. I ran toward the car and pounded on the window. Wayne Hanson jumped, startled, then leaned over and opened the car door. I was struck by the blast of his stereo. I rushed inside, slammed the door, and locked it. Hanson looked at me and tried to speak over the blaring music, then reached down and turned off the sound. Panting, I leaned back against the leather seat and tried to calm down enough so I could talk. Hanson looked at my straggly hair, the perspiration on my face, and the rip at the top of my shirt.

"Rough night, huh?" he said. With his uncombed hair and dirty sweatshirt, he didn't look much better than I did.

When I first tried to speak, nothing came out. My neck throbbed. I tried again. "Let's get out of here. Now," I said hoarsely.

Hanson looked bewildered. "Julie, what's wrong with you? What happened?"

I looked around the garage to make certain my attacker hadn't followed me. I turned back to Hanson. "Listen to me. Someone tried to kill me just now in the computer room. He could be coming after me. We need to get out of here."

Hanson's eyes widened. "You mean the Silicon Slayer?"

I didn't answer him. I didn't need to. He turned the ignition key, slammed the car into gear, and sped out of the garage leaving a trail of black rubber. Whoever attacked me wouldn't be able to catch me now unless he was traveling by jet.

"Holy shit," Hanson blubbered as he jumped the Ferrari over a median and ran a red light. He turned onto an empty street traveling at least ninety miles per hour. I looked behind us and saw that the road was empty. No one was following us. I breathed easier. I had escaped a murderer, now all I had to do was survive the trip with Hanson. Looking around the car, I saw piles of trash, including empty Cracker Jacks boxes, wrinkled computer printouts, torn textbooks, and various unidentifiable paraphernalia.

"Are we okay?" he asked in a frightened squeak when we were a safe distance from ICI. His hands were shaking.

"We're fine. I just need you to take me home." I didn't dare return to my car that night. Whoever attacked me knew me well enough to know I was going to be in the computer room. Maybe he knew where I had parked my car as well.

"What did he look like?" Hanson asked after he had calmed down. I had given him directions to my house, and we were on Highway 101 heading toward Palo Alto.

"I couldn't see him. It was too dark. The lights were out," I said. Then a question hit me. What was Hanson doing in the parking garage alone, late at night? Could he have been waiting there for the killer as an accomplice? The security guard patrolled the outside lot, but perhaps not the garage. I had been so desperate for help I had run out the first exit door I saw and to the first person I came across. I should have run to the security guard, but I hadn't been thinking rationally. I had only wanted out of the building as fast as possible. My body tensed and my hands instinctively went up to my throat.

"Wayne, what were you doing in the parking garage?" I asked slowly. Hanson stiffened. I calculated how I could fight him if he veered off onto a lonely road. Hanson was such a wussy, I was sure I could take him in hand-to-hand combat.

"Answer me, Wayne," I pressed. He shifted uncomfortably, loosened his death grip on the steering wheel, and slowed the car to eighty.

"It's just something to do, I guess."

"Just something to do, Wayne?"

He pushed his shoulders up to his ears. "I go there pretty often and park and just listen to the car stereo," he said, his voice sounding feeble. "I've told you that before. It's no big deal."

"Why sit in a parking lot?"

Hanson looked embarrassed. "I didn't have anything else to do. I go crazy sitting at home alone. Of course, I'm not really alone. The housekeeper is there all the time. But I don't think she likes me."

I looked at Hanson's sheepish face, his body awkwardly hunched over the steering wheel. My instincts told me he was telling the truth. I had always thought of him as an arrogant, brash, unbearable genius, but at that moment he looked like a scruffy dog nobody wanted.

"I'm not exactly Mr. Popularity," he added. Then Hanson brightened. "I consider you a friend, though."

"Of course we're friends," I said, feeling maternal toward him. I gave his arm a reassuring pat.

His look turned somber. "I'm really sorry if I've caused you trouble at the office. I'd undo it if I could, but I've already spoken to the executive committee. I'm sure they won't do anything to you. You're very well thought of at headquarters, you know."

I laughed. "Don't worry about it, Wayne. I just escaped

the Silicon Slayer. The executive committee doesn't scare me anymore."

Hanson smiled. "I've always liked you because Max used to tell me how smart you are." Hanson sighed and mouthed the word "Max" as if the word held some voodoo. "I miss Max. I always had plenty to do when she was around. I still love her. She doesn't realize it yet, but I'm the right man for her. At least I could learn to be. She and I are alike. We don't fit in with the rest of the people around us. We can't be labeled. That's why we belong together, and she'll wake up to it one day. Don't you think so, Julie?" he asked as he exited the highway toward my home.

But I couldn't answer. I was staring down at my hands and fighting off nausea. Underneath my fingernails I saw blood and human flesh.

CHAPTER 17

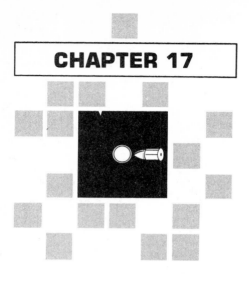

I opened my eyes the next morning and pretended it had all been a nightmare, just another of my ghoulish dreams that lately entered my sleep so frequently. But when I looked into my bathroom mirror, the marks on my neck, large and purplish, were a grim testament to the reality of what had happened the night before.

Someone had tried to kill me. I turned the thought over and over in my mind to try to place it in the proper perspective, to reduce its importance and reason away the quivering in my hands, but the fact was there, and it both frightened and excited me. *Someone had tried to kill me.*

I pulled on a skirt and a sweater then went into the kitchen for coffee. I turned on the radio, poured my orange juice, scooped the instant coffee into a mug, trying to create some normalcy, a sense that things were all right. But they weren't.

Closing my eyes, I leaned back against the kitchen counter and remembered the hands around my throat, how tightly they had squeezed. I remembered feeling my life slipping away from me, but I also remembered fighting back and winning. Part of me was still frightened, part of me was relieved because the attack had made me less suspicious of Max. I was also excited, for the killer had exposed himself to me in a way. He had made a serious error, for he had failed to kill me and now I would find him.

I lifted the cup of black coffee to my lips and tried to focus my thoughts on the work day ahead of me, but something nagged at me, the memory of a muffled sound, a barely audible groan of my attacker when the rack of tapes fell on him. There was something familiar in its tone, a timbre in the voice that I recognized. I couldn't be certain of it or identify it, yet I knew I had heard it.

When I glanced at the clock, I saw the time and raced around the house looking for clean panty hose. I guess some things never change. Shouldn't there be some unwritten rule that if you survive a murder attempt you get to forgo panty hose the next day? I keep one drawer filled with nothing but various forms of hosiery. I was ripping the plastic wrapping off a new pair of control tops when the phone rang.

"Good morning, darling. I'm glad I caught you."

Charles. He sounded cheerful and so different from my own state of mind. It was as if he were calling from a another planet where people didn't lie, steal, and murder.

"Are you still in Seattle?" I asked.

"Yes. I'm not sure when I'll be back. The meetings here have been dragging. What's been going on with you?"

I hesitated, not knowing if I should tell him the truth. Oh, not much, Charles. Someone tried to strangle me last night, but other than that, same old grind. I needed to spill my guts to someone, but that someone wasn't going to be Charles.

"Julie, is there anything wrong?"

"No, everything is fine, really. I just didn't sleep well last night and I'm a little groggy."

"Can't sleep without me, right? I'll try to be home tomorrow. I miss you."

"I miss you too."

We exchanged good-byes and I heard the *click* that disconnected us. I placed the receiver on its cradle and looked down at it for a long time. I should have told him what happened, but I felt too drained to get into an argument about why I had been in the office again at night. Besides, he would have immediately called Mother.

I wiggled into my panty hose, grabbed my coat, and left for work.

■ ◻ ■

"Well, la dee da, don't you look sporty? I like you in that turtleneck. You've looked so snappy lately with your new hairdo. I just love it loose," said Mrs. Dabney, standing on her tiptoes to reach inside a high file cabinet. She grabbed the file, slammed the drawer shut, then walked, high heels clicking, back to her desk.

"Here's a memo from Joshua in the computer room." She handed me a slip of paper.

"The tape rack fell over last night and the tapes are all over the place (no corpses, though). Should we worry?" the scrawled note said. I handed it back to Mrs. Dabney.

"Send Josh a note saying that the tape racks are unstable and a safety hazard. Tell him we're going to convert them all to cartridges. Any other messages?"

"Just these." She handed me more message slips. "And that secret agent's been skulking around looking for you. When he comes back, should I get rid of him?"

Something caught in the back of my throat. "Uh, no. Send him in."

I walked past Mrs. Dabney into my office. Everything

seemed the same as yesterday. It annoyed me a little that somebody could try to murder me and the world would go on turning as if nothing had happened. I sat down at my desk and was unlocking my drawer when I heard a rap on my opened door. I looked up at Paoli.

"We had an appointment, remember?" he said.

"Of course I remember. Have a seat."

He shut the door behind him, sat down, shifted in his chair a few times, looking like someone waiting for a root canal. It surprised me. I guess I expected him to swagger in and call me baby.

"We need to decide what our next step is. That is, if you're still interested in working on this with me," he said slowly, faking nonchalance. He sat stiffly back in his chair, giving the impression that the chair didn't fit him. I pondered the source of his discomfort. Did he worry that I would throw myself at him, play the shameless vamp, or sob at his feet and profess undying love? Well, he was wrong. Even though the sight of him filled my mind with unbusinesslike images. I saw his hands and I remembered him touching me. I heard him speak and I remembered kissing him. Even the faint scent of his cologne drifting toward me made my body temperature rise five degrees. Keep your cologne on your side of the office, Paoli. It makes me feel weak in the knees, makes me want to curl up in your lap for about thirty years.

"Yes. Still interested," I replied.

He smiled and his blue eyes crinkled up at the corners. Don't smile at me, I begged silently. I was feeling flushed and the room grew uncomfortably warm. Instinctively I ran my hand across the neck of my sweater, pulling the itchy wool away from my neck.

"Good God, Julie, what happened to your neck?"

He jumped out of his chair and over to my desk. I quickly moved away from him and closed my office door.

"What are you talking about? Sit down," I told him, but he wouldn't move. He reached over and pulled down the neck of my sweater.

"Get your hands off me."

"How did that happen?"

I couldn't think of anything plausible to say. How could I answer? I got my neck caught in a car window? I kept quiet.

He grabbed my arms and turned me so I faced him. "I'm not moving until you tell me what happened, do you understand? I'm not budging."

We just stared at each other a moment. Paoli looked rooted to the floor.

"Okay, I'll tell you, but you have to promise not to repeat it."

He nodded.

"I was in the computer room last night. I was trying to log on to Larry's security files, to compare them one more time to Gershbein's code." I paused. "And someone attacked me."

"What do you mean, someone attacked you?"

"He tried to strangle me."

A look flashed across his face like maybe he was going to yell at me or throw me out the window. I didn't understand him well enough to know what it was he was mad at.

"Who was it?" he asked.

"I don't know. It was so dark."

He looked steamed and little veins were popping up on the side of his neck. I could tell by his face that he cared that I had been hurt, and I guess the prospect of a confidant made the words come tumbling out of me.

"I was so scared. I almost didn't get away from him. He had his hands on my throat and he—"

Paoli had pulled me toward him and put his arms around me, holding me close to him. I could feel his face in my hair, his heart pounding. If I had been the type to cry, I would have, but I wasn't the type. Still, the more I described my terrible experience the closer he held me, so I described it some more.

"He tried to strangle me. He turned off all the lights then he came into the computer room and tried to kill me.

I couldn't see him because he was wearing a ski mask. But I guess he'll remember me for a few days. I fought him. His face probably looks like he's been in a cat fight."

I looked up at Paoli. He was momentarily speechless. I liked him that way. He continued to hold me for a while, stroking my hair.

"Have you told the police?" he finally asked.

"No, and I'm not going to. I'm not telling anyone. If Elkin or Garrett found out that I was in the computer room last night I could be fired. The least they would do is bump me off the project."

"It would be best for you if they did, Julie. Someone out there is killing over it. You can't take any more risks."

"But that's just it," I said, pulling back from him. "Someone tried to kill me last night because I was going to log on to Larry. It's just like the time I tried it before when Larry was powered down. It proves that the data leaks and the murders are connected. It also proves that the secret to the whole thing is inside Larry's code."

Paoli's arms dropped away from me. "Are you crazy? Someone tried to kill you last night, Julie. Doesn't that tell you to back off this thing?"

"No, it doesn't. It tells me to press harder because I must be getting closer to the answer. Don't you get it? Whoever it was last night didn't want me accessing Larry. That's why he tried to stop me. That's why he killed Gershbein."

Paoli looked doubtful. "But several people had access to Larry's security code until two weeks ago when they revoked the passwords. He would have had to kill half a dozen people to protect that software. Why select you and Gershbein?"

"Because it wasn't *what* we were accessing. It was *why*. Whoever it is realizes I'm on to him, that I know something is screwed up in that security code. Gershbein knew it too, and that's why he took the code printout home. He wanted to study it to understand what was wrong."

I watched Paoli's expression for signs of agreement. I

guess I expected him to jump up and throw his arms around me and shout, "By George, you've got it!" But he didn't. He looked thoughtful. He walked over to the window and looked out at the street.

"How did you get a password into the security code? Yours was revoked."

"Easy. I programmed in a trapdoor password four years ago when I wrote the program. I originally did it for testing purposes and luckily just never got around to taking it out. I needed some way to get around that stupid decision to revoke the passwords."

He turned toward me. "That was my stupid decision."

"Yours? Why?"

"Because I guessed from the beginning that Gershbein was suspicious of the security code and that maybe it was why he was killed. I couldn't be sure. I'm still not, but after Wu was murdered, I asked Garrett to revoke the passwords, just in case, so no one else would be in danger."

"But Wu didn't have a password to the security code. Why was he killed?"

"I'm not sure yet. I do know that he was probably selling project data. Those large cash deposits he made in the three bank accounts are too suspicious. You don't do that with money you've come by honestly."

"So maybe Wu was going to double-cross somebody so they snuffed him."

"Julie, where do you get words like 'double-cross' and 'snuff'? You're starting to sound like a cheap detective novel. You know, you're hard to figure out sometimes. Someone tried to kill you last night and now you're all excited. Do you have some bizarre sexual tastes I should be aware of?"

"It's just that we're closer now to the answer than ever before. The closer we are to the answer, the closer I am to completing Project 6, and that excites me."

"That's about the only thing that excites you," Paoli muttered, as he once again turned away from me.

"What do you mean by that?"

"I guess I mean I don't like being used," he said. He had his hands stuffed in his pockets and he avoided my eyes.

"And exactly how have you been used?" I asked, now ready for a fight. "I don't care about taking any credit for solving this thing. You can take it all. I just care about the project."

"How typical of you to reduce everything to business. I was talking about you and me and the night we spent scrambling the sheets in my hotel room."

"Lower your voice," I told him. I could imagine Mrs. Dabney with her ear to the door. "I'm still not getting you."

"What did you want from me? Did you think that if you slept with me I would work harder on the case? Or was it insurance for the future in case you needed my protection against Garrett?"

I just stared at him. His Italian heritage showed as he paced across the office, his arms and hands gesturing wildly with each sentence he uttered. The whole scene reminded me of some old movie except he was playing the Sophia Loren part and I was Cary Grant. It made me like him even more. He stood there in front of me spouting out his insecurities, and the words were so familiar, as if they were coming from me.

"I spent the night with you because I wanted to. It meant a lot to me."

"Then why did you jump up and leave the other morning without saying a word to me, and why have you turned into this ice bitch lately?"

"Because I've been feeling the same things you have, that you might be using me, that you might write my phone number in the men's room with 'For a good time call' written over it."

"You mean you went in there and you saw it?"

"If you did, I'll—"

"Of course I didn't. You're acting like somebody in high school."

"And you're not?" I asked.

Paoli stepped much closer to me, so close I could feel the warmth generated from his body, could smell the faint scent of his skin. I read somewhere that physical attraction was chemically based, the primitive reaction of one molecule to another molecule. If so, right then our molecules were dancing the mambo.

"If I wrote anything about you in the men's room it would be a picture of a big heart with both our names in it. Now, Julie, how's that for high school?" he said with a grin. He moved his face closer to mine. "I'm crazy about you. Let's go steady," he whispered as our molecules whipped themselves into a sexual frenzy. I looked at his face and used all my willpower not to kiss him.

"Or better yet, meet me at the hotel tonight," he whispered.

I leaned back against the wall for support. I forced myself to think of Charles—warm, caring, wonderful Charles who needed me, who cared for me, who wanted to marry me.

"I'll be there."

"Great. We'll have dinner," he responded, kissing me before I could object.

■ ◻ ■

"The Soviets have even newer versions of the molecular memory designs," Paoli said as we both lay naked and happy in his rumpled bed. At least I had been happy. I quickly pushed the sheet down and sat up.

"How new?" I asked.

"The designs are current up to about eight weeks ago. Eleven weeks more current than the previous designs that were leaked to them."

"How do you know this?"

"Our main office in Washington. They got it from the same source as last time."

I got out of bed and threw on Paoli's robe, too nervous to sit still. "Why did you wait until now to tell me?"

"I wanted to tell you yesterday morning as soon as I found out, but if you'll remember, you practically threw me out of your office."

I wrapped a bath towel around myself and walked around the room a few times. Paoli sat in bed looking sexy and watching me, the white sheet pulled to his waist.

"How long have Garrett and Elkin known about this?"

"They don't know," he replied. "And I'm not telling them, at least not for a while. I wanted to give us a chance to work on it first. As soon as I tell them they'll kick you back to the East Coast, won't they?"

"That's if they're in good humor."

"Now what are you doing?"

"Getting my clothes," I said.

"What for?"

"I need to go to the office."

"To do what?"

"I'm not sure, but I can't stand around here wasting time," I said as I headed for the bathroom. I shut the door behind me, but I could hear Paoli talking through the door.

"First of all, I don't consider what we're doing here wasting time, but second, there's nothing you can do tonight," he pleaded.

"There's always something you can do. It's just going to take a few minutes to think of what it is."

When I walked out of the bathroom, Paoli was getting dressed. He saw my surprise. "I intend to spend the night with you. Spending it with you at your office isn't exactly what I had planned, but if that's all I can get, I'll take it," he said with a smile.

CHAPTER 18

Mrs. Dabney dipped one finger into a pink cocktail and twirled the ice cubes before she drank. After savoring a lingering sip, she smacked her lips with satisfaction.

"Lord, I do love a party," she drawled, pushing her rhinestone glasses down her nose and peering over them to survey the scene around her.

I used my napkin to dab away a drop of gin that perched upon her nose. Everyone looked forward to the ICI anniversary cocktail parties. Employees began discussing the event days in advance, rehashing tales of drunken revelry from previous years, anticipating the coming celebration. It was their once-a-year opportunity to drop their corporate façades, to really let loose at the office, to tell dirty jokes, to grab the behind of the programmer at the next desk.

Once a year ICI transformed the cafeteria with crêpe paper, banners, an open bar, and a large framed photo of our founding father, and my usually quiet, industrious employees dropped their corporate shorts and transformed into swinging party animals complete with paper hats and lewd dancing. Even Mrs. Dabney was wearing a satiny purple cocktail dress with a daring neckline that gaped threateningly as she shimmied her shoulders to the piped-in music. I wore my favorite navy dress with a scarf draped artfully around my neck to hide my bruises.

"I could sure stand a rhumba right about now," Mrs. Dabney said, grabbing the hand of an innocent male passing by and dragging him onto the dance floor.

I walked over to the bar to refresh my orange juice and watched Mrs. Dabney teach the rhumba to a data entry clerk thirty years her junior. I hummed to the music, thought of Paoli, smiled inside and out, then stifled a yawn. I had gone back with him to his hotel the night before where I had gotten plenty of everything but sleep. I would have gladly passed up this office celebration, but I had been looking for Max and I knew she would be at the party. There were questions I needed to ask her. Besides, the cocktail parties were a command performance for managers in order to give employees the opportunity to rub elbows with management. Suddenly I felt a hand trying to rub more than my elbow.

"Hi there, cookie," slurred Steve Burmann, a shortish, dark-haired man in his late forties. He was a manager on a project in another department. I didn't know him well, but he had always seemed okay. At least until now. He was sotted. I removed his hand from my hip. He moved his face close to mine. He reeked of gin and miniature meatballs.

"You know, you're a very attractive woman," he muttered as he sniffed my neck.

One thing I didn't like about company cocktail parties was that sometimes people felt that because they were allowed to drink on company premises they were also allowed to vent their most unprofessional, primitive instincts. I did not share that assumption.

"It's only nine-thirty, Steve. What are you going to be like by midnight?" I asked, backing off from him.

"I'll sober up by then. But first, let's you and me go in the parking lot."

Burmann started pulling me toward the door. I refused to move. Luckily Elkin walked toward us and Burmann quickly dropped my hand and got lost in the crowd. I saw Mrs. Dabney, drink in hand, rhumba-ing her way, alone, out of the room. She was going to have one hell of a headache the next morning.

"You don't look like you're in the party mood," Elkin said when he reached my side.

"I don't feel like a party tonight, Brad. Too much on my mind." He looked handsome in a dark suit and an aqua silk tie that brought out the blue in his eyes. I wondered if that was why he wore it, but it was hard to imagine Elkin prey to such vanity.

"It's Thursday, Julie. You know your two weeks is up."

I felt my body tense. I had been avoiding him all day and had failed to return one of his calls. I knew I would see him tonight, but I wanted to put this off this confrontation as long as possible.

"I'm aware of that," I answered.

"I gave you the time you asked for. Now I expect you to accept the terms of our agreement. We're closing down the project. It will be official tomorrow. I'll expect you to cooperate in turning over your files."

"You don't have to worry, Brad. I live up to my agreements."

"I know it's been tough on you, but remember, I offered to you an escape hatch out of this problem," he said.

"I know, but I don't like to escape from problems. You taught me that, remember?"

He smiled. "I guess I did. We'll pull through this thing." His eyes scanned the room. "Garrett is over there and I need to talk to him. Go mingle a little and try to enjoy yourself. That's an order from your manager."

He glided off and I stood there a few moments nodding, smiling, and chatting with people like a good hostess. Then Max walked up. She was wearing a black sheath cut to the waist in back. She looked fantastic.

"Having fun?" she asked. I made a face and she laughed. "Me either. How long do you have to stay here?"

"Until about ten, I think. Things start breaking up when the food runs out. Mrs. Dabney mentioned earlier that she saw you at ICI today. What's up?"

"Negotiations. I'm working with your people on a marketing agreement between ICI and Comtech for when and if molecular memory is manufactured."

"Isn't that a little premature?

"Sure it's premature, but ICI likes everything spelled out in black and white. It's possible the project could be completed tomorrow if that computer of yours would just spit out the right design," said Max.

"It will. Give it time."

"Meanwhile I've got to do this grunt work with your marketing department. God, they're stuffy."

I smiled. "But they're supposed to be stuffy. That's our corporate image. Speaking of our corporate image, I need a break from it. Let's take a breather."

Max nodded and we weaved through the crowd toward the door. There were people in the hallway, so we headed up the stairs where I knew there were empty offices and we would be alone. Max had grabbed a bottle of wine from the bartender, which she placed in the middle of the desk. We sat down and she filled our glasses.

"Max, I need to ask you something."

"Excellent. I'm full of answers tonight."

I took a deep breath. "That comb of yours, Max. The black one with the pearls. How did you lose it?"

Max cocked her head to one side and looked at me quizzically. "You were going on about that silly comb at lunch the other day. What's with you?"

"I just need to know."

"Why?"

I drew in a long breath. "Because I found one just like it on the computer room the other night. I'd like to know how it got there."

Max looked perplexed a moment, then burst out laughing.

"So that's what happened to it. I've been looking for it. If you must know, I was having a little amour in the computer room, and I guess in the tussle the comb fell out."

"You had sex in the computer room?"

"No, I was making love in the computer room. It was around eight-thirty, I think. We had had a few drinks and just got this crazy idea. So we came back to ICI, got in the computer room, and sort of pressed ourselves against Larry. God, I could feel him vibrating against me. Larry, I mean, and then—"

Max was interrupted by the sound of sobbing coming from down the hall. We were both startled a moment, then I jumped up and ran toward the sound. Max followed. As we turned down the corridor I saw Peggy, who was working second shift, running toward us. Her hair was flying, her face white. I grabbed her by the shoulders.

"Peggy, what is it?" I asked her. Her expression was frantic. She choked off a sob.

"Come . . . come look," she said. Max and I glanced at each other, then followed Peggy down the hall to the computer room. My stomach twisted into a knot. When Peggy opened the door, Max and I braced ourselves, but when we walked in I didn't see anything that looked out of the ordinary.

Peggy pointed to a wall where backup power packs and tubing from the water cooling system were located. From a distance everything seemed in perfect order. Peggy pushed me ahead of her toward the wall.

Then I saw it. On the wall ran five plastic tubes that brought chilled water from roof tanks down to Larry. Normally that tubing wouldn't be exposed in a computer room, but prior to Project 6, ICI brought customers and students into our research facility for tours. The tubes were exposed to show the cooling procedures for supermainframes. One or two of the tubes were usually empty because not all the tanks were used. Under normal circumstances it would be difficult to tell which tubes actually held the water, but this time it was easy, for through one of the tubes dripped a thick reddish liquid.

Max gasped and put her hands up to her face when she saw it. I moved in and inspected the tubing more closely.

"It looks like blood," I said, stating the obvious. "How do we get to the roof?" I asked Peggy. She shook her head.

"Peggy, stay here. Max and I will check this out." Peggy nodded quickly. Max gave me a dubious look, but I grabbed her hand and pulled her with me. I didn't want to go up there alone.

We walked outside and I could see through the windows of the cafeteria that the party was managing to go on without us. Someone had put a crêpe-paper mustache on Harold T. Gordon's picture. I looked around the outside of the building and saw a metal ladder attached to the wall between two windows. After checking to make sure it was sturdy, I kicked off my high heels and put my panty-hosed foot on the ladder's first rung. Max stared at me, open-mouthed.

"Now listen, Jules. I'm a firm believer that certain things are best left to professionals, like manicures, housework, oil changes, searching for bleeding bodies. Why don't we just call the police? And for chrissakes, get off that thing. Someone will see you and it will start a panic," Max whispered as I started up the ladder.

I looked down at her. "No one can see me. Just stay in between the windows and be quiet."

I climbed up the ladder as quickly as I dared. When I reached the roof I looked down at Max.

"Throw me my purse," I told her.

"This is no time to refresh one's lipstick," she said, then threw my handbag with a wild underhand toss that I barely caught.

"Now get up here, Max."

She looked at me like I had asked her to strip naked and run down Broadway. In fact, she probably would have preferred it.

"These shoes are Charles Jourdan, honey. They're made for treading lightly across thick carpeting, not for playing fireman."

"So take them off. Just get up here."

"Shouldn't we at least get some help before we tackle this?"

"Are you going to be a wimp?"

Max scowled, kicked off her high heels, and started gingerly up the ladder. She gave me her hand when she reached the top and I helped her onto the roof. I took a penlight out of my purse and shined it around the gravel surface. Three water tanks sat near the back.

"Follow me," I said. Max walked behind me as we moved slowly toward the tanks.

"Ouch!" Max yelped.

"Be quiet."

"But this gravel is digging into the soles of my feet."

"It's digging into mine too. Toughen up, Max. What would you do if they started drafting women into the army?"

Max cursed but continued to follow me. We reached the first tank. Max and I exchanged a look, then I handed her the penlight as I lifted the heavy metal lid to the tank.

"Give me a hand," I told her. Max put the penlight between her teeth and helped me lift. When the lid was raised about a foot I took a deep breath and looked inside. It was filled with water. We quickly lowered it shut.

"See? Nothing. Let's go back to the party," Max pleaded.

"There are two more tanks, Max. Let's go."

We walked over to the second tank and together lifted the lid, but once again found only water.

"Jules, these things are obviously filled with *agua puro*.

The blood must be coming from someplace else, maybe a disk drive that committed suicide. I think we should go call security right now."

"The freon in the water corrodes the sides and causes leakage, so we usually keep one of the tanks empty as a backup. It's got to be this one," I said, pointing to the last tank. I pulled Max with me.

"I don't like this," she whispered. I didn't respond. We put our hands under the edge of the lid and lifted.

"Oh, shit, I broke a nail," Max said with a snarl, dropping the penlight.

"This one is empty. Quick, give me the flashlight."

She picked it up and handed it to me. I pointed it inside the tank toward the side. The light revealed two large feet clad in wingtip shoes.

"Holy shit," Max muttered. With a grunt, I gave the lid a push. It slipped over the side of the tank with a loud *thud*. I moved the flashlight slowly up the body and saw a large pool of blood. Max grabbed my hand and I could feel her quivering. When the light from my flashlight reached the throat of the body we both gasped, for it was slit across with a bright-red slash. Max turned her head away. I moved the flashlight to the face. Its flesh was a startling white, the eyes staring up at me with a glassy look of surprise. I cried out, dropped the flashlight, and covered my face with my hands. Max turned to me quickly. She looked down into the tank where the flashlight had fallen on the body and illuminated its bloody neck and pale face. I heard her yelp, and then she threw her arms around me. The body in the tank was Charles.

What she didn't know was that the three long scratches across his face had been made by me.

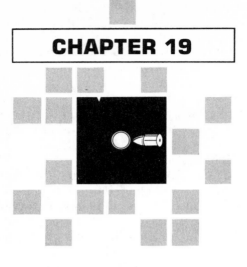

CHAPTER 19

I stood there shivering, staring at Charles's distorted face and bloodless pallor. Like dull glass, his eyes stared back at me with an inhuman blankness, the three red scratches streaked down his left cheek. I had left those scratches there two nights before. Last year Max had talked me into growing my nails longer. I never knew they would come in so handy. My hands raised involuntarily to my throat and I recalled once more the muffled groan I had heard that night in the darkness. It had a quality that sounded so familiar, a sound that somewhere in the back of my mind I remembered. It was the sound of my lover as he made love to me. It was the sound of my lover as he tried to kill me. At that moment I was really pissed off at men.

Max and I held on to each other for what seemed a long time. Someone must have heard my scream, because a small group had gathered below. Max left me and shouted something down to them, and soon the night was filled with sirens and lights flashing, and I was surrounded by a throng of people. But I never moved, never spoke. I just stood there staring at Charles.

"Julie, you've got to leave here. Do you hear me?"

Looking up at Brad Elkin, I could see his eyes filled with sympathy, and for an instant I wanted to laugh. He looked at me as if I were stricken with grief at the loss of my fiancé. At that moment I wished it had been me who slashed his throat. At least I should have gotten the opportunity to tell him our engagement was off.

"We need to question Ms. Blake," a policeman said to Elkin.

"No one is going to question her, at least not tonight," he told him. He took the policeman aside and spoke to him. The officer protested at first, then shrugged his shoulders and joined his comrade in questioning Max, who was describing the scenario in technicolor detail. Elkin held my arm and steered me away from the others.

Elkin led me to the other side of the roof, where we took the stairs down to the main floor and then crossed back to the cafeteria and went out a side door. We stood there quietly with Elkin standing protectively by me. He said he wanted to wait for Max.

The police began dispersing everyone and the area started to clear. After finishing with the police, Max came to me with my shoes, a bottle of Beefeaters gin, and two glasses she had taken from the now-defunct party.

"Here, take a drink," she commanded. I shook my head but she poured the clear liquid into the cup and handed it to me. I drank it in a gulp.

She poured gin in the second glass and tossed it down her throat. One thing I liked about Max was that she knew when to be quiet.

"Could you drive her home?" Elkin asked her. She nodded. I put on my shoes and the three of us walked to the parking lot that was beginning to empty. Max unlocked the car door and I slid into her Porsche.

"I'll be back in a minute," she said after I was seated inside the car. After sitting there alone a few minutes, I twisted in my seat and looked around for her. About thirty feet from the car in a dark spot away from the lights I saw her wrapped in an embrace with someone. At first I couldn't tell who it was, but when they parted I recognized Brad Elkin. The night was full of surprises. So he was the one making love to her in elevators and computer rooms. It was a side of Elkin I had never suspected. He had been divorced for many years and I knew he dated occasionally, but he had always struck me as a strictly missionary-position type of guy. Now it all made sense why Max had been so secretive about her lover's identity.

Max and I drove in silence to her house. I didn't want to bring up Elkin and she didn't want to bring up Charles, and when you've just found your fiancé with his throat cut you don't feel like chatting about the stock market or the latest sale at Macy's. After we arrived at her house, Max gave me a flannel nightgown and a sleeping pill. After settling in the bed in her guest room, I lay in the darkness an hour before falling into restless sleep. I dreamed vividly that night, my mind filled with black visions of Charles. I dreamed I was at our wedding. We stood in front of the minister reciting our vows. I looked down and saw my white bridal gown covered with blood and I screamed, but the minister continued droning on about love and fidelity. I looked up at Charles and saw the blood flowing from his neck, his eyes fixed upon me. I awoke crying and sat up in bed, staring out my bedroom window. It was just before daybreak, and I was filled with confusion about my past and future.

■ ◻ ■

Mrs. Dabney blotted her moist eyes with a ragged Kleenex, then blew her nose furiously, emitting a honk that sounded like a dilapidated Chevy.

"It's so horrible," she muttered, shaking her coiffed head in distrust of the world. "You must be devastated. I can't believe you're even here." She looked up at me. Her glasses were fogged, but I was certain that past the haze lay an expression of shock and sympathy, the same expression registered on everyone's face that morning.

If Charles was looking up from his holy reward, I'm sure he was feeling smug. He always loved to be the center of attention. His bloodied corpse turning up at the ICI cocktail party had everyone in turmoil, all of them shocked and horrified and feeling very sorry for me. Even when I went home from Max's that morning to change clothes, phone calls came in from people certain that I was devastated by the loss of my beloved. Fortunately my mother had yet to hear the news. I couldn't tell anybody that my beloved tried to strangle me only three nights before. The bastard hadn't even had the guts to let me see his face. Part of me wanted to tell people about it because I couldn't stand feigning grief, but I didn't dare. I still couldn't let anyone know I was in the computer room that night. I still had too many things to do. What bugged me was how Charles's body had wound up on the roof. It would be too risky to carry a body through the building and he was much too heavy to have been lifted up the ladder, so he must have been killed after he had already climbed up it. But whom had he met there?

"I hate to burden you with this," Mrs. Dabney said, "but the police called, and they want to talk to you today."

That was the last thing I needed. "Could you tell them that I just can't talk about it yet?" I paused dramatically, trying to seem frail. "I'm not ready. Tell them to talk with Max. I'll go down to the station tomorrow."

Mrs. Dabney took my hand and gave it a pat. "Don't worry. I'll put them off," she said. I smiled gratefully. I knew I would eventually have to tell the police about Charles's attack in the computer room, but I wanted to stall them.

I thanked Mrs. Dabney for her sympathies and went into my office. As soon as I sat down the phone buzzed. I answered it. It was Garrett.

"I'm surprised you came into the office today," he said with fatherly concern. I wondered if it was real.

"I guess it's best for me to keep busy. Besides, there's work to do."

Garrett cleared his throat. "Yes, well, could you meet me in my office right away? If you're feeling up to it, of course. I'd like to have a chat with you."

"Of course." The term "chat" sounded ominous.

I walked down the hallway and around the corner to Garrett's office, trying to ignore the stares. On several desks sat the *Chronicle* bearing the headline "Silicon Slayer Slashes Again." As I approached Garrett's office I saw his secretary, Ida Franklin, lodged at her station directly outside his office. As soon as she saw me she began shaking her head and looking weepy-eyed. I steeled myself.

"You poor, poor child," she said when I neared her desk. "How are you holding up?"

"I'm managing. Is Garrett ready for me?"

"Charles was a wonderful man."

I could think of a few flaws. "Thank you. You're very kind."

"You're so strong," she said, clasping my hand. "He said to show you right in."

"Thanks." It took some effort, but I managed to tug my hand from Ida's grasp. As I walked through Garrett's door, I could feel her pitying eyes follow me. Garrett sat behind his desk looking corporate, the front page of the *Chronicle* laid out where I couldn't miss it. He looked up.

"Julie," he said with a somber tone, his hands clasped in front of him. There was a falseness about him that crystallized for me why I never liked him much. "Let me express my sincere sympathies over Charles. I always thought he was a fine man and a team player."

So did the Russians. "Thanks. You're very kind, but if that's the reason you wanted to see me . . ."

"That's not the reason," he interrupted. I could tell the warm-up was over and that we were about to play hardball. "Have a seat," he instructed, and I did.

"You know, Julie, the past few years have been exciting ones for all of us. For a long while Project 6 progressed beyond all our expectations, and of course we owe a great deal of that progress to you. You set our course, stood firm at the tiller, guided us through."

Garrett's boat-in-the-storm analogy always made me seasick. "What's the bottom line, John?"

He shot me a nasty look, hating my interruption of what he surely considered an insightful and blow-softening metaphor. "Project 6. It's over."

"Why?" I asked, my body rigid but my voice relaxed. I had expected this, but I wanted to fight.

"Because of this." He held up the front page of the *Chronicle*.

"But Charles wasn't even on the project."

"But the other two people murdered were, and Charles was obviously closely associated with you."

Garrett glared at me, his expression turning sour. I guess he didn't appreciate a confrontation from someone he considered an underling. He took a deep breath to compose himself. "Look at the bright side. You're going to be transferred to the large systems plant in upstate New York. You'll go at the same job level. Naturally ICI will pick up your moving expenses."

"And what happens to our five years of work?"

"We're going to dump all the data to tape and archive it."

Even though I had been expecting this, it still aroused my emotions when I heard it. I got out of my chair and leaned over his desk, my face only inches from his. "You can't do that! You can't just take five years of effort and lock it away somewhere. We could be only a few days away from completion. You can't just cancel the project and ship me off and pretend that fixes anything."

Garrett narrowed his eyes and bared his teeth like an

angry dog. "Let me tell you something," he said in a low and calculated voice. "We're sending you back east as a level sixty-two. It's practically a promotion."

I didn't jump up and down with glee.

"I guess you just don't understand," he continued. "Your project is months over schedule. You've let confidential data get leaked to another country, and several ICI employees are rotting in their graves for it. You're lucky you don't get transferred to a local jail. I'd have you bounced right out of here but I need to save face. You're just not too appreciative of how good you've got it, young lady."

"I don't like being called 'young lady' and I don't care about my job level or what you do to me. I care about the project and what it can mean to this company, to everyone. That's what I care about. I thought that's what you cared about too."

"Drop the Pollyanna act. I care about what everybody cares about, and that's the title that comes after my name. The executive committee is on my ass. It's embarrassed us with Washington and now it's embarrassing us with everyone who can spend a quarter for a newspaper. That's a lot of people to be embarrassed in front of. I'm going to be up for a directorship next year, and this project could drag me down unless I get rid of it. So it's gone. Do you understand?"

"I won't give up on it."

"Then let me put it this way. You go home and pack your bags for New York State, because if I hear you're on these premises after five o'clock today, you no longer work for this company. Do you understand me now?"

I didn't answer. I wanted to tell him to stick his level sixty-two job where the sun don't shine, walk out of ICI and into any of the hundred jobs with ICI competitors I could have in Silicon Valley. I didn't need ICI anymore. I had seen behind the surface and it all seemed like a nice corporate bedtime story with knights and princesses and dragons, all carefully concocted to conceal the power and the greed behind it. Yes, we want to be a good corporate citizen and contribute to society—as long as it doesn't interfere with job promotions and our stock options. But if I quit, Garrett would have every file in my office locked up immediately and I wouldn't have a prayer of accessing any of the project data. I couldn't let that happen, not yet. The urge to walk away from it all was enticing, but I wanted to fight back. And to do that I needed to be an ICI employee.

"I have a call to make now," Garrett said, returning his gaze to his paperwork to let me know our meeting was over.

I turned and walked out the door, past his secretary, down the hall, past the stares and the whispers, back to my office.

"I'm going to need some boxes," I said to Mrs. Dabney. She saw the look on my face.

"You're not going to try to hurt yourself, are you?"

"Do you think I'm going to put one over my head and try to suffocate?"

"The loss of a loved one can make you crazy."

"Don't worry about me. Please, just get me the boxes."

She seemed placated.

"By the way, he's in there again." She made a face as she said it, accenting the word "he." I tried not to gallop into my office.

"Why didn't you call me last night after it happened?" Paoli asked as I walked in.

"I'm very, very glad to see you," I told him. As soon as I laid eyes on him, the very moment I breathed in his scent, I could feel my body chemistry rearranging. A few days, even a few hours earlier, I would have felt awkward and would have struggled to relax around him. Not anymore. I walked up to him, pushed him down into a chair, sat on his lap, and kissed him as if he were shipping out with the Navy. I knew the door was open, but what the hell? I didn't work there anymore.

"At least you seem to be coping well," he said when our lips finally detached themselves. "Last night must have been awful for you. Finding your fiancé like that. Are you okay? Talk to me."

I got up and shut the door. "Ex-fiancé. I had already decided to call off the engagement. His dying just made it easier to break the news to him."

Paoli stood up and put his arms around me. "You can't cover up with a joke, Julie. I talked to the police. They think he was killed on the roof during the party."

"During the party? That can't be right. The ladder Max and I used to get up there was near a window. Anyone using that ladder or the stairs on the other side of the building would risk being seen."

He dropped his arms from my shoulders, but stayed very close, just where I liked him.

"You're right, Julie, but there was another way to the roof, a ladder on the south side of the building near a door to the cafeteria kitchen. Only someone who knew his way around the building would have known about that ladder. What I can't figure is why anyone would meet on the roof. It seems silly. Why not in an office?"

"Maybe because they couldn't risk being seen. The roof was the most secluded spot," I said.

Paoli shrugged. "So why not plan to meet somewhere else, away from ICI?"

I thought a moment. "Probably the meeting wasn't planned. It was decided on suddenly. The roof was the fastest, safest place to go."

"You're assuming it was someone at the party who killed him then?"

"It seems reasonable. Charles shows up at ICI because he desperately needs to talk to someone there. He calls into the cafeteria phone and asks to speak to someone. When he gets them he demands to meet them on the roof."

"Why the cloak and dagger? If these are all ICI people we're dealing with here, why wouldn't Charles just walk into the party and grab whoever he needed to talk to?"

I paused before answering. "Because he couldn't let anyone see his face."

Paoli looked confused. "You've lost me."

"Charles was the one who tried to kill me in the computer room that night."

"But, Julie, I thought you couldn't see the guy who attacked you."

"I scratched his face when we struggled. I scratched him hard, hard enough so that I found skin and blood under my fingernails later. When I found Charles's body he had scratches on his face. That's why he couldn't let me see him. Because then I would know it was he."

Paoli backed away from me and sat down in the chair in front of my desk. He looked funny.

"Don't you believe me?"

He looked up at me. "I believe you. I didn't want to tell you about this until I was certain, but we suspected he was the one selling off project data."

"To the Soviets?"

"No, to a company called ATB in Boston."

My thoughts started racing. Things were beginning to fall into place. "I know that company. But how did Charles get the data?"

"At first I thought maybe he had gotten it from you. But then, after my investigation got going, I knew that wasn't it. The problem is that I still don't know how he did it."

"Maybe Charles was the two-faced person Wu referred to in the note. It makes sense."

"Why would Charles be more two-faced than anyone else involved in stealing the data?"

"Because he was two-faced with me. Charles tried to murder me. He couldn't have been in love with me. Maybe he got involved with me because I managed Project 6. He needed me for information."

"I'm sure it was more than that," said Paoli.

"Drop the chivalry. It's true and you know it. You've probably known it for a while."

"I suspected it."

"Since when?"

"Since a week ago."

"Then why didn't you tell me before?"

"At first I couldn't. I didn't know if you were in on it. And I didn't have Charles connected into the murders, only the data leaks, so I didn't think you were in danger."

"What you're really saying is that you didn't trust me."

"No, not at first. How could I? But then I got to know you better and I decided I should tell you. That was the reason I wanted to spend the whole day with you staking out the building on Powell Street. I thought I could bring it up then."

"Then why didn't you?"

"It's tough to tell someone her fiancé might be a crook. I kept putting it off. Finally, when you got out of the car that night I tried to stop you so I could tell you then, but you slugged me with your purse."

"I thought you were going to kiss me."

"I know. When you hit me with your purse, that's when I knew we were destined to be more than business associates. So the next day I decided I had to be sure before I told you about Charles, so I let you think I was trying to jump your bones."

"That was nice of you."

"The strange thing is that after I did more investigating I found out that ATB wasn't the only company Charles was selling secrets to. Some of the initial molecular memory designs have turned up at several high-tech firms around the country, each one in a different city and each one in a different segment of the industry. For example, headquarters located the design at a bio-engineering firm in Chicago, a chip manufacturer in San Jose, and a fiber optics company in New York."

"What are you saying to me?"

"What I'm saying is that Charles and whoever else was in on this with him had sold the same information to multiple companies as well as to the Soviets, each group probably thinking it was the only one with the molecular memory designs. Actually it was a pretty gutsy thing to do. They cheated the Soviets."

"Are you watching Petrovsky to see who he's been dealing with?" I asked.

"Coleman had him followed, but he's made no contacts except with the prostitutes on Geary Street. He's still staying at the Soviet Embassy."

"Has anyone been able to use the designs well enough to create the finished product?" I asked, not sure I wanted the answer.

Paoli looked at me sympathetically. "No, not yet, but it's just a matter of time. Whoever gets it first gets the patent on it, and there's a good chance it won't be ICI."

We stared at each other a moment, each of us turning it over in our minds, then Paoli spoke.

"You were really going to break your engagement to Charles?" he asked softly.

"Yes."

"Julie, I'm crazy about you," he said, rising from his chair and coming toward me.

I raised a hand to stop him. "I'm crazy about you too, but we don't have time for that now."

"We don't?"

"No, we don't. In addition to everything else, Garrett has canceled the project and I'm being transferred to New York and—"

"Fantastic," Paoli interrupted. "It will be a short flight to Washington."

"It's not fantastic. Listen to me. They want to cancel the project. I can't let that happen, especially not now when there are so many other people working on our designs. We've got to come up with the finished product first."

"Good grief, Julie. Call me a worrier, but people around you are dropping like flies and you could be next. I think that's a pretty good reason to stop the project."

"That's because you're thinking like everyone else. The fact that people keep getting murdered is the reason to keep the project going. Somebody murdered Gershbein, Wu, and now Charles. The murders are all linked to the molecular memory work and the data leaks. If they cancel the project there will be no more data, so no more reason for our killer to stay interested. He gets to ride off into the sunset and we'll never catch him."

"But we can't risk him killing someone else."

"I can catch him before he has the chance."

"Don't even talk that way, Julie."

"But don't you see? Charles, Albert Wu, and whoever else were all in this together, and it's been going on a long time. Charles and I became engaged over a year ago. He and whoever else have been working on this for a couple of years at least. It took them awhile to figure out how to steal the data, then they had to wait for Larry to come up with a design complete enough to sell to the Soviets. Charles and Albert probably got killed because they got greedy and started selling the project design to other companies as well. Charles tried to kill me because I told him that morning I had a trapdoor password to Larry's security code. He knew I would be there that night and he knew the security code held the answer to how the data was being leaked. He also knew I would figure it out eventually. Gershbein was murdered for the same reason. The answers we need have to be in the security code."

Paoli looked exasperated. "But we've gone over that code and everything associated with it a dozen times. Nothing shows that anybody accessed it."

"The answer is there and I can find it." I paused. "Garrett said if I'm found on the building premises after five today, I'm fired."

"Would that be the end of the world for you?"

"A month ago it would have. Now I don't give a damn. I don't need ICI, but I do need to know that my five years of work meant something. And I need to know that whoever the murderer is doesn't get away with what he's done."

"But you don't have to consider yourself responsible for what's happened, and you don't have to solve everything yourself. You've been through a lot. It would have broken anybody else."

"I can handle it."

"And you don't have to act so tough. It's only human to be scared or unsure of yourself."

"But I'm not scared or unsure of myself. I'm just angry, and I know what to do, but I need your help."

"How?"

"I need you to stall them on unloading the project data from Larry. Garrett says it's all going to be dumped to tape and archived. You have to stop that."

"I can't do it. What reason would I use?"

"Tell them you still need the data for your investigation. Tell them you need it for two more days."

"That would be pretty hard to pull off, Julie. I got a call from Washington this morning about shelving the project, and archiving all the data was a joint decision between Washington and ICI."

"So tell Garrett you're putting in the request to Washington. That will impress him. He'll have to hold off at least until you get an answer. That would give us a day."

"But what good is it going to do? You can't even get on the premises after five today. You can bet that the first thing Garrett did today was cancel your password that gets you in the outside doors."

I moved closer to Paoli. "I can get around that. Just promise me you'll do it."

Paoli rolled his eyes. "All right, I'll do it. It will take some time. I have to call my supervisor and he's out the rest of the day. And there are other people I'll have to contact."

"You can start this afternoon."

"You know, you're getting very pushy," he said. "You said before that you were crazy about me. You meant that, didn't you?"

"Yes."

"Then could you at least call me by my first name?"

I laughed. "I'll try. I promise," I said, then I put my arms around him and kissed him once more.

"I'll be busy tonight making the phone calls," he told

me. "I want you to stay at home with your doors locked. You need a rest. We can start in on Larry's code again tomorrow."

I nodded.

"I'll call you tonight," he said. "And I want you to promise me that you'll stay at home."

I smiled and nodded as he walked out of my soon-to-be former office.

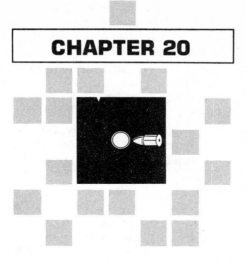

CHAPTER 20

"So you're just going to walk out of here with your tail between your legs?" Mrs. Dabney asked, her arms crossed and her eyes tracking me as I lugged a cardboard box filled with books and files through my office door.

"It looks that way," I answered, out of breath from the box's weight. A book on fourth-generation computer languages slid from the crammed box onto the floor.

Mrs. Dabney picked it up and put it back on top of the pile. Her eyes met mine and I saw the disappointment in her face. "This just doesn't sound like you. Ida told me everything that happened today with Garrett, and I expected you to fight back, give 'em a taste of their own medicine."

I put down my box and hugged her. "Good-bye, Mrs.

Dabney. It's been great working with you. I'll miss you. If I can ever help you with a reference, let me know."

I picked up my box and headed toward the lobby. News traveled fast at ICI, and by two forty-five almost everyone knew about my sudden and involuntary transfer. My office was like a morgue all day, with few phone calls and no one stopping by to see me. I had the corporate plague and no one wanted to catch it.

I was struggling to get my body and my box out the front door when I heard my name called out behind me. Turning, I saw Joshua running through the lobby waving a paper in his hand.

"Don't worry, Julie. Look at this," he said, and pushed a document in front of my face. "It's a petition. All the programmers signed it. My name is first on the list, you'll notice. It says that if the project, along with you as manager, isn't reinstated by next Wednesday at five o'clock, all the programming staff is staging a walkout."

I looked at the list of names, then at Joshua's beaming face. "I want you to throw this away."

"But why? We can't just stand by and let them throw you out."

"Josh, if you give that to management they'll fire all of you. These days jobs aren't that easy to come by. It wouldn't help anyway. My job here is over and a petition isn't going to save it."

I watched his expression fall and his face get a puppydog look that I used to find annoying. At that moment it made me want to kiss his forehead.

"But what's going to happen to you?"

"Things will be great for me. The job in the New York plant sounds good. It'll probably even involve some research. So don't worry about me, okay?"

Joshua stared at me with a sick expression. I put down my box and hugged him, then he helped me carry my belongings to my car and placed them in the trunk.

"So long," he said sadly as I opened the car door.

"See you." I didn't look back at him as I got in, started

the engine, and steered out of the parking lot. It hurt to do it, but I had to let him think I was really leaving. I couldn't let him or anyone else know I had no intention of going to New York.

In spite of the traffic I made it to San Francisco in a little under an hour. It took another twenty minutes to find the building I was looking for, but there was a parking place in front, and I took that as a good omen. I was due for one.

The Soviet Embassy, an older stone building, looked stern sitting in the middle of the block in a well-bred neighborhood. I walked up a short flight of stone steps to a heavy black-lacquered door. A foreboding brass knocker shaped like a lion's head faced me. I noticed a small buzzer on the right wall. I opted to use the buzzer, always preferring technology to manual labor.

"Yes. How may I help you?" a female voice asked with smooth politeness. I jumped, startled, then noticed a small speaker on the wall partially obscured by a large azalea bush.

"My name is Julie Blake. I need to speak to Professor Petrovsky."

"One moment."

A cold gust of wind blew up my skirt reminding me that the fog rolled into San Francisco most afternoons. I wrapped my arms around myself and shivered.

"Mr. Petrovsky is not here." The voice had lost its silkiness.

"He is there. He must be there. I have to talk to him."

"Mr. Petrovsky is not here. Good day."

I heard a *click* and the speaker was silent. Grabbing the brass knocker, I banged it against the door. Five minutes of my pounding passed with no response and my arm was getting tired. Finally a woman wearing a drab green suit and a face to match opened the door and motioned me inside. I walked into a foyer appointed with carved paneling and antiques, surprisingly opulent for a bastion of the communist state. The woman left me there and I saw Petrovsky standing in the hall wearing his dark overcoat and a black felt hat pulled low on his head. Two large suitcases stood at his side. He smiled at me.

"Ah, I thought you would come, Miz Blake, but alas, you come too late."

"I need you to help me."

He chuckled and wagged a fat finger at me. "Helping Americans is not why I'm here for. What do you want?"

"Tell me the name of the person you worked with to get the molecular memory designs."

Petrovsky threw his head back and laughed. I walked up to him, grabbed one of his shoulders, and looked him in the eye. He stopped laughing, and I saw something in his face that was compassion or amusement or maybe just the desire to grab my behind.

"I need that name," I told him. "Whoever it was cheated you. You're bound to know that. What do you care what happens to him? It's simple. All I need is the name."

The smile evaporated from Petrovsky's face. "It's simple, you say. I'm leaving your country now because I fear for my life. You Americans kill for money the way we kill for ideology, but the blood still flows. I'm going to make certain that it is not mine. I recommend you do the same."

I opened my mouth to speak but he held up his hand to stop me.

"I haven't told your security agency or your FBI. Do you think I would tell you? You are pretty but not that pretty. I will say no more," he said. He opened the door and pushed me onto the steps. "Still, I would have liked to know you better. You American women, you have fire," he said, grinning, raising his eyebrows lustfully, then slamming the door in my face.

■ ◻ ■

I reached home about six. I carried the box inside, opened it and dug past the ivy, the books, the Rolodex, finally reaching the confidential files that lay on the bottom. Flipping hastily through the pages, I came to the list of building passwords for my project team. All managers kept the password lists for their department so they could revoke the codes if the person left the company. It was standard procedure, so I knew Garrett had revoked mine as soon as I left his office that morning. If I was going to get into the building that night, I was going to need another password. I was halfway down the list of employees when I realized that even if I could get into the building it wouldn't matter, because all of the passwords to get inside the computer room had also been canceled. I slammed the folder shut, feeling as if the air had been knocked out of me, chiding myself for my stupidity. But then I opened the folder once more. ICI was very thorough in managing passwords, but maybe they wouldn't think to revoke the password of a dead person, especially in the midst of the confusion of a murder investigation. Running my finger down the list, I stopped when I found Gershbein's name. Before his death, Gershbein had access to the computer room. I wrote his building and computer room passwords on a piece of paper and slipped it in my pocket. All I had to do now was wait.

■ □ ■

My hands gripped the steering wheel too tightly as I drove to ICI. It was nine-thirty. Highway 101 stretched before me and with each mile I passed I felt more tense, more eager. All that time combing through details and yet never seeing the truth. That night was my last chance to find it.

It was Friday and the parking lot was empty. Even before the murders nobody ever liked working late on Fridays. I knew only the guards would be there.

I parked in the back lot and walked toward a side entrance. When I reached the door I slowed down and considered turning back. Standing in that cool night air brought back frightening memories of the night I fought Charles's hands off my throat. I remembered the air being choked from me, and for a second I thought I couldn't breathe. I forced myself to get air through my mouth, slowly inhaling, exhaling to calm myself so I could think clearly.

I could get back in my car and drive home, I told myself. It would take a few days to get my things packed, then I could move to New York and leave all of this behind me. There would be other projects, other opportunities that would get my career back on track. But I knew it wasn't the project or my career that was going to make me walk through that door. It was much more than that. It was knowing that somebody at ICI was a murderer and that I had the knowledge to find out who that person was. I placed my hand reassuringly on my purse, feeling the outline of a small revolver. Guns frightened me but I had bought it when I first moved to California, feeling it a necessary precaution for a woman living alone. It had stayed untouched in the closet for years, and I wasn't even sure I knew how to fire it, but I felt more comfortable just having it with me. Sitting next to my gun was my Maalox. I took a swallow like a drunk takes his bourbon.

I pressed my security code into the keypad, and as I anticipated, my code had been canceled; the door refused to move. Next I tried Gershbein's code, holding my breath as I slowly pressed the digits. The door *clicked*. I smiled at my victory. If no one had thought to cancel Gershbein's building code, his computer room password was certain to be intact. I opened the door and felt my way down the dark hallway, moving quietly in my aerobic shoes that at last had been put to good use.

I reached the corner of a lighted hall and heard voices. I pressed my body against the wall and listened. It was only the security guards' portable TV. I moved quickly down the hallway, up the stairs, checked the hallways on that level, then walked cautiously to the computer room. The fact that no guard was there surprised me. I pressed Gershbein's code into the keypad, opened the door, and stepped in.

My heart stopped when I heard movement on the other side of the room. Fear shot through me and for a second I stood frozen, but then I slipped behind a disk drive, crouching to hide. The sounds stopped. I tried not to breathe.

"Who's there?" I heard a man's fearful voice question. I peeked out and saw Fred Sanders, a field engineer.

"It's Julie. Julie Blake," I answered loudly, and then I saw Fred standing there with a large wrench in his hand, looking as scared as I was. Fred was responsible for performing regular maintenance on Larry. When we recognized each other, we both laughed out loud.

"You gave me a start, Julie," he said with a laugh. "With all the things going on around here, I guess we're all jumpy. I didn't realize anybody could still get in here."

"Well, there are just a couple of us," I replied, not comfortable with the lie. I lucked out, for Fred obviously didn't know about my banishment from the premises. Field engineering was in a separate location from the research complex. They spent most of their time at customer sites and were out of the mainstream of corporate politics.

"Where's the guard?" I asked Fred. "I thought there was supposed to be a guard here at night."

"Not anymore. Not since they decided to take Larry down. That's why I'm here. To start his reconditioning," he said as he walked to the rear of the machine. His words jolted me, but I didn't want to sound like it was new news.

"How long will reconditioning take?"

"A couple of weeks. I'm going to do some preliminary work the next few days, then Larry's being shipped back to the plant for the overhaul. But I guess you know that."

So that was Garrett's plan. Reconditioning Larry would be like giving him a frontal lobotomy, with every bit of his microcode dumped out of him. There wouldn't be a telltale scrap of Project 6 left to tarnish Garrett's illustrious career.

But the idea of the microcode stuck in my mind. Suddenly I saw it differently than I had before. I had been so busy examining Larry's software that I hadn't thought to check what had been hard-wired inside of him. Microcode was instructions that weren't part of any software but were actually wired into the computer. I always thought of a computer's operating system and microcode as its brain, which gave the computer the intelligence to read the instructions given by software and produce the desired results. The chances of anyone being able to change Larry's microcode were small, since few people had the technical skills. Still, it was worth taking a look.

"How much longer are you going to be, Fred? I'm going to be doing some work in here and I don't want to disturb you."

"I'm done for tonight. It's almost ten and I want to get home in time to watch the news. You shouldn't be here either, Julie."

"I'll be fine."

Fred didn't look convinced, but he just shrugged. I guess he assumed it wasn't his job to tell managers how to take care of themselves.

"I've got to come back and finish tomorrow morning, so I'll just leave things the way they are. Usually I wouldn't leave the back of the machine open like this, but since no one is going to be in here . . . Except you, of course. Just be careful."

"Don't worry. I will be. Larry is turned off anyway."

Fred grabbed his coat and headed for the door. "See you Monday," he said cheerily, then walked out, the door closing behind him.

I pushed a control unit against the door so it couldn't be opened from the outside, then I walked to the back of Larry to make sure Fred hadn't disassembled any part of him that might make him nonoperational. Everything looked okay.

I walked to the other side of the machine and flipped on the power for the main processor, the control terminal, and the storage units. The familiar *whir*ring sound filled the room as Larry's brain slowly awakened. The sound calmed me; it was like being joined by an old friend. I sat down at the terminal, my purse close by my side, and I began entering the necessary commands to operate Larry. My body tensed as I asked Larry to produce a readout of his microcode. After a pause, the statements flashed brightly on the screen. Using a ballpoint pen as a pointer, I examined each statement. They all looked normal.

I clenched my eyes shut, the glowing green words on the screen beginning to blur. I opened my eyes to look again at the terminal. That's when I saw it.

I examined it closer to make certain I was reading it right. The microcode alteration was subtle and wouldn't have been noticed except under the closest scrutiny. I now knew how the Project 6 data had been leaked, but I still didn't know who had done it. I needed more time, but time was one thing I didn't have.

I had to stop Larry from being shipped back to the plant. I considered calling Garrett and telling him what I had discovered, but I knew he wouldn't listen. And I didn't trust him. He was the one who threw me off the project, the one who must have authorized Larry's reconditioning. I thought of Paoli, but it would take days for him to get through the necessary government and ICI channels. I needed someone else.

I picked up the phone and dialed Elkin's home number, praying that he would be there. He answered on the third ring.

"Brad, it's Julie."

"What's the matter?"

"Nothing. I'm at ICI."

"How did you get in?"

"It doesn't matter. You have to get over here. Brad, I know how the project data was being leaked. I also know where all the correct memory algorithms are. They're here, Brad. They were here all the time," I said in a rush of words.

"You're not alone in there, are you? It's dangerous."

"Fred was here doing some maintenance on Larry, but he's gone now."

"Don't let anyone in but me, Julie. You scare me sometimes."

"Don't worry about me. Just get here quickly," I told him, then hung up. Elkin lived about ten minutes away. I dialed Paoli's hotel several times, but his extension was busy. I could hardly wait to show him what I had found. He was right, someone had put a virus in Larry, although not the way he expected. I moved the control unit away from the door and waited nervously for Elkin. The next fifteen minutes dragged, then I heard the door *click* open. Elkin walked in. He was dressed in a jogging suit and his hair was out of place. He saw me and frowned.

"I don't usually let myself get dragged away from home on a Friday night, but I couldn't stand the idea of you being alone in here. And you know I'm going to have to report your being in the computer room to Garrett."

"I don't care."

"Even if he fires you?"

"Especially if he fires me," I told him. "I want to show you something. Sit down."

He pulled a chair next to mine in front of the terminal.

"Here it is. I've spent the past two weeks going through the security code over and over again, thinking that the problem was there. But it wasn't. This is a readout of Larry's microcode," I said, pointing to the screen. "Here are the instructions hard-coded into Larry that hooked into the security system and retrieved output from the algorithm calculations. You see, no one had broken into Larry to steal the Project 6 data. Whoever was responsible programmed Larry to store the data on a specific memory chip that could be retrieved physically from the computer. Whenever Larry came up with an equation that was even close to the correct one for molecular memory, he stored it in a separate place that couldn't normally be accessed. In a sense, Larry was stealing the data himself and hiding it. We were getting only the bad results. Someone else was getting the right ones."

Elkin examined the screen closely. He looked puzzled at first, but then appeared to understand.

"You could be right," he said. "Congratulations. Only you could have figured this out."

"Not quite. There's someone else who figured it out, and that's the person who did this in the first place. It had to be someone who had easy access to Larry during the last few years, someone who was technically proficient enough to make the microcode changes."

"It could also be someone from outside the company who simply paid someone at ICI to do it," Elkin suggested.

"That's possible, but I doubt it. Whoever did it had to have continuing access to Larry to keep retrieving the data on a regular basis. That's why Gershbein was murdered. He knew there was something strange about the security software and he kept tinkering with it. But because the actual instructions to steal the data were in the microcode, the security software didn't indicate the real problem. Still, it was the one element that made Gershbein suspicious."

"What do you mean?"

"I'll show you." I hit keys until I was back to the initial screen used to log on to Larry's security code.

"You'll need my password," Elkin said.

"Not really." I typed my user i.d. and the word "rawdata" into the password field. Elkin looked surprised. "This is a trapdoor password I programmed in for testing four years ago," I explained. "The term seemed appropriate. You always taught me that the best way to tackle a problem was to gather the raw data, analyze it from as many different perspectives as possible, design a solution, then implement it. If I had used that approach in this situation, I would have found my answer sooner."

I pointed to the security code on the screen. "You see, I didn't look at the problem from enough different perspectives. This security code had some minor irregularities that in themselves meant nothing to me because I couldn't connect them to the microcode. Gershbein saw the irregularities and tried to change them. When he made the changes the microcode could no longer store the algorithms. It's all obvious to me now, except for one thing."

"And what is that?"

"This one line of programming, 'EXEC 11,14.' It's nonsense. I've studied back levels of the software and it wasn't there before Gershbein's death. From checking the control logs for the past few months I'm certain that Gershbein put it in the night he was murdered, but I can't figure out why. It doesn't do anything," I said. "Unless it was never intended to do anything. Unless it was some sort of message."

I stared at the screen in silence. Yes, it was a message. It had to be. Perhaps an abbreviation of some sort, but what can you abbreviate with numbers? I was a programmer and I thought like one. Gershbein and I would have written the message in the same way. The key was the numbers. When working in certain programming languages, you use a base 16 numbering system. It was the standard method of arithmetic with computers that every programmer knew from the first day he wrote a line of software. In base 16 some numbers were represented by letters of the alphabet. The number 11 represented "B" and 14 represented "E." But what did the command "EXEC" mean? EXEC B.E. They could be initials. Gershbein died while sitting at the terminal. Someone held a gun to his head and forced him to change back the security code. Did he identify his killer and the person who was stealing the data in the only way he could, with a line of programming?

I started to blurt out my discovery to Elkin, but I stopped. "EXEC B.E." "Executive Brad Elkin." My body became rigid, my face flushed hot. He had access to all of Larry's coding from the day the computer arrived. He had the technical knowledge.

"So you said earlier that this was what killed Gershbein. Tell me how," said Elkin.

Looking back at it, I should have run out of the room after I realized I was sitting next to a murderer. But something held me back. I guess I couldn't let myself believe it was true. I had looked up to him for such a long time.

"He suspected the problem," I said slowly, looking only at the screen in front of me. "That's why I found a printout of the security software at his house. He was making some minor changes to it, changes that kept these microcode instructions from executing properly. Whoever was behind it noticed that he was no longer getting the data and reasoned that somebody was tampering with the software."

"But how did this person know it was Gershbein?"

"It had to be someone fairly high up at ICI, someone who could have checked log-on times and i.d.'s and figured out who was tampering with the code. Then he forced Gershbein at gunpoint to change the software back to its original state, and then that's when he shot him."

Elkin's hand was lying on the desktop and I saw his fingers slowly curl into a fist.

"But if this person was technically proficient enough to make changes to microcode, wouldn't he or she be able to change the security software without Gershbein's help?" he asked. His voice remained calm.

Now I looked at him. His face was dispassionate. "But the person couldn't risk logging on to the security code with his personal i.d. and having it show up in the control log. Gershbein would have known that the security code had been tampered with again, checked the control log, and eventually figured out who was responsible. The killer had to eliminate Gershbein to protect himself," I said. My eyes never left Elkin's. Tiny beads of perspiration were now breaking out on his upper lip and forehead. "Why did you steal from a company you've devoted over twenty years of your life to?" I asked him.

The dispassion was now gone from his face, replaced by a sudden flash of anger and sadness. The corners of his lips trembled, and for the first time I could remember, he didn't look strong.

"Yes," he said. "I devoted twenty-five years of my life to this company." He laughed, but there was no amusement in its sound. "You know what this company does to you after you reach fifty? ICI assumes that once you've reached a certain age your creative years are over, that you need to be replaced with fresher blood, so they give you a so-called promotion and move you to some innocuous administrative job with a flashy title where you can't affect anything."

His voice became hoarse, and his eyes turned moist.

"What are you talking about?" I said. "You oversee several big projects, including Project 6. Everyone knows you're in line for a promotion to head this whole research facility. You can't call that an innocuous position."

"I used to think that too. But one of my connections at headquarters told me when I began this project that the executive committee considered me too old for research. It's too fast-paced and competitive. They wanted someone younger and more energetic. A fast tracker." He laughed softly. "You know who was going to get that job as head of the research facility? I'm sure you can guess, Julie. When did you first start going behind my back to maneuver for it? You set your sights on it from the moment you started working here, didn't you?"

I couldn't believe what he was saying, but there was no denying the pain in his eyes. The muscles in his face were contorted into a venomous expression.

"That's not true, Brad. I was never interested in taking your job from you. I assumed I would step into it when you moved up, but that's all."

"Don't try and placate me. This isn't the time for it."

His features had twisted into a face I hardly recognized. How could I have not been aware of the anger inside him? I had only seen the cool, calm shell around him. And behind it he had been white-hot with rage. I had missed the truth in everything. I had seen only the surface, only the façades, and now my ignorance infuriated me.

"I want to know more," I told him.

"You're not in a position to be making demands."

"I need to know more," I repeated. The beginnings of hot tears seeped into my eyes and I felt my cheeks burning. At that moment my anger was as much at myself as it was at Elkin. How could I have so ignorant and not seen what was going on around me? "Tell me how you did this," I continued, my voice faltering. "I understand how you could have initially tampered with Larry's microcode, but as the project moved along I made maintenance changes in the software that would have affected it. As I altered the software, you must have altered the microcode as well. How did you know what changes I was making and when? They weren't all in the documentation. I never told you or Charles or anybody else everything I was doing with the software."

Elkin's lips turned up into a small, tight smile. "You're just like Gershbein, concerned about the technical issues right up to the very end. Even when I had a gun to his head he was asking me questions about how I changed the microcode. I don't know if it was because he was mad at himself for not figuring it out sooner or if it was because he didn't think I would really shoot him."

My body froze as I envisioned Elkin pulling the gun's triggrer.

"How could you have killed Gershbein? He was your friend," I asked when I was at last able to make my mouth move. I spoke the words carefully. We both sat there motionless for a second, like two animals, one knowing the other was about to attack.

I inched my hand toward my purse, which lay on the desk next to me. My fingers grazed the leather but Elkin placed his hand on top of mine. He knew me well enough to know I wouldn't enter the computer room that night without protection.

I jumped from my chair and bolted for the door, planning to open it and scream so the guard would hear me. My hand was inches away from the door handle when I felt his grip on my shoulder. He pulled me back and shoved me to the floor. The blow knocked the breath out of me for a second, then I raised myself onto my elbows and saw him lean down toward me. He pulled out something from his pocket. I couldn't distinguish it at first, but then I saw the thin wire. He wrapped it around his hands and pulled it taut. He was positioned in front of the door, and when he heard it open, he turned quickly away from me and toward the new visitor. He looked surprised when he saw Mrs. Dabney walk in and shut the door behind her.

"Get out!" I yelled at her. "Get help!"

Elkin spun back toward me. Still on the floor, I grabbed a chair and pushed it at him, hoping to knock him off balance. I didn't see Mrs. Dabney's knife at first, only the look of shock that burst across Elkin's face and the blood that spewed from his neck. He fell to the floor and looked up at the small figure of Mrs. Dabney. Still holding the knife, she looked back at him with an expression that I can only describe as one of profound disappointment. He tried to speak, but collapsed. I knew he was dead.

"He called me half an hour ago panicked that maybe you had discovered something. I warned him not to blow up and act impulsive, but he told me to stay out of it, that he would take care of everything. And look what happened," she said to me as she stepped closer to Elkin and peered down at him, shaking her head as if she were inspecting a stain on new carpeting. "Men are so stupid, aren't they? They don't think. They have no patience. Everything has to be now, now, now." She straightened herself. I stood up and leaned back against a desk, trying to regain my senses.

"And they're so goddamn easy to manipulate," she continued. "They're driven by lust and power and guns that go bang. That's what started this whole mess. I told him that guns are loud and messy, that bullets can always be linked with individual weapons, but would he listen? Of course not. Big executive. Has to do things his own way."

"No," I said, the word dragging itself out of me slowly. "You're not involved in this, Mrs. Dabney."

"Do you think these idiots could have figured this all out? I had to teach them how to do things like they were little boys. Even that fat little Russian was stupid as a post. He had no business sense. Not like you and me. You wouldn't believe what they offered for the molecular memory designs. We would have gladly sold for half the amount. Charles and Albert were beside themselves."

She looked so calm, as if she were discussing some petty office gossip. That's when I noticed the pearls, the fake pearls she always wore. So that was the "pearl" Albert Wu had referred to. And she was small enough to fit inside the air-conditioning duct. The possibility of it being she had not crossed my mind until then.

"Mrs. Dabney, did you kill the others?"

She rolled her eyes and looked at me as if I were very stupid. "God, no. I didn't have to. They were too busy killing each other."

Suddenly she looked irritated, as if I had offended her. "Wipe that look off your face. You look so shocked, like a Girl Scout seeing someone cheat to get a merit badge."

"What part could you have played in this? You have no technical background."

She stiffened, and pointed the bloody knife at me as casually as if she were pointing a pencil.

"Never underestimate the power of good clerical help, my dear. You never gave me credit for anything, did you? You think of yourself as such a feminist, but because I'm not young and I don't have a fancy job you look right through me like I'm nothing. That was my advantage. That's why they needed me. All these big executive types needed little Mrs. Dabney. You see, you left your notebook lying around, your desk unlocked, your files hanging open when I was there. I photographed every note you ever took. I knew every idea you had, every software change you planned. I couldn't understand all the notes myself, but Brad and Wu did."

A tiny drop of blood slid down the handle of the knife and landed on her pink dress. I waited for her to notice it, for it to take her attention for just a moment so I could make a move against her. But she never took her eyes from me. She wanted to savor every moment, for at last she was in control.

"You know, I got so familiar with your notes I could even tell by your doodles when your spirits were low. I'd tell Charles to buy you flowers or dinner. He was so cheap, he never wanted to do it. But I made him. I told him to think of it as an investment. Charles was a greedy, two-faced little bastard. How I wanted to tell you. I couldn't stand the thought of you marrying such slime. He'd cut somebody's legs off for a quarter, including yours. It was bad enough when he and Brad killed Albert just so they could get more money for themselves, but when I found out he tried to kill you that night, well, I was quite ticked off. That wasn't my idea, you know. I want you to be aware of that."

She puckered her lips and sighed. "I'm lying a little. I did kill Charles. Brad just held him for me. I did that for you. I've almost liked you, really, even though you treated me like a grunt. You and I are so different from the rest of them. We have intelligence and integrity. We know what we want. We know how to set goals, how to strategize. There was always this unspoken connection between you and me. Can you feel it?"

"No, I can't," I told her.

Her lips twisted with rage at my remark. "Then feel this." She snapped her hand out quickly toward me and the knife sliced my cheek. I screamed, raised my hand to my face, and saw the blood on my fingers. I backed away from her and tried to locate my purse out of the corner of my eye, but I couldn't see it. I didn't dare take my eyes off her. I just kept backing up and she followed me with every step, the bloody knife held out in front of her. Finally I was next to Larry. My body touched his metal siding and I knew I could retreat no further. I yelled for help, and she giggled. We both knew the soundproofing of the room was impregnable. She paused and stared at me for a moment, as if to savor the sight of my cowering in terror of her.

"Can you imagine what it was like being patronized and looked down upon by you for the past five years?" she said as she waved the knife in front of me. "You, little Miss Yuppie Queen, Little Miss Goody Two Shoes, always feeling superior, like nobody knew anything but you. Brad even suggested once that we bring you in on our deal, but Charles and I laughed at him."

I could taste my blood trickling from my cheek. I used my hands to brace myself against Larry, and I could feel him vibrating beneath my fingers. My hand touched a metal edge and I quickly drew it back, remembering that Larry's door was open, exposing his circuits. I calmed myself enough to assess my situation, and it did not look good. I was caught between two thousand volts of electricity and a crazed woman with a knife. It was then I felt the fear drain out of me, and it was replaced with the clear-headed objectivity that comes from having nothing to lose. I was probably going to die. I could accept that. But I was taking that bitch with me.

I reached for one of Larry's internal cables, pulling it from one side of its connection with a sharp jerk. It made a crackling noise as I held the bare end toward Mrs. Dabney.

"I'm going to give you a choice, Mrs. Dabney. You can throw down the knife and we can both walk out of here, or you can stab me. But if you do I'll make sure we both fry. The electricity will go through you first, then through me. It will ensure your so-called connection between us."

Mrs. Dabney's petite body shook with fury. She knew she had lost her advantage, and she didn't like it. She thrust the knife closer to me.

"Just throw down the knife, Mrs. Dabney, and we'll walk out of here. I'm telling you to throw down the knife."

Her eyes turned hot; her face reddened with anger and saliva bubbled at one corner of her badly rouged mouth. This had been her chance to best me, and I had ruined it. Suddenly she lunged at me, the knife outstretched before her as if the power of the blade itself dragged it toward me. My survival instincts took over, and when I saw her advance, I dropped the wire and dove to the floor, sliding like a base-ball player into home plate. My head hit the side of something hard, and after that I didn't see much. I just remember hearing a sizzling noise and Mrs. Dabney's scream.

When I came to I saw Mrs. Dabney's body crumpled on the floor, her arms tangled inside Larry's wiring. The hideous expression on her face and the odor of her burned flesh will stay with me the rest of my life. Somehow Larry was still humming. I know this is crazy, but at that moment I was convinced Larry had saved my life.

I walked out of the computer room, found the security guard dozing in front of his portable TV, and told him to call the police. Then I sat down in a chair and cried.

CHAPTER 21

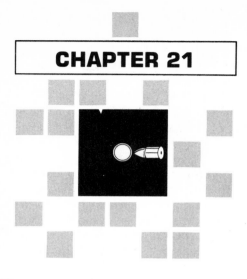

I dipped one finger into my margarita, then dangled it over Paoli's face until a drop of the icy liquid slid off my fingernail and rolled down his nose. Lifting up his sunglasses, he gave me a glance that was pleasantly reprimanding. I licked off the offending drop then returned my attention to the phone.

"Yes, Mother. I'm fine. I'm just taking some time off to relax. I deserve it, don't I? Don't worry, I've already had several job offers. Good ones."

I held the phone away from me for a moment while Paoli kissed me and my mother's unceasing stream of chatter faded into the distance. Then I returned my ear once more to the womb.

"Of course, Charles was a beast, a terrible person. You were right all along, Mom. No, I don't miss him."

Paoli smiled with satisfaction.

"Gotta go, Mom. Love you too."

I picked up the suntan lotion and began rubbing it on Paoli's chest. He purred. It was unseasonably warm and we had decided to take advantage of the sunshine by lounging on my patio. We had accomplished nothing all day except for the detailed preparation of a pitcher of margaritas and the beginnings of golden tans.

"I find this display of sloth quite disgusting. After all, it is a weekday. Decent people are working."

I looked up and saw Max marching toward us. She looked cool and crisp in a white linen suit and hot-pink high heels that sunk precariously into the lawn as she walked.

"Yes, it is Wednesday, so shouldn't you be at Comtech making Hanson more money?" asked Paoli.

"Since ICI and Comtech got the molecular memory patent, Wayne is happy as a clam. He's too busy giving interviews to notice whether I work or not. Of course he's claiming all the credit."

"That doesn't surprise or bother me," I said, pouring a drink for Max.

"Oh, yes, I forgot. You've joined the listless ranks of the unemployed. Rumor around the Valley is that Garrett calls here every day, weeping and begging you to come back."

I grinned. "He doesn't weep."

"Well, don't give in, whatever you do. You don't need ICI anymore. Besides, I have an intriguing offer for you."

"I'm burned out on intrigue, Max."

She pulled a chair next to me and sat down. "Not on this kind, Jules. Picture this. A new company called Hantech. Wayne and I have, shall we say, rekindled our relationship, and out of this new collaboration Wayne has this idea for developing and marketing a new technology for artificial intelligence using molecular memory as a basic design. Wayne will be CEO, naturally. I'll be V.P. of marketing, and, now listen to this, Jules, you'll be President. How do you like that for a title? Impressive?"

"I'm not interested."

Max frowned. "Why not?"

"Because I want to take time off from computers and business in general. That's the whole idea of my leaving ICI. Vic's on a leave of absence and I'm unemployed and we both intend to stay this way for a while."

Max looked dubious. "How long is a while?"

"I'm not sure. Three months, six months, maybe even a year."

Max laughed. "I know you better than you know yourself. How long ago did you quit ICI? A week? By the end of the month you'll be crawling the walls. You'll be computerizing recipes, your wardrobe, drawing flowcharts on the ceiling and—"

"You're wrong. I want to relax."

"Relaxation to you is a forty-hour work week. You're not a relaxer, my dear. You're a doer, a confirmed workaholic, a classic Type-A personality. You can't stay out of the business for more than a few weeks because if you did, when you got back, all the technology could be different. You wouldn't be on top of things and you couldn't live with that. You have to be in the thick of it."

Paoli had taken off his sunglasses and was sitting up in his chair taking in our conversation. I had to admit, I had been restless the past few days, but I reasoned that it just took awhile to learn to do nothing. Paoli and I had made a pact about not discussing anything technical, but just that morning I found myself sneaking an issue of *ComputerWorld* into the bathroom.

"Artificial intelligence," Max said slowly, dramatizing each syllable. "It hasn't been perfected yet. Lots of people have tried. No one has been able to do it. We could though. Vic, how would you like to be in on this company? We could always use a technical V.P. Of course, if Jules would rather sit at home and watch Phil Donahue, whip up casseroles . . ."

"What would we need to get started?" I asked.

Max's face lit up. "Venture capital."

"Venture capital? I thought Hanson was rolling in cash."

"He's a firm believer in using other people's money. He says he wants investors for forty-nine percent of the startup capital before he'll begin. But we won't have any trouble coming up with investors, especially if word gets around that you're in on it."

"Why should that matter?"

"Jules, your name is as good as gold around here. You solved the Silicon Slayer murders, uncovered the data leaks, and completed the molecular memory project. You're practically a folk hero. Why, they're probably going to write ballads about you and play them years from now on computerized music synthesizers. With you involved in Hantech people will be throwing money at us."

"I'm still not interested."

"Just think about it, ponder it, muse upon it while you bake your brain in the sun. Well, I don't want to burden you hedonists with too much business talk. I'll get back to you later. Just remember these words—artificial intelligence. Bye now," she said as she maneuvered her way back across the lawn.

Paoli and I sank once more into our lounge chairs, closed our eyes, and lifted our faces toward the noonday sun.

"Julie?"

"Hmmm?"

"Are you interested?"

"In what?"

"In Hantech."

"I don't know. I guess I could be. But it would take a lot of money to put a deal like that together."

Paoli sat up and grabbed my hand. "Then what about this idea. You and I made such a great team working on the data leaks and the murders. You have to admit that we made an impressive pair. Why don't we start our own agency specializing in detecting computer fraud? You and me. Imagine a sign reading 'Blake and Paoli. Investigations.' "

"You and me? Detectives? Besides, even that takes startup money, which is something neither one of us has. You're a government employee and I'm currently in between opportunities."

"But you know as well as I do that Max is right. We'll both go brain-dead sitting around and drinking margaritas every day."

"I'm willing to switch to mai tais when we need a change."

"Come on, Julie. Let's at least consider really breaking out of our molds. I'm perfectly willing to dump the NSA job and embark on something new, and whatever it is, I want you with me. It would mean we could really be together."

I picked up my cellular phone and started dialing.

"Who are you calling?" he asked.

"I have a friend who's part of a venture capital group in San Jose. I can check it out and see if I can come up with some investors."

"But for what? Are we going to be in the computer or the detective business?"

I smiled. I kissed him. Then I dialed San Jose.

980